When You Promise the Dead

ALICE THÜRST

When You Promise the Dead

Published by Jaime Munt

Cover Design and Photography by Jaime Munt

ISBN-13: 978-0692552605
ISBN-10: 069255260X

Printed in the United States of America

To My Niece and Nephews

May you, one day, find peace with the ghosts of
your pasts and satisfaction with your lives.

Know that you are loved.

CONTENTS

...

When You Promise the Dead

ALICE THÜRST

Non mortem timemus, sed cogitationem mortis —

We do not fear death, but the thought of death...

~ Seneca

PREFACE

. . .

PINCH to GROW an INCH

"The detective was fat. Fatter than fat. Depression and a decent fee kept him rolling in the dough. Bread dough, that is. And cookie dough, and donut dough, and doe-a-deer doe. Venison steaks piled up to his third chin. He knew he'd be in trouble if he ever had to catch somebody—by running, that is.

"He caught people all the time. Made some enemies, in fact.

"He hoped his mental more than compensated for his physical, which it did. He was smart, too smart. In fact, being smarter than his enemies made him a lot more enemies.

"But none perhaps more than Reginald Storm—or Reggie, as his customers called him—"Vaginald" or "Gina"—as his wife, Bettie, called him when she thought he was being a weak little bitch. He was particularly a Gina when it came to our man, Detective Walter "The Wall" Douglass—with two s's, thanks.

"As it goes—'Of all the somewhat classy, all-you-can-eat seafood banquet buffets in New England, he had to come into mine.'

"The detective was fat and thanks to Reggie, a real connoisseur of the omega-3 kind—the unguilty kind. The all-you-can-eat kind. The, you make the Nips look gentle on the sea, kind.

"It certainly wasn't gentle on Reggie's income after the IRS did its own all-you-can-eat. And Gina had no balls when it came to someone with a badge, and a gun, and over four-hundred-and-fifty pounds on him. So all that hate could only fester and Bettie was just a pickin' at any scab that tried to grow and she, like Bettie Bacteria, only makes a wound worse.

"They wasn't the only ones dreaming concrete and deep waters for "The Wall". When he was young and in his prime physically, and already too damn smart, he put a lot of really bad men to the clinker and more than one to the great zapper too and once, or twice, to the great firing squad in the dark, when his client was the less of two evils, sort of speak.

"He found people that wa'nt supposed to be found— some of um fugitives, some of 'em dead. Even so, "Stormy Sea All-You-Can-Eat" may rank highest on wishing *they'd* never been found by this bottomless pit gumshoe.

"So it was no surprise when one day *he* couldn't be found…"

While the pages lowered from the English teacher's smug face, her dark red penciled eyebrows went up. Her lips, that if not for lipstick would have otherwise not existed, puckered around the last word she read, like seeing an egg laid in reverse.

"Well, Bailey," came a voice ruined and masculinized by almost fifty-years of chain-smoking, "What do you have to say for yourself?"

The trembling strawberry blonde, so small she barely cast a shadow, had nothing to say for herself. Ever.

"This was *supposed* to be a story about your father."

Like ripping duct tape off skin, the scrawny girl pried her glassy blue-green eyes off her feet to meet the dark pair glowering at her. Bailey licked her dry lips and opened her mouth as something came up her throat. It would either be a response or vomit.

"It is," she tried to tell the monster towering over her.

The teacher's left eyebrow raised a bundle of five chubby looking wrinkles up to her thinning hairline and stared condescendingly down her impossibly small nose through glasses that almost had to be glued to stay on her face.

The girl looked everywhere, but at the teacher.

The odor of cigarettes pushed through the smell of a pungent flowery perfume and the stink of cats when the teacher leaned in to inform the twelve-year-old that it was nothing more than lies and vulgarity.

"Do you want me to call your father?"

Bailey's blue eyes jumped to the face that always frightened her.

Ms. Seles' face bloomed with wrinkles when it smiled, feeling triumphant and, as always, enjoyed seeing fear in a student, because she interpreted it as respect and accepted it as power at the school, if nowhere else. The same way she exhibited her fluency in Latin and Gaelic languages, no one understood when she scolded them in tongues they didn't understand, but it certainly made the teacher feel superior—which sometimes seemed more important than doing her job. A single contradiction or argumentative question would lock the entire class in a match of "Who's Smarter Than Who?" Should the pupil have made a valid point and argued it to the last—Final Jeopardy answer always was: If you're so smart, then a ten page report, due Friday, won't be a problem for you."

The teacher's most common threats involved telling the mother or father, always delivered in a way that suggested a secret alliance between the pedagogue and parents.

"You wouldn't like that, *would* you?"

You wouldn't like that, the girl thought, if Ms. Seles didn't like lying and vulgarity.

What Bailey wouldn't like was being exposed as an inconvenience. Her dad didn't like to be interrupted by anything that had to do with her. He wouldn't appreciate his adolescent daughter doing anything to make him be a part of her life.

The twelve-year-old didn't imagine "The Wall" would care what she'd wrote about him or give a flaming shit if Ms. Seles had a problem with any of the language. The vicious and somewhat androgynous teacher was apt to hear a lot worse if she called him.

Bailey knew there would be no reprisals for upsetting a teacher. It wouldn't be discussed—like everything else between and about them.

Discipline required too much interaction for a man who kept a child out of obligation and not because he's her father—which he never claimed to be. He cringed when called "dad". Everyone said her mom must have been holding onto the hope that the baby would come out looking like her, instead the baby looked like neither of them.

Bailey heard the rumor that her mom fled the maternity ward in the middle of the night—for fear that the bad-tempered gumshoe, with connections in high and low places, might hurt her, or worse.

There was a little girl named Trisha, who always told "The Wall's" mousy daughter that the real reason her mother left was because Bailey was so ugly—among whatever other similar insults children make up to climb the social ladder on the backs of any other child's weaknesses, but Trisha made upsetting Bailey Jacobs a personal mission.

The plethora of rumors surrounding her mother's absence and being the daughter of a, popularly reputed, vicious scumbag certainly didn't improve conditions at school, where the quiet and reserved adolescent had and would spend the previous and future six years a virtual ghost.

At home, though never blatantly expressed physically or verbally, Bailey was well aware that her existence might be the most painful part of her father's life. The insults, the teasing, made her feel a lot worse for him than for herself.

Should the wrathful teacher bother "The Wall", he would collapse on the haughty woman. Bailey would suffer the consequences in school—whether in English class or not—Seles would get the girl back for the bitching out she wouldn't be wise enough to feel lucky was all she received.

So, Bailey decided to submit to the accusation.

"I'm sorry about what I wrote for my theme. I didn't know what to write."

The truth was, she didn't know what she *could* write. Everything about her dad's "other life" was both shrouded in mystery and blabbed about over too much Scotch or dark beer. Occasionally the single parent would have an acquaintance over to share in the libations. Then Bailey heard stories about how the—sometimes former cop, former CIA agent, former S.E.A.L., former bakery owner—met her "old man". Every one of them seemed to know a different version of "The Wall". How could she write the truth when she didn't know what it was?

The only truth she could write about was that she was afraid of losing him, because she, literally, had no one else. She tried to romanticize or satirize something happening to him because he often said, "it could happen any day". He *had* been a damn good cop and was an even better P. I.

"Your old man's made a lot of enemies."

To say nothing of any other foes a loudly racist, foul mouthed, dirty talking, heavy drinking, neighbor hating, quick-tempered, trigger happy, arrogant, rude and mean man would make.

Part of Bailey wanted her dad to see what she wrote, which might only happen if she got in trouble. Even if she felt like she could bother him with it—even, or maybe *especially,* because the theme was about him—it would never be read.

If the paper was posed to him as problematic, vulgar, or a bunch of lies by an infuriated teacher, only then Walter Douglass might be tempted to see what the girl had written about him.

Getting her father to read it might be the only way to let him know she was afraid of losing him. That he need remember, in carelessness or the making of enemies, his life was not the only affected. Bailey was pretty sure she cared more about him than he cared for himself.

Once she'd said, "I love you", to him. He left the house without a word and was gone until Bailey was supposed to be sleeping. As far he knew, she was. For the whole of that miserable night he would have been wrong to suppose that.

"I can't give you a passing grade," Ms. Seles tried to sound vaguely apologetic.

"Okay."

"And I want a proper theme on my desk Monday morning or I *will* be calling your father."

Bailey nodded, looking only at her feet.

The teacher closed her gnarly fist around the offending sheet of paper and threw it on the floor—a last second reconsideration, having intended on hitting the twelve-year-old.

The girl was surprised, when she looked down at the crumpled piece of college ruled paper, that Ms. Seles hadn't kept it as evidence.

"I hope you've learned something from this."

I tried to.

The air thickened as impatience became anger. Bailey didn't know what the woman wanted. Another "okay" might be more than Seles could take, but it was also more than the girl thought she could force out of her mouth, so she just looked at the ground.

The teacher stared hotly at the twig in cheap clothes who appeared to be ignoring her.

"*Well*—if you've got nothing to say," the hot and damp voice of roses and nicotine wafted against the girl, "then I'm not going to waste any more of *either* of our time."

The frail student guessed that meant it was now okay to leave, but she was afraid to move and be wrong.

The adult stared unblinking, skin blotching, at the petrified creature.

Bailey wavered, having almost talked herself into leaving and then thought she didn't dare, just yet. If the teacher was anyone other than Barbara Seles, Bailey would have asked or would have, at least, been able to look at the adult enough convey the uncertainty, but she couldn't even glance up again.

After an unbearable span of silence, the teacher flew into motion, grunting and sighing hugely as she gathered her belongings, driving home the message of how put-out she was. The student recoiled from the sudden, startling movement, edging closer to the desk as the teacher surged past, trying to be small, invisible, so to not provoke any other interaction or hostility.

Bailey was used to feeling inconvenient.

The classroom door connected loudly with its metal frame—making the small girl's heart feel pinched and then racing from the sudden, violent noise. The door closed with enough force and speed that, rather than marry into the latch, it bounced open again.

The ball of paper was swiftly snatched up and pocketed under the heart-pounding fear of Seles' return and reconsidered interest in it.

Everyone entering the 7th grade dreaded English.

When the girl pulled on the threadbare gray sweater it snagged on the short zipper on the back of her washed out periwinkle dress. After a brief struggle, she freed it and fed its oversized buttons through the limp slits with shaking hands. Her face was burning at the mere possibility that someone might have seen the ordeal.

The tall rectangular window on the classroom door was void of nosey peepers. The room was on an upper floor, thereby safe from outside interest. This may have deserved a sigh had she not the halls and stairwell to survive before actually feeling safe and utterly free of the institute.

When the class was told, "Bailey Jacobs will *not* be reading her theme, because if she did, half of your parents would be calling to complain about it. On that note, Miss Jacobs, you can count on staying after class to discuss it with me," most the class turned to look at the miserable waif who, in roughly fifteen minutes, would be catching hell from Satan's Schoolteacher.

So when Bailey peeked through the window, before exiting the classroom, she feared any number of children waiting to see how much trouble she was in. That's what happened to other kids. She guessed, this time, she was lucky she was so "different". A much less interesting target than Davis, the lightweight with apparently chronic allergies or Jenna Loch, who had lice at least once a year and was the youngest of seven in one of the most impoverished families in Lanester, Massachusetts.

With a sigh of relief, Bailey slipped awkwardly through the partially opened door, her book bag snagging on the handle when she thought she was free and clear.

A few other students lingered in the halls or were visiting at their lockers. There were a couple who wondered what horrible things the bookworm dared write in a theme. Others considered what they should do or say to make it worse.

Probably it was safer to ignore her than take the chance she'd snitch and her fat old man would come after them—not that she ever told her dad about any of the things said or done to her. Not that he ever had or ever would fight her battles for her.

There had always been a lot of talk in Lanester about her dad—it might have been literally impossible not to personally know or know about, someone like Walter Douglass in a town of only some thirty-thousand people.

Everything she wrote about her dad's career was true, as far as she knew. The few times when he had people at the house they always bragged to her about how smart he was and that she should know— nobody gets away with anything around "The Wall". They told her about awards he received, once upon a time, and "shitloads" of bad guys he caught.

They'd play cards with stacks of cash, get drunk, and tell racist jokes while dirty videos played in the room kitty corner from the kitchen table.

There were other reasons "The Wall" stood out.

The sea takes a lot of husbands, these days most couples end up divorced, and a lot of pregnant women are left to fend for themselves. In Lanester, some eleven percent of the population are single mothers. Single fathers are few and far between, so the small community takes particular interest in them, especially when the father is notorious for being a bastard who, many people thought, was too mean, ugly and fat for any woman to be interested in, even if he had money, which no one knew one way or another.

The few times "The Wall" mentioned Bailey's mother, it was the closest to affection she ever knew, because he spoke like her mother was their enemy in common:

The bitch who left them.

People liked to talk about her mom almost as much as they liked to speculate about her old man's money.

Walter Douglass and his daughter lived down by Mill Pond where almost half of the residents live under the poverty line. A lot of people automatically assume when there are that many low income families that they all must be suffering financially.

Now, even though the Douglass's lived in a self-proclaimed shithole, Walter "The Wall" spent money lavishly when it came to restaurants and take-away while otherwise being as stingy with money as an ATM with no power.

Bailey only wore second-hand clothes, neighbors thought her worrisomely thin, and she had very little personal belongings besides the necessities. At Christmas, she was asked what she wanted and she would get it. It never crossed her mind to ask for anything more than a book or doll she liked and she was hesitant to tell her dad what she wanted, even though he asked.

Having "wants" felt like complaining.

This wasn't the case for every holiday. She saw very little of her dad around her birthday or Father's Day, which she guessed was okay because, when he was around, he was morose or drunk. The energy he gave off, when he was like that, drove her out of the house until she needed sleep and then, hoped everything would be better in the morning…the energy made her feel like his nemesis.

When Bailey was four, at Easter, he bought her a preassembled Easter basket, an event that for many years after brought tears to her eyes at the memory.

When she was five, he bought her a grocery bag full of candy—she'd just started school and he figured she'd want to go trick-or-treating. The candy was to sate the desire to go door-to-door, to neighbors he didn't like, for treats he didn't trust. He said if she needed to get dressed up it was her concern, but she wasn't to talk to strangers and sure as hell wasn't going to take anything from anyone but him.

Jake Winterbrooke, seventeen, remembered a frightened blooming adolescent paying for a pack of maxi-pads with a one-hundred dollar bill. The change and receipt went into an envelope she licked and sealed before putting in her pocket. He said *he* was usually the one mortified when he had to ring up feminine stuff, but this once he felt worse for the one buying it.

Bailey left school, still trembling from the confrontation with Ms. Seles. All she wanted was to get home and rewrite the stupid paper so she could spend the rest of the weekend finishing the Richard Matheson collection she picked up at the thrift shop.

She hurried down the steps of the Middle School and turned left. Her scuffed tennis shoes crunched leaves between them and the clamshell white sidewalk. The phantom of a hopscotch game lay faintly on the last section of concrete before she changed direction and abandoned cement for tar.

She cut across Washington to take Poplar all the way up to the point where Washington and Veterans almost intersect. Her dad told her not to take Washington, it was too busy and there are too many strangers. Bailey never crossed her father—if he bothered to tell her something, she took it as having dire importance.

On her first day of school, "The Wall" walked her to and from. After that, he told her she should know how to do it on her own.

There were few alternate routes home, her dad didn't suggest any so she figured them out using the phonebook's map of Lanester and a small amount of "I wonder where this alley goes".

That day, Bailey picked the one nearest to water.

At almost a mile, this longest route took almost half an hour to walk home. Since she was kept after class to discuss the theme, she already had a late start getting home, but she thought a walk along Mill River would make her feel better.

The largely untamed vegetation, interesting rocks and trees were seductive enough, but the sound and smell of the water was addictively soothing and the primary reason she chose this way, as she almost always did.

The culture of mariners may be strong in most coastal cities, but it's not just in the air in Lanester, it's in the blood too. And while Bailey's family tree left more roots in Midwestern states, something in the water spoke to her—maybe it's being so close to the ocean and the possibilities hundreds of thousands of people saw in the endless reaches of such waters—an option to get far away.

Bailey walked on the shoulder of Poplar Street, pressing the leaves into the damp earth, leaving them flattened, clinging, and, she thought, very pretty. The pinxter flowers, she sadly found, had submitted to the colder autumn weather, leaving their man-sized bushes like dark sentinels, the majority gathered on either side of the bridge spanning Mill River.

On the other side of the guardrail, the tall beach grass swayed softly, vying to be stroked. A cluster of bluestem brushed her calf as, leaning against it, she slid along the matte gray metal, answering to the gently bade wishes to run a hand across the feather soft blades—like any child would.

A stiff breeze came up and a cascade of crispy gold and copper foliage poured across her path and with it an odor that turned her stomach.

Spinning on the bald heel of one dirty shoe, the girl sniffed and scoured without spotting a likely source of the smell.

All at once the tall swaying grasses looked threatening and concealing. The tall reaching trees that leant their beautiful leaves to be pressed under her feet were now twisted and ugly vessels offering only shadows and whatever their darkness and shape invoked.

What happened to the sun?

When the breeze came up a second time she caught the odor again, but fainter and struggled, at first, with turning around and going back or not. Bailey was seldom late and, though she liked to think her dad would worry, she didn't ever want to make him worry either.

Consumed with curiosity, Bailey decided, just this once, it would be okay. The odor wasn't completely unfamiliar, but never had she smelled the sour redolence of death so strongly.

No more than a block back in the opposite direction, she spied a small figure on the mudflat which water would completely cover when the tide came in. It looked like a doll was thrown out there and repeated to herself it could be nothing else. She even tried to get herself excited about the discarded toy, though she was well past playing with dolls.

Leaning her stomach on the guardrail, the girl swung her legs over first and rotated her body, like a helicopter propeller, and stood up when her feet were on the right side of the rail. She lost sight of the small pale figure as she negotiated a path down the bank, losing her footing once and spilling into the tall flowing grasses.

When she gathered herself and stood, she was so near the mudflat she could almost taste the wet earth when she breathed.

A cold, numbing feeling crept into her.

She decided to go back, but something deeper than consciousness overruled this and her growing horror.

When Bailey started across the flat, she began to doubt how far her legs would take her.

The smooth and dully shining mudflat stretched out before her apprehensive eyes. The distance, impossible, she suddenly felt.

Each labored step had to be consciously demanded. Her knees knocked together. She tried to only see the tiny pockets where clams lived. Tried to guess what kind of soda or beer was buried under the silver circle of aluminum glaring at her near the weak streaming water's edge.

Over and over she kept thinking of what her dad said when he saw her reluctance to do something—like walk to school when it was storming or go to school at all—so often that, rather than repeat himself, one morning with two feet of drifting snow piled up the opposite side of the front door she discovered a note taped to the door that read: "*Cogi qui potest nescit mori.*"

It would never be taken down.

Its meaning:

"She who can be forced has not learned how to die."

He knew she was learning Latin at church and even if it was a tongue in cheek way of showing how little he cared about faith and about her, before, like now, Bailey drew strength from it.

As terror mounted, she needed all the strength she could muster.

Then, it was over.

All at once, the scrawny twelve-year-old reached the sprawled and broken thing.

She almost wished she *had* fallen, farther back, and simply been unable to continue—this might have been the case if the *need* to get to it hadn't forced the skinny legs, that felt of little more than clay and water, to take each miserable step. The fortitude to cross, came not from the possibility there might be some wonderful if not foolishly discarded toy, but because, in the back of her mind, or even nearer to conscious thought, she needed to reach it because she knew it wasn't.

Bailey stooped to smack small crabs away from the graying blue flesh of the bloody little doll laying out in the plant silted mud bed.

There were little bites where small aquatic animals fed, but there were countless clotted puncture wounds all over the little doll's torso and what was left of the face.

The privates both on top and below were cut off, but years later she'd reflect on how little, if anything, could have possibly been to even cut from the little body's breast.

The fingers and toes were gone.

The lips and teeth were gone.

The water washed most of the blood away, leaving pale, colorless masses where the limbs and tissue should have been. Small skinless patches revealed little yellowish bubbles of the thin layer of fat that once protected the small person from cold and getting bumped around.

Bailey thought she might be able to figure out how to check for a pulse, but didn't. She was less afraid of touching the body than finding out that nothing could be done for this little person—a person only a few years younger than herself.

She wondered if she knew this boy or girl.

Only later, she remember wondering, as she stood on the verge of shock looking down on the cold and naked sexless child full of strange black holes and horrors, if they had known what they wanted to be when they grew up.

Tears welled up in her eyes. Stained with grass and dirtied by the fall, one hand moved to cover her mouth from whatever threatened to come up.

The first quality of justice people understand is fairness. Though never manifested in words or thoughts, Bailey felt in her whole being the injustice of this. She felt the offense to reason and the crime's abhorrence to normalcy.

She was overcome by a sense of its wrongness. It made her whole body hurt.

The whisper of water's ebb crawling nearer drove the fear-stiffened girl to act, but first Bailey knelt, touching the strange, waxy feeling skin of the dead child's upper arm and said to it, as near to the blackish ear as she dared, before running to call the police, "I'm going to help you. I promise."

1

...

PRIORITIES

Bailey paced her small apartment like a kenneled dog. Her blue-green eyes fixed on the little silver and black phone standing in its charger.

After almost a dozen consecutive calls to the same number, she decided to let it cool off and give them a chance to call back. Even though it had only been seven minutes and eighteen, nineteen, twenty seconds, she kept thinking the word "ridiculous" and applying it to the wait.

Outside was a night diluted by city lights. The steady sound of motors and occasional passersby talking loudly carried through the walls. The room's pale green walls would be eating the fluorescent yellow light from the post almost parallel to her bedroom window, if not for the heavy gray blackout curtains.

A Peeping Tom need only climb that post to look in on the pretty woman living there—who only changed clothes in the bathroom, where there were no windows, and never wore anything skimpy, because her mother—and the way her father despised her—made the attractive thirty-two-year-old conscientious of terms like slut, whore, bitch—if not for a curtain that never opened, a man or woman with such an inclination could surely steal a perve at the woman living there.

Bailey was only too aware that predators often use rituals and routines against their victims. They get a lot of that information just by looking through windows—like watching TV. Predators can see if your door is unlocked, or watch you enter your code. They can see when you lay down to sleep or go to have a shower—if you're alone. When they're not just a Peeping Tom, that's *all* they need to know.

Bailey was also aware that most major criminals start out as petty thieves, animal abusers or Peeping Toms… no one wants to be a victim of that person's first escalation.

Her experiences as a cop and, most recently as a detective, had nothing to do with, what some might describe as irrational fears, that *others* might describe as being overly cautious. Walter "The Wall" Douglass warned her, more than once and bluntly, of what can happen to "stupid women."

She didn't want to be stupid, not just because of the consequences, but her dad also told her, "Stupid women deserve *whatever* happens to them."

That also applied to stupid men.

And stupid animals.

And groups, organizations, and even countries that he believed were entirely stupid.

If Bailey hadn't already known better, several early criminal cases demonstrated the validity in taking extra precautions, because she saw what happened to people that hadn't.

It was a shame, she always thought and always meant. How one thing, that should mean almost nothing, ends up meaning the difference between that person seeing another day or not. One blind spot unchecked. One window unlocked. One simple online post that says "Gonna have the place all to myself this weekend!"

It was a shame.

Even though the light indicated the phone was working, the detective checked it anyway, again.

The dial tone sounded too loud against her ear and she checked to see if she'd turned it up accidently. She hadn't.

She thought about trying the cell phone, but what if he called back on it instead of the house phone and she was occupying the line.

Her left wrist came up in front of her, but it was bare. She'd taken the watch off half an hour ago after telling herself to stop looking at it. That didn't keep her from checking every other clock and then re-checking to make sure all of them showed the same time.

Her pace quickened.

Her heart was beginning to pound.

She imagined what she was going to say when he finally called back:

"Where have you been you bastard? Don't you check your messages? You've had me worried to death!"

But she couldn't really say any of that.

She could never call someone a bastard when her own mother ran out on her in the O.B. ward and she didn't have a paternal last name.

And, if her phone rang that meant that he obviously *had* checked his messages, because he would never miss her enough to call by merit of his own compulsion.

Finally, telling him she was worried would only start a chain reaction of berating and criticisms to deflect the affections he didn't want from her and certainly didn't want any pressure to return.

The tall-slender shape that moved to stand at the window was completely hidden through the curtains, but she wanted to feel the street outside as if that gave her some insight to where he might be or what he might be up to.

When Bailey Jacobs was on a tough case, getting out, going for walks, helped her feel open to possibilities she couldn't come to staring at evidence. It let her pay attention to her own instinct and intuition—which some people regarded as uncanny.

She didn't talk to a lot of people about her dad, because back home most people didn't want to. By the time she was in first grade, she'd already learned not to mention him.

Having very little that was hers except plenty of self-doubt, "The Wall" made up most of Bailey's world and so she had very little else to talk to other people about. If they didn't have something to say about her old man there were always those, besides her father, who tried to impress how much of herself she should be ashamed of and how little she was worth.

There was rarely a moment Bailey didn't feel like her father blamed her for her mom leaving. He never said, but for as long as she had memory, Bailey lived with the feeling she'd wronged him…

…so she'd never be able to blame him for the worry he was causing her by not calling.

Since she left Lanester to enroll in Boston University's criminal justice program, Walter Douglass's daughter had called home every Sunday night. This *wasn't* the first time he hadn't been home, but by the time she got back from school or work, Monday afternoon or evening there'd be a message from him—usually irritated that she would leave a message and then not even be home to be called back—it had been three days since Monday.

"The Wall" thought Bailey went into law enforcement as a last ditch effort to put herself in his good graces—the truth was that it started out as a last ditch effort to understand him and had morphed into an all but consuming career. She lied to herself about how much influence finding the murdered child had on these decisions, because if the detective allowed it to be a conscious part of her life, then she opened herself up to remembering what she'd whispered into the sand and water filled ear. Even though she'd brought help, Bailey always had the lingering feeling she'd lied and to a person unmatched in helplessness.

The case went cold roughly a year later. The only help that could be offered the slain never came.

Though no death on the news or papers, no fleeting mention of someone passed, or any murder Bailey later investigated failed to conjure memories of the unchampioned victim—the homicide detective told herself it had little, if nothing, to do with why she went into law enforcement.

Bailey believed in her work. It was the only time in her life when she felt she had purpose.

At college nobody stared at her for being "The Wall's" daughter, though her looks often earned second and third glances.

Though most thought it unlikely, Bailey Jacobs had grown into a striking woman, with hair that shone like copper, stalling blue-green eyes, and a sad mouth on a determined jaw that gave her lips a gentle, but perpetual pout.

She hadn't inherited any portion of her father's body type, or even her mother's, some said. Still others pointed out the impossibility that she should resemble "The Wall" at all.

Bailey was willowy and somewhat tall for a woman at five-foot-nine. Her hips were only slightly rounded and so was her bosom—which she was grateful for in her work, but not so when she was still in junior and high school and the only boys who showed interest were the ones who thought she'd be an easy score.

She watched them take off with the fat girls, the troubled girls, the ugly girls, and any girls who were naïve enough to think that something lasting could come from laying down for one of those pigs.

Her dad, perhaps seeing Bailey's transformation before others, informed her at fifteen:

"If you go to bed with a pig, don't be surprised when you end up covered in shit."

The heavy curtain swayed, when her elbow incidentally brushed it, as Bailey turned away. She switched off the heat to the scented wax and went to boil water for tea. She only bought one scent after finding one she liked. She was the same about perfumes too. She only wore *Curve Appeal*. Bailey didn't look around for new things to like once she found something that worked.

Sometimes police and detectives work cases like that—someone sets their mind on one suspect and likes them so much for the perpetrator that they stop looking at anyone else.

When something bad happens, there are two main types of cop people want to respond—that being:

One who always makes the right decision, takes risks that always work out and enforces justice with disregard for the bullshit that too often lets bad guys go and locks up the innocent—and the wisdom to know the difference. The cop vigilante who would get justice, no matter what. The *Dirty Harry* type.

The other is an earnest, hard-working, God-fearing, give-a-shitter with a careful conscience, common sense, and a little bit extra when it comes to instinct.

Bailey was the second kind.

She didn't think too much about the kind of cop she was, but grew up learning quickly how she didn't want to be.

The end justifies the means.

She'd called bullshit on that with a strong, "When?"

That policy makes for clumsy and ruthless business. When your business is people, there's no room for clumsy and ruthless.

And those cops who sniff out a possible perpetrator on gut instinct and hold to that theory 'til death do us part', so perhaps that they might boldly and arrogantly claim that he'd caught the prize fish on his first cast—"his gut told him he was right"—and for that, many innocent people go to jail or prison, lives are ruined after lives have already been ruined—it would be too shameful to throw the fish back and admit they were wrong…even though it obviously means letting a criminal run around freely.

Instinct is a tool—it doesn't promise anything factual.

If being born ruined her father's life, that was one too many lives ruined, to Bailey. So her investigations were painstakingly accurate. Her documentation, immaculate. The consequences of error to a victim's family and friends, society, and suspects' lives was ever present.

Ruling out to the point of utter certainty means never having to say you're sorry.

The silver teapot made a rough, grating sound when it skimmed over the black coiled element of the burner—the sound prickled across her scalp and made her teeth hurt to the point she had to rub them with her tongue.

On the green marbled laminate countertop she placed a bag of black pekoe tea and a spoon.

"Come on, dad," she murmured.

While waiting for the boil, she checked the magnet-backed Shopping and To-Do lists on the fridge. Both lists were short. She was going to need eggs again and bread. She needed to change the spring and seat on the bathroom sink's cold water.

She added "socks" to the shopping list. It was late August, soon it would get cold, and work was as hard on socks as it was on shoes, so she knew she'd be needing them soon.

Years ago, she'd thought, in the long run she'd actually save money by buying more expensive shoes, socks, underwear, winter clothes—that somehow cost implied better quality... the damn things wore out just as fast, if not faster in some cases.

When her pager went off, Bailey's first thought was a fire alarm in her apartment, which she didn't understand because she only heard the alarm when she tested them, but heard the pager incessantly, it sometimes seemed. Why had she thought the alarm first? Her gut response to the sound, this time, was "Trouble".

The pager was sitting beside her keys and badge wallet on the island dividing the kitchen from the living room and had vibrated itself dangerously close to the edge.

"Damn," she muttered as she read the number.

She turned off the stove—no point now.

The clamshell clip came off the freezer door handle and gathered the full length of long, penny-red hair in a tidy coil low on the back of her head.

The drawer nearest the end of the island rattled as she pulled it open. She took out her Beretta and pulled on a limp vest holster. Badge and cuffs went on one side of her belt, the pager on the other. She snatched up the cell phone in her left hand—the set of keys closed inside her right. Bailey went to the closet for her jacket.

Then, the phone rang.

She swore under her breath.

The pager was going off again.

"Goddamn it."

Ring. Ring. Ring.

She slung the coat over her elbow.

Beep-beep-beep-beep-beep!

She checked the pager.

RING! RING! RING!

The keys jingled like change as she stepped out into the gray and cream coordinated hall and locked the deadbolt and door. She could hear the phone's last ring interrupted when the caller hung up.

She pressed the cell phone to her ear and listened to it ring. It sounded too loud too.

"Nate here," said the man with the thick northeasterly accent that always made her miss home. To her, he always sounded like he was trying to talk around food. Her father's accent was similar but a little more Jersey, that being where she always suspected he'd spent a lot of his life, after leaving Michigan

"You paged me," she stated breathlessly as she sailed down the stairwell.

"What are you doing for dinner?"

"What?" she froze, stepping hard and unsteadily as she braked on the worn gray linoleum steps. Before momentum spilled her down the remainder of the flight, she grabbed the handrail that was, before this moment, too disgusting to touch.

A ringing sound quietly, but unignorably, permeated her head which whipped back to look over her shoulder, passing through countless layers of paint and drywall until her thoughts reached the small silver and black phone sitting quietly on the nightstand.

She had to sit down and she was surprised that, more than anger, tears were rising in her eyes and it made her feel stupid.

And she wanted to be angry.

"Bail?"

He heard her swallow, but couldn't hear the phone shaking in her hand.

"Hey, I was foolin'. I only asked because we have a mess out here and I need my partner. Just wanted to make sure you weren't planning on going home to sloppy joes after."

"That bad?" she asked, composed, while she worked on getting the rest of herself there. She was heading down the stairs again.

"Not really sure yet if it was punks doing a stupid stunt or vicious bastards with a creative flare."

"Okay. Where are you?"

"I'm on the scene, Bail. We're at the Beacon Park rail yard."

"Alright. I'm on my way."

"Hey—Bail?" he jumped in before the phone was far enough away that she wouldn't hear.

"Mm-hmm?"

"You okay, you sound funny?"

"*You're* telling *me* I sound funny?"

She could almost hear him smile, she never meant it to become a running joke or an insult. He was good natured about it, regardless of which.

"Yeah I am," her partner said.

"I didn't hear you laughing," she remarked dryly as she emerged onto the first floor hall of her apartment building.

"It doesn't make me feel like laughing," he told her.

"You took me off guard with your 'dinner' question."

Nate was silent for a moment before apologizing, "Maybe I should have *concluded* the conversation that way."

Silence answered. He heard the sucking sound of the heavy front door opening into the gusty evening air and her footsteps eating concrete as she rushed to her vehicle.

He was hesitant to finish his thought.

"But, you know, maybe sometime we—"

"I'm well out the door Nate, I'll be there ASAP."

"Sure, Bailey."

Nathaniel Treuer heard the line go dead and shoved the phone back into his pocket.

Stupid, he thought.

Bailey parked behind the CSU van and started across the long abandoned rail yard through the strobing lights of police and emergency vehicles.

She was surprised to see ambulances still there. There were no good conclusions to draw from that, even if they'd only just arrived too—she'd arrived in the shortest, safest amount of time possible—even that would've been a long wait for anyone needing emergency care.

A lean male figure, with carefully combed brown hair that never stayed tidy, separated from the people working on the other side of the yellow tape—the enclosed area was vast compared to most crime scenes she, or anyone, worked. In street clothes, he stood out from all the uniforms on site. Under a half-zipped cotton hoodie, he wore a dark tan t-shirt and deeply faded dark blue boot-cut jeans. Casual even for casual. Obviously having shared the impression Bailey had that the work day was over.

She stopped and made him breech the distance by merit of his own black oxfords.

"Jee-sus! I thought only my mother had the power to make a guy feel guilt just by making him come to her," he smiled a little as he reached his partner.

"Was it that or did you know you were going to be punished once you got to her?" Bailey walked past him. He turned automatically so they were walking together. He handed her a pair of sterling gray latex-free gloves.

His mouth bowed in a lazy, but agreeable smile while he nodded slowly, "Good point."

"So what are we dealing with here?"

"Well, the easy part is them two—" he pointed at the two ambulances with the fore and middle finger of his left hand, so his arm wouldn't go across his partner's face.

She looked over at Nate after seeing where he pointed.

"—see those guys in there are responsible whether this is manslaughter of premeditated. That's the good news. EMS is checking them out right now. Guy on the right said he just ran because he was scared, but the officer who was called to investigate the strange sounds down here had to take him down like a linebacker while his partner watched the other guy."

When they crossed the old railway ties Detective Treuer instinctively supported his partner's elbow, should she stumble. Bailey was familiar with these compulsive little acts of chivalry. She'd warned him once that the right wrong woman might call that sexual harassment, so he immediately stopped doing things like that until she later told him that she only wanted him to be aware of it. Bailey didn't tell Nate that, to her, she felt like he was being respectful not chauvinistic.

When the difference between those is lost and good intentions are punished, that is when good men stop telling their sons to treat women decently.

Rarely did her partner receive a "thank you" anymore, but he almost preferred it that way. This way it was treated just like part of his nature instead of an act that required thanks, which he found a little embarrassing, even before he got the sense Bailey Jacobs wasn't accustomed to being treated well or, perhaps, at all.

This time she thanked him, because the flashing lights and fallen night made negotiating the tracks a little more difficult. The limited number of work lights CSU sat up had to be picky about what they were going to illuminate in such a large area.

"Tell me what you saw," Bailey said.

That was something he'd heard her say a lot, to him, to suspects, witnesses, EMT's, whoever was at the scene before her—with little deviation in her wording.

She wanted Nate's first reactions and breakdown of the surroundings before too many conclusions were drawn from deeper investigation.

"When I pulled up there was one squad car and a guy in a maroon sedan who was a first responder, retired RN, who got the call through the fire department dispatch—and appeared to be treating one of the victims over on the far left. I could barely make him out over there, but his cream colored sweater drank up just enough light that he kinda glowed over there, where he squatted.

"The cops had two suspects handcuffed and sitting beside the squad car waiting for buses. The wrecked cars are as they were, over there, sandwiched, but the lights were still on. Over there—" he pointed to a small yellow tent card with a "1" on it, sitting near the edge of the police border "—that was where I found the boot shoe with a foot and half a shin still in it."

Nate lifted the police tape for Bailey and followed.

"There wasn't a significant amount of blood there. Just what was still cycling through what was left of the limb, yeah, but otherwise there was just spatter. I found more tissue as I walked in the direction of the wrecked cars," he pointed to another yellow card. "I saw fresh tire tracks over and under the blood."

With the back of his wrist, the detective rubbed at the stubble growing in on his jaw, then fell away to point in the direction of another card, "As I approached the vehicles I saw something pale over there. It was most of an arm—well, up to the elbow."

"What were they doing?" Bailey wanted to know as much as she wanted him to walk her through the scene.

"Like I said, there are two possibilities."

They were getting close to the wrecked cars.

One was a black Dodge Charger, the other was a dark blue Mitsubishi Outlander, but it was on the farther side of the accident and in too bad of shape for her to tell without circling around it.

The area around the mangled vehicles had recently been the site of much chaos. Any evidence in a six-foot parameter would have been disturbed or destroyed. Getting to the victims, should there be anything yet that may save them, was an obvious priority. She hoped Nate had seen the site before emergency people arrived.

The prints left by the firefighter's boots were an all too familiar mark of a crime scene. A lot of people don't realize how closely police and the firemen end up working together, at least initially. If someone is hurt, or could be hurt, they respond. If there is an accident, fire, someone unresponsive, left somewhere... even domestic disputes.

Bailey was not so far removed from her days with the police department—since she started working for the homicide department their presence was evanescent, if at all. Most the time, by the time the scene was turned over to homicide, the only evidence of the firefighter's presence was standing water and the tell-tale marks of their boots.

Four members of the Crime Scene Unit were combing over the wreckage, several more meandered the cordoned off area, occasionally stooping to pick up something, set up cards, or take pictures. The detectives and four CSU investigators at the wreck moved around each other consciously, while she was taken through the scene.

Near the mangled vehicles, the air was thick with the odor of engine fluids. Underneath it lay the smell of dirt and of blood.

"This door was open," Nate indicated the driver's side door. "The interior was—*is* clean, but smelled of alcohol."

Vodka, Bailey internally agreed.

"Came around the side and that's about when I could hear the first responder crying over there—" the detectives were close to the place Nate had pointed to from the other side of the yard "—I had thought he was treating somebody, until I came around the door. Then, I saw the boot shoe's partner hanging from little more than a tendon next to that bumper."

In order to get between the vehicles, the firemen forced the collided vehicles apart. From the depth of the crater in the front of the blue car, it almost looked like the Dodge made a strong attempt at driving right through it.

What was left of the fronts of either vehicles was clotted with bloody tissue, like someone had taken hundreds of pounds of red-velvet cake and packed it into the grill, bumper, broken lights, crimped hoods and engines. There were spatters and droplets of blood here and there on the walk over, but there was little else than blood before them.

"What do we know about the victims?" she asked Nate.

"White males, aged mid-twenties—they were able to recover the driver's licenses from the remains. They were tied horizontally across the front of the bumpers with their arms over their heads. Victim one, on the Outlander, Officer Collins thought he recognized a gang tattoo on the left side of his neck. The poor guy on the Charger was six-foot-five on a roughly six-foot, two-inch bumper."

Nate compulsively moved to fold his arms across his chest, but, remembering his gloves, stopped himself just in time, as usual.

"EMS did the best they could to separate one from the other," he added.

"Do you mind if I walk for a bit?" she asked.

He told her, "Be my guest."

There were times that Nate wished he was just a gawking bystander, hanging out to see "what happened", instead of being so completely occupied by responsibility. There was something fluid and android-like about the way his partner moved through a crime scene. Her narrow chin seemed solely responsible for the purposeful pivot of her head and direction of her gaze—the way she looked at points of interest seemed more like a diagnostic scan than even a studious observation. He felt like he could watch her all day.

Nate was leaning against his own car when Bailey finally returned to him. Officer Collins and his partner had taken the suspects to lock-up after the paramedics said they were okay. The ambulances left, so it was just detectives and forensics in the vast and considerably darker lot.

"Not too far from the collision the Dodge lost control—do you think they might have revised 'chicken' for hazing and accidently collided?" she was asking as soon as she knew he could hear her.

"That's what I meant by 'stupid stunt'," he answered with a shrug. He had taken his gloves off and his arms were crossed.

"The evidence supports it," Bailey sighed. "The vehicles appeared to have been in pretty decent shape—CSU didn't think the victims or suspects appeared to have really expensive clothes or jewelry—they probably didn't want to wreck those cars. The tracks, where they drifted at the end of the yard, because they turned so hard, and the dismembered foot and hand suggest that the vehicles made multiple passes—"

"—do you think the driver of the Outlander wouldn't have noticed if he clipped the poor bastard tied to that bumper?" her partner interrupted.

"Against a dark vehicle, at fast speeds, at night?" it was Bailey's turn to shrug. "I dunno. He *must* have screamed—did the person who reported the crash say anything about hearing any screaming?"

"The victims were tied up, but it doesn't look like they were gagged. Toxicology will tell us if those guys riding bumpers were wasted—they might have been unconscious. The fellas inside might have had their stereos up loud. But, the alternative is this—the drivers walk away from this deal with a few bruises and abrasions. Too many normal, average commuters don't buckle-up, but these punks did?"

His partner was nodding, "A limb or two gone might have just been a bonus on passes intended to terrify the victims before finishing them. Would appear to be a pretty costly way to kill someone."

"Unless it wasn't *their* loss. The cars weren't reported stolen, but it's late—the owners might not even be aware yet if they were. Hold on, let me check something…" Nate went back toward his car, flipping through his notepad with the thumb of the hand holding it—in the other, he was taking out his phone.

Bailey looked back at the braided vehicles. The volumes weren't up. They were turned all the way down, in fact. If she had to guess, they might have wanted to hear every one of their victim's cries. Other than blind rage, there was only one reason she could think of why people would think so little of demolishing those vehicles.

When she looked back at Detective Treuer, her chin brushing her right shoulder as she simultaneously stretched her collarbone and shoulders while finding him with her eyes. The bones crackled like crushed potato chips, but she felt a little less stiff when her shoulders sank.

She didn't like playing catch up and, at the moment, felt the only reason she was there was to verify the conclusions her partner already came to. He must have been really close by when the call came—especially because traffic was abhorrent. She also felt cheated out of an opportunity to learn, having only a fraction of Nate's experience in homicide. Treuer was brilliant. She aspired to be better—no—she felt she *needed* to be.

Detective Jacobs sighed as she drew her eyes away from the more experienced officer and lay them where they were needed most.

Bailey had no idea her partner sometimes resented playing second fiddle when she reached the stage first. If a crime scene were a dinner table, a person would swiftly starve on what she'd overlook.

Most of the time, while Nate was on the line, he was waiting and looking down at one open page in the pad. His eyebrows went up slightly and he cast a look over his shoulder at the woman waiting nearby.

Finally, he hung up and put away the phone before he turned around—he was shaking his head.

Bailey nodded ever so slightly as he said what she already expected:

"They were the victims' cars."

The desk lamp was starting to feel pretty hot by the time Bailey finished writing her report. Periodically throughout, she made calls or received them. An hour ago, Nate brought her an Irish cream cappuccino when he got sick of the stale brew left over in the department coffeemakers. He went to their favorite coffee shop, the same she went to after only weeks on the police force—since the coffee was good, she didn't go looking anywhere else.

The only time she drank cappuccino was when they were getting drinks at this particular shop, otherwise she took her coffee black. Nate drowned his in whipping cream and honey when it was available—if not, then it was any plain creamer and tons of sugar. Bailey always thought he was addicted to the effect of coffee, but didn't really like the taste of it. The job was probably responsible for that.

She imagined, when Nate first started, that everyone around him was guzzling it and started drinking it himself either as a way to fit in or someone suggested he start drinking it if he was going to last.

Bailey meant to ask him about it sometime, but guessed she probably never would. They'd been partners for almost five years—she saved most her questions for interrogations and didn't want him to feel like he was in one. She hadn't even asked where he was from. Asking questions is also an invitation to receive them and she didn't like to answer questions any more than she wanted to pry.

There were just a few i's to dot and t's to cross and she'd be able to stop. She was grateful. Most the time things don't go so smoothly, but the district attorney wasn't going to have any trouble making a case against the drivers, the only thing missing—

There was no time to react, once she noticed footsteps approaching her.

Suddenly a man's hand closed on the left side of the burgundy office chair's back and she stiffened. Something touched the back of her neck, just as Bailey caught the scent of aftershave and knew what was touching her were hoodie cords.

Her shoulders lowered and she was, otherwise, outwardly unstartled.

"I'm through with this till *mañana*. I don't suppose you're up for a hoagie before calling it a night?"

She sighed thoughtfully and let her pen drop to the legal pad underneath it. When she looked up, Nate smiled at how flushed the right side of her face was—he reached past her and shut off the desk lamp.

"Tanning?"

"I know…I need to move it somewhere else or use a lower wattage," she excused.

"So, wha'd'ya say?" he wanted to know.

"I'm waiting to hear back from Dan Hansen. He and Collins felt like they should be the ones to inform the families. He must have caught on to something when he was there because he told me he'd call back when he got a chance."

Nate nodded and leaned in until he was close enough so he could smell the fragrance of her shampoo, "He did.

"Well, actually, I called him when he was about to call you."

His presence fell back from her and when woman detective turned the chair to face him, he was leaning proudly against the end of the desk, with one hand on the desktop and other on his side. He was smiling ever so slightly.

When it was apparent she wasn't going to ask what he found out or even yell at him to just spit it out, Nate explained:

"We have a motive. I think the realm in which those rejects decided to murder was 'Let the punishment fit the crime.'"

"How's that?" Bailey asked immediately.

"The boys on the bumpers were lovers, Bail. About an hour and a half before the murders, the driver of the blue car and our victims had a few words in one of the south side pubs. Apparently, because there are bars for gays, he thought all the rest are, or should be, segregated. The bartender had said driver thrown out, but our victims were done with the joint and decide to leave minutes later. The rest, we know."

"How did the other driver get involved?" Bailey frowned.

"Apparently he was called by this outraged friend who asked him to cruise the area for a couple of fags on the lam. I've turned over my report to the DA. Is that all you were missing?"

She nodded and turned back to her desk, looking over the array of notes, officer's and EMS reports, suspect's statements, and files she'd pulled on the drivers. Having been deeply involved in the work, the disruption made returning to it disorienting.

"I guess that's the last of it."

"I know a place that makes incredible hoagies and they're open totally indecent hours, because of all these years feeding sailors and factory workers. I used to go there all the time when I lived by the docks. Interested?"

"I am hungry, but I need to get home. I was expecting a call."

"Why don't you check your messages?" Nate suggested. His face brightened, "I'll be right back."

When her partner was out of earshot, Bailey took out her cell phone. Fear and tension crawled up and coiled around her like tentacles as she punched buttons through the directions to reach her messages.

"Press '1' to play new messages. Press '2' to save mes—BEEP—" she heard herself tapping the desktop with the pen in her free hand.

"There are no new messages. To hear"—BEEP!

Her face dropped against the back of the hand holding the pen while her thumb found the sequence of numbers she knew by heart since she was four.

The phone pressed to her ear.

The ringing sounded louder still, underneath the synthesized tones she heard her heart beating, all else was the stuffy sound of deafness.

"Dad?!" she called into the mic.

His voice came on the line:

"If you don't leave a message then it wasn't important enough to call. Wait for the beep and tell me what the fuck is so important that you're bothering me."

BEEP!

"It's almost five am…where are you, dad?"

A tremble worked up her chin to her mouth. Jaw set and body stiffened to resist the inevitable. The drawing of a breath was denied, as if that was the deciding weakest link. The hot wetness of tears ran down her cheeks even before the sensation of them stung in her eyes.

When Nate returned, her chair was empty.

2

. . .

OBLIGATION

Bailey ignored the sound of the phone going off in her pocket. What little reserve of concentration she had was spent wholly on driving—the rest was being scattered and scrambled in the place of her mind where problems go to be solved.

Probably someone was murdered. Probably it was Nate or someone at the scene calling. Maybe something happened with one of her other cases. Even the possibility that her father may be calling was lost to the overwhelming sense of being late to save him—wholly expecting to whip into the driveway and pass her headlights over his still and crumpled body and the silhouette of the one responsible, still hunched from delivering the fatal blow. And, if she could get there a moment sooner, everything would be okay.

A headache was blooming between her eyes and she was crying so hard she could barely see.

I shouldn't be driving, she thought.

I can't stop.

There's no excuse for anyone to drive in this condition, blared an angry voice of common sense so far away in the back of her mind it was barely audible, like a dog-whistle.

It's different when it's you.

How fast would you drive to the hospital if you heard a loved one was in a horrible accident and is fading? When they tell you to come say your goodbyes?

How fast do you drive when you wake to a phone call in the middle of the night and your daughter or son is screaming for help—*HEEELP!*—because mom and dad's is the first and only number she or he can think to call?

How fast does one drive when the thing they fear most might have happened and there's an unignorable feeling in your gut that if you can *just get there* in a concrete, but undisclosed amount of time, that everything will be just fine?

You're going to kill somebody.

The small white Ford suddenly jerked onto the shoulder, raising angry horns from drivers who almost had to brake, even though she hadn't until she was all the way over.

A woman spilled out into the misting rain and the thump-thump of the slender black wipers slapping water from the windshield. Closing the door with her whole body, Bailey clung to the roof with one hand and buried her face in the crook of the other arm.

"Where are you?" her breath fogged the cool exterior of the car.

"Where are you!?!" she reeled on the night as though it were caught sneaking up on her.

A car laid on its horn as it switched lanes, motivating her to move to another side of the vehicle, even though she'd pulled over until her left wheels were off pavement and was nowhere near traffic.

Then she sat against the hood, collecting herself. She'd stopped crying. Breathing was just becoming regular when she started to think about every time, growing up, when she'd unlocked the front door and was afraid something would have happened to him. Afraid he would have a heart attack—staring at his sleeping form for the rise and fall of it breathing. Afraid of him falling in the tub and being too heavy to move himself or falling at all and being crushed under the weight of himself. Afraid for him when she went to school. Afraid that she'd wake up and be without him—forever. Thousands of days, nights, mornings of fear…because everyone in the world seemed to hate him, but her.

A wail burst from her mouth and raked her throat until it was raw. She screamed until the fists she clenched punched slender moon shaped slits in her palms. She screamed until her lungs felt as small as unfilled water balloons twisted by the ends in the fingers of a child.

The bumper drove itself roughly into her back as she slid onto the blacktop, pulling her knees up to her chest.

The headlights of the next passing vehicle lit up the sign for the off-ramp to Interstate 95.

You can't do this, she thought as she stared at it. In her heart the sign read "One Way" while the fear in her was chanting "tick-tock, tick-tock".

"Nobody's going to look for you, dad," her voice sounded pleading.

"They're going to notice you're gone without looking and they're not going to look when they know it—they're not going to report it," she heard anger thicken in her throat.

"Just so damn *stupid*!"

The ground on either side of her bottom was slowly illuminated as a vehicle pulled up behind her car. Amongst the blazing yellow light were the intermittent flashing of red and blue.

Through the pouring rain, the state patrol officer didn't hear her announce her position when he looked through the driver's side window, so he was surprised when the flashlight's beam caught the front of her face looking back at him from where she was sitting and now rising with her hands out and visible, but conscious to only appear that she was using them for balance.

"Ma'am? What are you doing down there?" the beam of light lit on her face again, then he was really looking at it.

"I was upset, I thought the rain would clear my head."

"You should have turned on your hazards," said the officer.

Bailey nodded regretfully.

"I need to see your license and registration."

"The registration is the glove compartment," she told him. "I don't want you to be surprised when I retrieve the license, because you're going to see a gun. I'm a cop."

They looked at each other quietly while the highway patrol considered this a second or two.

"Here's what I'm going to do, just keep your hands out like they are," the officer took out his own gun, "and I'm going to ask you to slowly remove your piece and set it on the ground in front of you and step away from it before you get me that license."

She followed his directions slowly, well aware that the other officer in the patrol car had removed himself from the vehicle when he saw his partner draw a weapon.

After studying Detective Jacobs' I.D. the patrolman asked her to follow him back to his car so he could call in and make sure she wasn't disgruntled or suspended.

"Would it be alright if you picked my gun off the ground?"

She kept her distance until the piece was in his hand and he was standing straight again, then followed him back to their state vehicle, and sat in the back while they made sure she wasn't dangerous.

After a few minutes he handed back the license and gun and apologized.

"Don't apologize for being safe. I understand."

"Are you alright?"

A line pressed between her eyebrows like an aftershock and fought back anything else that wanted to happen.

"Just had a rough day," she offered.

"Will you be okay to get where you're going?" he worried.

She shook her head.

The sky was turning a dull gray and in half an hour the sun would be rising.

"I think I'll just go home and do this when I'm feeling better."

"That sounds like the right idea," agreed the officer, who was able to itch his hairline from the back of his gray-blue patrol hat.

Concern of a different kind read across the older officer's face when the distressed woman transformed into a distressed detective. When Bailey looked at him, a man first impressions pegged as a kind and decent person, despite or because of this she saw someone who would not do the right thing for a man like Walter Douglass.

As Detective Jacobs slid dripping behind the wheel of the car, she caught a glimpse of herself in the mirror and averted her eyes like she could turn herself to stone.

She had responsibilities to the people of Boston and felt ashamed for abandoning them, if only for this short time, but in turning back, her reflection revealed someone who hadn't done the right thing for her father.

The only difference she saw between how her mother abandoned him and what she did now was that Bailey loved him.

And even that didn't stop her from doing it too.

*   *   *

Once collapsed exhaustedly into bed, she slept so deeply she didn't hear the phone ring.

When Bailey woke up, the sound of driving rain was rattling the windows. She smelled the rain in her clothes and hair and the phantom odor of new tar she remembered from the cracks patched on the interstate. Part of her expected to wake up in the ditch. Another part of her expected to wake up at home—*home* home, where she thought she was going to be last night. She imagined her dad asking what she was doing there. He'd ask her how a few missed calls justified a nearly forty mile drive in the butt-crack of dawn.

She wouldn't be able to answer.

She would want to, but never say, "I was just checking on you."

As much as she would never be able to ask:

Why don't I matter?
What did I do to you?
Do you hate me?
...
Then how come I feel like you don't?

The broad top seam of the flat sheet was balled in a fist under her chin, where she lay on her stomach staring dry eyed at nothing on the wall.

"Where are you dad?" she mumbled against the unmoving pressure of the hand beneath her jaw.

We have a motive…let the punishment fit the crime.

Thunder crashed almost overhead, the few dishes in the cupboard rattled. Bailey rattled.

When Bailey was seven she'd once walked past the church several blocks from their place and the priest happened to be sitting outside eating lunch and enjoying one of those days when the air, the breeze, and the light are just perfect.

She wasn't supposed to talk to strangers and later, when her dad asked how she ended up being talked into going to service, couldn't bring herself to tell him that she'd asked that man what people do "in *there*". And she asked what God is. The look on his face made her feel stupid and ashamed. He told her to come back next Sunday at nine and he'd tell her about Him then.

Of course, part of this was doing his job, but a greater part was because the priest knew who she was and felt bad for her, as plenty of people did. Over the next ten years the girl experienced an excessive sense of acceptance and support from the largely middle-aged and elderly attendants of the church.

Though it was never said outright, the congregation was concerned about what life was like living with the foul-mouthed, belligerent, godless bully. Because the child was a rail and the father was enormous meant he was starving her. Her quietness meant she was afraid. The uneasy way she accepted hugs goodbye, at the end of service, didn't come across as being unfamiliar with human contact—or that it was something her dad wouldn't want her to allow strangers to do—it meant he was abusive. Had they, along with almost everyone else who disliked him, not been so afraid of what he was capable of, social services would have been called. They always said they'd "be there if she needed them". A fat lot of good that would have done her if "The Wall" was any of those things.

She never understood how people who don't know anything always think they know everything. Or how they could feel bad for her, when she felt so bad for him. She felt bad he had *to be* him.

"It was no surprise when one day he couldn't be found," Bailey reflected, rolling on her back as her face pinched with worry. She was done with tears. How many were wasted on fears never founded?

The bed complained even as her small frame pushed itself up so she was sitting with her back against the pillows and headboard. Her eyes were flat and distant. Anyone who worked with Bailey knew she retreated to the farther reaches of her mind to process lots of information or to make big decisions carefully.

When at last she started moving, it began with the slow and slight motion of just nodding to herself. She was nodding to something apparent, but overlooked until that moment.

The homicide detective slid out of bed.

Lightning traced the outside of the windows and fought for room between the curtain panels as she stood there second guessing—not because she doubted herself, but because, even if the first answer is the correct one, you shouldn't believe it until you make yourself know it at least twice.

Why did she keep so distant from her colleagues—even those she sincerely liked? Why did she live so frugally—so immaterially? Why did her apartment look like a proxy—like it was just supposed to simulate someone living there?

"You knew you weren't going to stay."

Her damp shoes squished barely audibly as she crossed the almost perfectly dark apartment to the kitchen island where her laptop sat, largely neglected since college. In the back of her mind was a silenced voice remarking on wet shoes in the bedding.

Certainty felt cold and heavy like a blanket weighed with rocks and ice. Miserable. If this was truth she'd rather not know it, but it felt like truth, for now. It felt like someone she loved was on life support and the physician just told her the person's condition would never improve. It felt like accepting that kind of reality—one contrary to every want, hope, or dream. But inarguable.

The single foldable barstool was cool underneath her. She stared at the glossy black shell of the closed computer like it was a door to another world. She held the bottom of the laptop lightly as she pushed it open, wondering how to begin writing a request for transfer.

The screen cast an eerie glow across the otherwise unlit room, soon followed by the initially hesitant then rapid clicking of keys and, in the silence and storm, these sounded like the skittering of large bugs in the silent apartment.

Her lips formed words as they appeared on the screen—frowning deeply as she composed an appeal to leave the best place she had ever been. The proudest position realistically imaginable. If her subconscious had always known her stay in Boston was impermanent, she wished it had let her in on it before she got comfortable with her life and fell in love with her work. Simplicity had always felt normal for her surroundings—that in truth her "style" existed for easy escape would complement the unhappiness she almost always felt in Lanester.

She leaned back from the glaring screen, staring hard at what she'd written.

Never had she felt in Boston, the chronic doubt and sadness of living in Lanester. Never.

Her whole body constricted when the intercom buzzed, so much so that it took her longer than it should have to get up. Long enough for the person downstairs to buzz a second time.

She glanced at the microwave clock and was alarmed at the time and then alarmed that she couldn't remember if she had anywhere—like work—to be.

"Hello?"

"Buzz me in," she heard Nate say.

She considered asking him what he wanted or why he was there, but that would be treating him like a stranger—someone who might deserve distrust.

Déjà vu might not be strong enough to describe the force of memory or realization that struck her while she stood there at the door. She reeled around like someone catching a glimpse of something utterly terrifying pass through their peripheral vision.

She was in this exact position yesterday—and her phone had been ringing.

She depressed the "unlock" button with her thumb, giving her partner a few seconds to open the door, then went steadily toward the blinking red light in the other room. The "2" on the counter looked very bright in the very dark. Either blocking or ignoring the fact that she had checked for messages after she had to leave yesterday—a cruel part of her mind was saying one of the messages recorded was *the* missed call.

The sequence of dialing, listening, and finally entering the code to reach her voicemail again felt too long. The first message was only the click of a hang up. The second message said:

"Bail—Nate here. You need to call me. No, you need to *talk* to me. <long pause> Stop leaving me in the dark. <sigh> You know my number."

She didn't recognize the phone number that came up on the caller ID from the "hang-up".

At the door, Nate called her name before knocking.

"Bailey?" he repeated.

He listened to the deadbolts and chain lock moved, the light under the door came on only before it opened. Nate was, at first, just surprised to see her disheveled, but then also by the redness at her eyes and the worry in them—concern and empathy were almost always present, but not worry—at least nothing like this. This was despair.

"Where'd you go this morning?" he asked, dripping with rain.

"Go?" she was afraid whoever got the call from the state trooper, at the station, had called him after.

"I thought I'd talked you into conquering a couple hoagies?"

"Do you want some coffee?" she offered, stepping aside to give him space enough to come in.

His overcoat was dripping, so he gave it a stiff shake in the hall outside before hanging it up on the wall behind the open door. While it was raining generously, she doubted he got soaked racing between his car and the apartment building. So, she wondered, how many times did he change his mind and then change it again.

He'd gotten ready in a hurry, she noticed, because his watch was fastened too loose on his wrist. When time was of the essence, he fitted it to the first notch that took the buckle.

Then Bailey had her back to him. She'd tossed out the used filter and was filling a new one when he sat down at the kitchen table.

The other detective thought her movements seemed deliberately smooth, like a lapse in her concentration would be dangerous for the glass coffee pot—because if she wasn't trying so hard not to, her hands would be shaking.

Obviously, she deflected the question. Any detective, cop, crossing guard, or hall monitor would have caught that, but Nate felt particularly good at detecting a lie or refracted answer.

"You didn't call me back," he said.

"I only heard the message a second ago."

He felt she was being honest, but he also didn't think she would have called him back.

"Why'd you leave like that?"

The pot slid onto the burner and she clicked on the machine.

"I had to take care of something. I should have left a note, but it felt urgent at the time."

He studied her face as she slipped into the chair opposite him. He was bothered that she didn't look him in the eyes. She almost always looked away at some point, but she never altogether wouldn't look at him.

"It's late, did you sleep yet?" he asked her, but he was trying to look at the apartment.

Were there belongings askew or broken? Signs of someone else? Someone hiding? Someone scaring her? Signs something was troubling her besides what he read in her expression and movements.

His cousin, Marta, bought a new picture every time her husband put a hole in the wall...

"I did," she looked at him when she answered.

"Were you going to call me back?"

"Did you hear anything more from the DA?"

Nate slid back in the chair, his face tilted into the fingertips of the arm leaning on the rest.

"You know that's a done deal."

She nodded, more like remembering than agreeing.

The coffee was brewed enough that two cups could be poured. She put sugar on the table and placed the cream, she only used in tea, beside it before filling the cups.

"Is someone hurting you, Bailey?" he probed.

She sat down his coffee, it shook so slightly he wasn't sure if it was natural or a tremble.

"No."

Though carefully executed, that "no" didn't sound entirely true to the more experienced investigator.

"If the only way I'm going to get anywhere is by playing bad cop, I'll try it Bail. You look like twice-baked shit, partner. You go on a bender after work?"

The look she returned wasn't cast with dull or dreary eyes, but blue-green sparks of surprise and maybe a little anger or annoyance.

"Do you really think I'd do that?" she wanted to know.

"You knew you had the day off, how could I know? For all I know you get shit-faced every instance you get a chance, stuff yourself on humus, and walk shelter dogs in your favorite purple jumpsuit."

"Would I leave like that if it wasn't important?"

He threw up his hands, "How would I know, Bailey? In my world there's no proof you exist unless someone's been killed."

After a long silence she returned, "Have I ever done that before?"

"No," he answered after an extended delay of his own. "You don't give me much choice, but to be an asshole, ya know?"

Bailey frowned deeply as she looked back at him.

"You're not an asshole."

"Okay, but I'm not an idiot either. You *don't* just take off and it's obvious something is wrong."

"I never said nothing was wrong," she countered.

"Goddamn it, Bail, just—"

"I'll be right back," she promised as she stood abruptly.

He watched her leave the room, a skewed rectangle of light broke against the hall, and saw her silhouette swallowed by darkness and the sound of a closing door.

Bailey stared at the bathroom mirror and cursed herself for not using the time before Nate came up to see how bad she looked instead of wasting it on the answering machine.

Her hair was falling out of the almost tidy knot she'd made last night, when she left to respond to the pages. She looked pale—no, *pasty*—and like she'd almost literally cried her eyes out. The tissue around her eyes was puffy, shiny, and red against which her eyes look bioluminescent. The whites of her eyes were pink. Her sinuses felt heavy and full like the udders of a cow desperately needing milking. Even her lips were swollen and the feel of dried tears was like a film across her smooth cheeks. It had been a long time since she'd looked in the mirror and saw *this* Bailey.

No wonder he reacted the way he did...

She took out her hair, combed it, and assembled the lengths neatly at the base of her scalp.

After washing her face she filled a wash cloth with cold water and wrung it out before holding the cool square of cloth against it. The air she breathed through the fabric tasted cleaner than the air outside it. After a couple minutes Bailey thought she looked significantly better, but was unable to think of the right way to apologize for the worry so unnecessarily put on him.

When she emerged from the restroom Nate was standing on the living room side of the island, holding his coffee cup too low to possibly be considering drinking from it.

As soon as the bathroom door opened the handsome detective looked toward her. Then, as if just remembering he was holding it, put the cup on the counter. She could tell, from how he moved it, that it was still full, all but, perhaps, the few sips she'd seen him take at the kitchen table.

His upper lip curved the way children draw waves. Even when he was mad, it gave the slightest illusion of a smile which, at first, gave Bailey the impression that he was cocky. There was no such illusion at the moment and could have been no farther from smiling if he had no mouth at all.

"If it's something I did, just tell me, Bail."

Her glassy blue eyes flicked over to the open laptop practically in front of him.

"Nate…"

"Don't bullshit me—please. You're good at what you do. Whatever happened, don't let it drive you out of here. Is someone leaning on you? A perp?"

The woman in the hallway was little more than a mannequin, unmoving and unspeaking. She didn't like to answer questions about herself.

Her partner crossed the room, the concern in his face almost rivalled the strength of the guilt it incited. He reached out to hold her face, just to make her listen, but she recoiled ever-so-slightly that it stayed him, even if it didn't imply revulsion.

"Is someone threatening you?"

"No," she insisted.

"Then, Bailey, I don't understand…"

His gray-green eyes studied her as carefully, if not more, than he'd ever looked at a suspect or witness. It made a lot of sense to him that she should take off like that, look this way, or want to leave the department and or city, if a credible threat had been made. When a person goes up the river for murder, their life is pretty much ruined. People get mad at the police for that. Lawyers, judges, cops, witnesses are all subjected to the rage of the defendant's overzealous supporters.

"Do you have to?" she replied gently.

"You know what, I actually do."

They looked at each other for what seemed like a long time before she gave him something of an answer, because he really did deserve to know:

"I want to transfer to Essex County and work in Lanester, because I have family there. It looks like one of them is going to need a lot of my time and the only way that I can do that is to be there."

"Nah, Bailey it's like only forty minutes up the coast—I'll drive you there if that's the problem."

Bailey shook her head quickly, looked him straight in the eyes, but the "no" that came out had considerably less conviction. She just wanted to find her dad…she didn't want to talk about this.

"Nobody takes the time off they got coming—why don't you use some of them days, but don't kiss off the time you put in here, Bail. Take a leave of absence if you need one—or FMLA. You've got the stuff to make a career uh this. You really want to waste a master's up in Essex?"

"They don't murder each other up there?" Bailey slipped past him and went to close her laptop.

"Sure they do. Any horrible thing that anyone does to anybody anywhere is done *everywhere*."

The detective didn't feel like he could say he didn't want a new partner—you don't lay a guilt trip on someone you risk your life with every day. Nate felt closer to Bailey than almost anyone, even without knowing a lot about each other. Maybe it was because she was so respectful to him, to their work, and to people. Their understanding of how each other works a crime scene was verging on psychic. How couldn't he feel close to her? She was the best partner he ever had.

He felt like all he could do was throw up his hands. Her paperwork would show a clean service record, good record keeping, integrity, and a spotless disciplinary history, to say nothing of showing up with a master's in forensic psychology. They would bite, even if they didn't have room—they'd make it.

"You got friends and shit up there to help you out with this family stuff?" he sounded defeated and leaned back against the wall tiredly.

"Yeah," she answered.

Liar, he thought and sighed.

"You'll let me know when the transfer goes through if you need help moving or anything."

She didn't bother agreeing, they both knew she wouldn't do that.

Her partner moved to the door where he retrieved his coat and shrugged it on once his hands were in the sleeves.

His handsome eyes were clouded with mixed feelings and suppressed words he pinned with teeth over the insides of his lips. He felt a little mad and equally hurt. The only consolation he could think of was how he so often hoped he'd never see her wounded.

"See you tomorrow," Nate managed when he decided he should just leave.

Bailey listened to the sound of him move down the hall and stairwell. His steps sounded angry. She felt at a loss, but didn't see what else she could do.

It was her dad.

Sometimes it's just that simple.

3

. . .

HURRY UP and WAIT

Nate was right about how quickly the State Detectives Unit in Essex would make the transfer happen, though it felt like a long time to Bailey. The Missing Persons Department in Lanester didn't act so fast—just as she feared they might.

The morning of Nate's visit she filed a missing person's report with the Lanester Police Department. Their opinion was the same as Bailey's had always been—if a crime was involved, it could be anyone—though they'd never tell her so.

The first week she called every few days and once a week after that. Two weeks in, the response remained the same:

"Sorry Ms. Douglass," even though she introduced herself every time she called, "No one's at home. No one's seen anything. Give it time."

Bailey wanted to know if anyone had gone inside to check—a heart attack or fall seemed likely suspects for his sudden absence. She didn't want to be hasty and give up everything to find that he'd died naturally or by accident and was just inside the house, but if that wasn't the case she wanted permission to go, without altogether giving up her shield. The request gave her options, even if Nate looked at it as a done deal and she suffered the unshakable need to be in Lanester.

Missing Persons consoled her, told her they knew what they were doing, not to worry, and so on. Had they checked neighbors, places where he had accounts, airlines, buses, acquaintances…?

"Please don't worry, Ms. Douglass, we have it under control."

During the month and a half wait for transfer, there was still no word from her dad. Not a day passed without consideration toward making the trip home, but she knew it would raise more questions than answers. Until she could devote a reasonable amount of time to the investigation, it would be harder to go for just hours than to wait months. It seemed that every time she could no longer stand not knowing and not doing something herself, something urgent would come up at work. Doing the right thing by victims in Boston meant she had to sit by and count on Missing Persons do the right thing.

In every job there will be people you don't like, but of the officers serving Boston, Massachusetts— the overwhelming number were admirable, committed, give-a-damn'ers—maybe so much so that she gave credit to the Lanester PD they never earned.

At this point, Bailey was well beyond regretting the decision to trust her father's well-being to her home town. If the first two days are the most important in closing a case successfully—where would almost two months leave her? To say she was feeling guilty and stupid might parallel the understatement of comparing the Grand Canyon to a crack in a muffin top.

She knew she should have done more. How could she live with herself if something happened that could have been stopped earlier?

It was one week before she officially joined the Essex Detectives Unit and her last day in Boston Homicide. At the office there was a surprise sendoff.

Being her partner, Nate was told about the plans well ahead of time. He thought it would be embarrassing for Bailey. Everyone in the office knew everyone else, so they were well aware of how reserved the young detective was, but it didn't really matter. It's what you do for each other.

Sometimes it's just that simple.

Nate thought about not going—he didn't know if he could, but he didn't want to leave any hard feelings, just in case she came to her senses and backed out. He hoped the damage wasn't already done. After that night, her partner just couldn't pretend everything was normal. He'd be the first to admit he was being kind of a prick about it, but he wasn't happy and there wasn't a damn thing he could do about it, so it seemed natural to take his frustrations out on her.

At the going away party, Bailey *was* embarrassed by the attention, but was also moved by the festivities and laughter in the often heavy feeling office—it was also the first party she ever had.

For the most part, the quiet redhead sincerely liked and or admired her colleagues—it hurt to leave them and only more so by the thoughtfulness of recognizing her departure that—in many cases can be perceived as an obligatory gesture. She wasn't happy to leave them, if only this once, they knew it.

The office took a pool of money for birthdays, baby showers, and funerals to get a little something for the relevant person. When Bailey first started in the homicide unit, there was a birthday in the office and she was nervously approached by one of her co-workers to ask for the three dollars he said each person contributed. She thought it was the beginning of some kind of initiation and was waiting for someone to tell her she was stupid to fall for it.

The "Good Luck" and "We'll Miss You" balloons glared loudly as they swayed on their red and blue metallic lines over matching flowers. Around her, men and women whose joys and losses would thereafter pass without her quiet inclusion in the department's acknowledgement of either. She felt undeserving and a traitor.

She wanted to be there for those things—she spied the heavily pregnant belly of one clerk, who sat laughing and pushing her third piece of cake into her hormonally greedy mouth—an efficient worker and para-angelic human being. The lieutenant by the water cooler talking seriously to their captain—a veteran on the force who would retire in only seven months. She fixed her eyes on the young officer trying to be social while nursing the worry for a partner laid up in an ICU. She wanted to be there for them… and for everything else.

More than once she had to steal a private second to blot a determined tear and smiled through those she fought back. Nate wasn't surprised to see her sneak off when a few of the other detectives were called away and some others showed up who had been busy.

He also wasn't surprised to find her sitting in her cubicle, collecting herself while the flush slowly waned from her face, to come rushing back with full force, and then some, when she realized someone was there to see it.

"I won't tell nobody where you're hiding," he comforted and reached out for the second office chair, turning it the wrong way to sit down so he could fold his arms across the top of the back.

She nodded appreciatively.

"You come back to Boston, give me a call, okay? I still owe you that sandwich."

"Okay," she said with the same nod.

Her reply read flatly on his internal lie detector.

"Bail—I know why you're goin' to Lanester."

Her eyes lifted and met his.

"We got a missing persons notice and someone said it was your old man."

"Who would know that?" Bailey frowned deeply.

Nate was surprised by the question.

"Well, the captain knew who he was and he asked me how you were—I had no idea what he was talking about...I told him I bet that was why you were checking out—cap said the same thing I had, about you just taking time for it. Your desk hasn't been filled yet, Bail."

Her whole body trembled and she looked down.

"You're not going to be on his case, Bail, it's with Missing Persons—"

"It's a homicide," she put flatly.

"No doubt in your mind?"

She looked up at him again—she looked uncertain—probably because everyone reserves a degree of hope for people they love, even when there's no justification to. One thing was certain, Bailey was going to treat it like life or death.

He grabbed the edge of the desk and pulled his chair closer.

"I called up there to see what those folks are doing about it and they had a lot to say about your old man, Bailey—and it really doesn't look good.

The police have a million issues with him. The local no-goods have a million issues with him. There are Everyday Joes, just trying to live a life he seems hell bent on destroying. Instead of throwing all of this away, maybe you should accept that to most people the world is a better place without him."

The emotion in her eyes read hurt as clearly as if he'd raised it with his own hand.

"Do I have to accept what anyone believes if I don't?"

"You know, the captain didn't know Walter Douglass because they were old friends or something and he hasn't exactly got a huge fan club in Lanester—from the shit I heard in just a few minutes of blabbing and citing incidents, I can only imagine what he was like at home—how can you even care if he's dead?"

She leaned back in the chair, her glassy blue-green eyes suddenly hard and penetrating like lances when she responded stiffly, "If we only care when we like someone how can we even do this job?"

"We don't have to care to solve murders," he shrugged like it was obvious.

"Don't you think it helps?"

"*No.* It's logic. Forensics. Science and deduction."

"Maybe you should care because someone out there needs you to care."

He opened his hands and returned, "What if nobody misses them? Then who *needs* me to care?"

A personal injury read in her eyes.

Bailey tried twice before an answer came out.

"That's *never* true if we give a damn about our work. You haven't forgotten what that is, have you?"

"—and besides," she continued without letting Nate answer, "if that *were* true—then someone died or was killed and no one cared—if you realized that—how couldn't you feel for them?"

"It's not my job. I have to deal with the mess of people not caring, I'm not going to take home the guilt that should have been felt too."

Bailey stared at him blankly. He could feel frost forming between them—deadening her to him.

Why should I care about someone who won't care about anyone they don't know? Why do we need reason for empathy? he heard her voice or thoughts project almost accurately what she wouldn't say so couldn't add—*After all, I don't know you—I* really *don't know you and you sure as hell don't know me—not really—not at all.*

Bailey got up to leave. Nate didn't remember her being so tall. Her Pacific blue eyes were dark as the north Atlantic when she looked away.

"You're going to break yourself feeling that way," he warned her seriously.

"I'll take my chances," she muttered as she turned her back on him.

"I wouldn't do *that* for strangers either!" he retorted—he wasn't sure if he was going for a laugh or a winning attack.

She shot him a look of such grave disappointment that he was suddenly aware she wasn't going to waste any empathy on him.

After his partner of five years was out of sight and the door she passed through stood so still it'd no visible memory of her leaving, Nate was left struggling with his choices.

"Way to make it easy for her to go," he mumbled, then dropped his face into his hands and shook it, feeling helpless and stupid and unlikely to ever see his partner again.

4

...

A VICIOUS CYCLE

While Nate lay awake wondering if he should try to reach Bailey or not to apologize, she was driving down the same interstate where, not even two months earlier, she'd raced in desperation and fear to find her missing father.

With the radio off Bailey thought she could better recall people she knew despised her dad or had outright threatened to kill him, in the past, but when her thoughts were inundated with possibilities it started drifting back to what happened at the office.

Before things got out of hand, she'd decided to discuss some of it with the captain. She had no idea he knew her father and wondered if he'd known all along "The Wall" raised her. And if he, like the people at church, gave her too much credit and consideration because they had none for her dad. Captain Heintz apparently didn't have a very high opinion of the man, since Nate walked away from the conversation with those hastily forged opinions.

She tried to restrict her thoughts about Nate to who might be assigned as his partner and if she should have approached the situation with transferring differently, but she couldn't help but think about the things he said. He'd always struck her as a brilliant and well-meaning detective—one she was proud to be assigned to and grateful, because she thought she could learn a lot from him.

Disillusionment washed over her and it was all the detective could do not to reevaluate everything she remembered him saying about victims, perps, and anyone else for that matter.

Bailey knew that his behavior over the past seven weeks had everything to do with her leaving— it didn't hurt or anger her—she felt guilty. But she had no idea that he distanced himself so much from the victims—was it true, or was it just self-defensive? Lord knows, if you care, you are going to be hurt.

After twenty minutes of dwelling on, what was now inconsequential, she turned on the radio.

In twenty more minutes she'd be home.

She thought she'd just stay at her dad's while looking for a place of her own. It would give her a chance to start working on tracking him down.

There was always the possibility that he took off somewhere with a broad and had been shacked up for all these weeks. She remembered every so often there being strange women in their house when she got herself up for school. He stopped bringing them home when he assumed she was old enough to understand they were hookers—probably, this was much later than when she actually knew it.

Afterwards, her dad would occasionally leave for a day to bring them back where he found them.

Sometimes he took off for weeks to "Vegas" or "Reno" to gamble with his "pals".

She knew they never went to Vegas or Reno and he wasn't there to meet friends.

He bet on dog fights and played some cards, because he sometimes mentioned this on the phone. She overheard him book flights to Minneapolis, Detroit, Chicago and other places he always said were Reno or Vegas when he told her where he was going.

Maybe he got sick of telling her—that she was damn well old enough to have her own life, after he had spent about three decades trying to have his. Had he cut her off? Abandoned her? Run all the way to Puerto Rico, maybe he was in the Keys, Cancun, or Honolulu.

What would happen when he came home and realized his daughter had been through every inch of his house?

She was prepared to be angry about it too.

It had been a long time since she visited Lanester. Twice a year, at most, did she feel there was little he could say about her wanting to be there with him—not that it kept him from saying things about it. Like bitching about the commercialization of Christmas and that Thanksgiving had no meaning. Making jabs at how devotedly she'd attended church and the naiveté of people who believe there's anything but nothing after they die.

Fed up, she'd once almost responded that, with no better prospects than eternal damnation to look forward to, it's beneficial for assholes to vote for nothingness instead.

But even the idea of her father suffering what the priest described as Hell, made her more miserable than the berating.

Once her career was going well, Bailey brought Thanksgiving dinner from the same deli in Boston every year. She bought her dad a little something for

Christmas, usually a sweater or those "As Seen on TV" gadgets. Even though he said they were just a bunch of cheap crap imports, he actually did use them. Sometimes until they broke, which they usually did, because they were just cheap crap.

Bailey kept telling herself that one of these years she'd buy him a couple cases of his favorite regional beer and a bunch of really nasty skin magazines. Then he would have to keep his mouth shut, because he'd have nothing bad to say about that kind of present, or at least, it might take him a while to come up with something—he'd surely try.

When she pulled onto Washington Street, her childhood home was just a few doors down. The only one with no personality.

Some of the houses had solar lights, flowers, shrubs, a few statues, were littered with toys, seasonal décor or at least displayed an American flag. It's like the inhabitant of this one house had no interest in existing there.

The first thing the detective noticed when she pulled up was her dad's car in the small dirt driveway. She looked at the tan Oldsmobile sedan and could almost see the massive man squeeze out of it like a kiwi dropping an egg.

His size was frightening to most.

He looked fragile to Bailey.

When she was just starting out as a police officer, quite a few of the older officers remembered when her dad was a cop, decades earlier. They heard she was from Lanester and asked about him, when she nervously admitted he was her dad they apologized. He was not liked—he was a mean bastard. Everyone was scared of him, whether they knew him or not.

Why was that, she pondered. *What makes someone be such a piece of shit—even to people they don't know?* Especially *to people they don't know?*

People were intimidated by him.

That she didn't understand either.

Like Jabba the Hut, what could he do, other than bark and holler at someone—one swing and he would be too tired to take another.

Did no one else see this?

He was helpless.

Every step was labored. A gentle shove could knock him over and he'd be like a turtle with no legs. So his anger held no weight with her—except that it meant she was wrong again.

In the presence of his ill temper and long angry tirades, against whoever, she learned to be calm.

What else was there to do?

Every once and a while, for no reason apparent to his daughter, her dad would change the locks on the door, so Bailey was glad that last year's spare key still worked, and let herself in to a musty smell like a human kennel.

The door's familiar creak announced the daughter's return. The delayed light from her car's headlights, after turning it off, was the first and only light against the space little changed since her childhood. The spot on the rug, to the right of the door, where Bailey put her shoes, remained vacant.

The detective swallowed hard and stepped across the threshold.

Despite how crappy a human being he was and that no one knew him or wanted to, his daughter immediately recognized his absence, as she would anyone's—or any*thing* gone amiss.

She saw the coffee cup—a film on the surface, not from sitting long, though it had, but because the cup had not been cleaned in all its life. She took no pause at that, but the unfinished—and now grotesquely spoiled—breakfast was noted and totally unlike him.

Habits a person would never break. These were so important in knowing something was wrong and *how* wrong. How often she heard from witnesses, friends, and families, "They would *never...*"

Then the detective found out if the witness would really know if the person "would never".

"I know everything about you," Bailey murmured, like saying so would scare evidence to the surface, because she would find it anyway.

"Everything but where you are."

The daughter knew that the names and numbers in her dad's address book were coded so you would only ever find a contact's monograms in the phone number and the phone numbers were all hidden in the addresses. The "name" for that listing might be "Vet"—that would probably be his dogfight contact or perhaps the ex-S.E.A.L. who, when she was nine, told her how to restrain someone just by holding their hand a certain way.

Walter "The Wall" Douglass always put medicine in candy or breath mint containers, for convenience and for allowing the medicine to pick up the flavor.

Her dad preferred black girl on black girl videos, but was outwardly racist against almost every ethnicity, especially African Americans.

He puts chili powder in his mac and cheese. Saffron in his coffee.

The only odor that bothers him is foot odor and blows through hundred or hundreds of dollar shoes the way other people go through gallons of milk. Foot powders and sprays are for sissies. His left foot is slightly smaller than his right and the only shop in the world that he claims to make a comfortable belt is in Texas.

She knew that nine out of ten plastic bags, crammed into the one hanging on the coat hooks by the door, were from discount-dollar-marts, because the man was cheap—not out of obsessive frugality, but because he thought it gave him an image and he hated people too much "to waste his hard earned greenbacks on a bunch of no-good welfare junkies and thieving corporations."

Which was why one of the ten bags said Wal-mart or similar company, because "those sneaky bastards sell everything for one dollar when that's *ten cents* more than I can get it at so-and-so".

"The human race is nothing but a bunch of cannibals—" she remembered him say as she dropped down onto a kitchen chair that was turned out, the cushion sighed through an open seam.

She saw his porno mags and DVDs clustered beneath the living room couch.

"—one way or another," the words came out monotonous.

Bailey leaned heavily onto her fist, with her chin resting in the bowl her thumb and forefinger made.

It's breakfast time, that's nine or ten in the morning. He's eating, drinking coffee...

Bailey glanced over at the coffee pot. It was shut off and looked like only the unfinished cup, left sitting here, had been drained from the pot.

There's a knock at the door. If there was a phone call he wouldn't answer when he was eating...

His long dingy trench coat hung limply and forgotten on its hook two down from the plastic bags. It could be ninety degrees out or negative twenty and he'd still wear that jacket, she knew. The only time he went outside without it was to get the paper or yell at someone.

The paper would have been delivered before breakfast. It used to come around 7:15.

Bailey checked the date on the issue spread open on the kitchen table. It was the Friday paper from before her weekly call. If there had been piles of papers at the front of the house she would have noticed, so someone was taking them, or...

She quickly made some notes in the pad she always kept handy.

Bailey rose to look at the answering machine.

How many calls she made over the past weeks, she couldn't remember, but the count was maxed out at ninety-nine. Her dad didn't trust automatic bill pay, so she imagined some of the calls might have been from the utility companies.

She pushed down on the button to scroll through the list of missed calls. One of the last numbers on the caller ID was the same as the "hang-up" call. She stared at it, running a second scan through her mental databank and found the number wasn't even remotely familiar. Whoever it was called her less than a week after they called him.

The number might turn up again once she turned over the contents of the small building.

The private investigator's daughter started at one side of the house to the other, making mental notes of anything that seemed out of place or otherwise "not like dad". There was very, very little to raise concerns and she hoped that meant he really had just taken off on vacation somewhere. She'd find out tomorrow if he took a cab, paid his bills, had a mail hold, was hospitalized somewhere, and she'd visit with the neighbors to see if they remembered anything.

It seemed a plausible scenario, should he have planned to leave town, that the cab to the airport was late, and he'd decided to make himself breakfast. When the ride showed up in the middle of the meal, being angry, turning off the coffee pot, and exited thinking of little else than to lock the door behind him. Forgetting coat. Forgetting food left out.

Enough time had passed that the police, who were looking into his disappearance, should have been able to tell her, "Don't worry, we checked your dad's credit card and phone record—it looks like he's in Tahoe we can give you the number of the hotel." Missing Persons should have answers to everything she was about to look into herself, because most the answers would, one way or another, give away clues about her father's disappearance. If the police had answers, then she would have liked to know.

People count on the police to do the looking for them and Bailey hoped she'd never regret entrusting her father's life to other people…anymore than she already did.

She thought of what Nate said about not caring about people and she knew the police in Lanester weren't like that—they *weren't*—with *other* people.

Walter Douglass wasn't like other people.

Was any job or amount of money worth losing someone you care about? Was losing the respect of people she also liked and respected so important that you would forfeit your responsibility to someone when you know that something is wrong? Do you trust someone you love to people you don't trust?

"I should have just left," she smelt the odor of him waft out of the almost flat cushions when she sat on the smoke stained couch.

That stain marked where his armpit always hung over the arm. When he got up there would always be a damp spot. The threadbare portion of carpet was from his feet. Burn marks from cigars. Shriveled black nubs on the discolored carpet from where ashes landed. The dingy television and satellite remote with buttons polished spots at the power, play, and channel scrolling buttons.

That's the blood stain on the floor from where Bailey tripped and hit her face on the coffee table when she was four. She used warm water instead of cold to try and clean it. Her dad said that was wrong. Whenever she was cleaning up the house, it seemed like a good time to remind her—pointing at the brownish stain—that it was her that made it a mess.

But that spot, in front of the far left side of the couch, in front of the arm stained with sweat, below the matted and flattened cushions, was where he'd slid off the couch and held his handkerchief to the small bloody nose and told her, "If some stupid S.O.B. says you 'tip your head back' when you have a bloody nose, it's bullshit."

She remembered that the dark blue paisley cloth was crusty with snot and sharp against her face. And that his hand felt huge against the back of her head and the smell of the hand holding the handkerchief to her face was of Irish Spring soap, ketchup, and bacon grease.

Mostly, she remembered that she felt loved—she so very rarely did, that she remembered every detail of every instance when the weight of whatever contempt or hurt he felt that her mother left them was noticeably absent.

Sitting on the floor beside the counter, Bailey listened to every message on the machine. Her knees pulled up and arms held out like beams across them, holding her right thumb with her left hand as she waited for something unexpected to play. There were a few hang-ups and one call from the police department asking that he call them back as soon as possible, should he receive the message—this was a week and a half after she filed the missing person's report.

There were calls from utilities. A guy named "Al" called once to ask where the hell he was. He sounded drunk. Bailey remembered him as one of her dad's Detroit dogfight pals. He probably wanted advice or a loan—neither of which "The Wall" offered without conditions.

The detective was still awake when the sky turned gray with dawn. She made a fresh pot of coffee and sipped at only half a cup while making plans about collecting what evidence might still be there and who she was going to need to call or visit today, including looking for a place to rent or buy, because staying at home wasn't something she could plan to do long term.

When her dad came back, he wouldn't be happy about her going through everything and he made it seem like she wasn't welcome anyway. How violated would you feel to have someone unwelcome touch every single thing you own? Douglass relished his privacy—this wasn't going to improve father and daughter's relationship.

When she was growing up, Bailey was really confused by his coldness, because it seemed they were all each other had.

The door thumped solidly into its frame as Bailey closed it behind her. Any footprints or tire tracks would be long, long gone and a professional—the only person who would dare to do what so many people had threatened—would rap the door with his knuckles and would only put his hands on the victim, hands that would be gloved anyway.

She locked the door and pushed the screen door closed.

The only thing Bailey had in common with her dad was being tall—she stood five-foot nine while her father loomed over the majority at six-foot four. She tried to imagine how someone could overpower the man. Even at gunpoint she *knew* her dad wouldn't just go with someone.

The rule is: the next location is always worse.

You never submit because being on their terms obviously protects them, not you. A perp's going to take his victims somewhere he can do what he wants with them and dump them where they can't be found. If he wants to move you, then you are somewhere he's vulnerable, and you fight like your life is at stake—it most likely is.

There's no way her dad would be led away at gunpoint.

She thought it unlikely someone overpowered him—even though there was little he could do once he was on the ground, she'd like to see what it would take to move him once he was down, because he weighed more than six-hundred pounds.

Bailey was standing at the mailbox when the paperboy came down the street, whipping rolled newspapers in clear, construction orange bags, at subscribers' front doors. The skinny blonde, under baseball cap, stared at the stranger and strange white car parked where everybody knew everybody.

"Hi," she said as he came close and slowed down, even though he seemed like he was going to ride past and hadn't gotten a paper ready to throw.

"Hey," the kid answered.

"Isn't Walter Douglass still getting papers?" she poked the handful of mail at the house—she noted that the postmarks indicated mail that would have been sitting there for more than a month.

"Naw," the kid shook his head. "Cancelled his subscription."

"Do you know when?" Bailey leaned against the mailbox, thumbing through the top envelopes like it wasn't really important if he remembered or not.

"A long time ago. Like more than a month ago."

She could find out for certain at the newspaper.

"By any chance are you related to Alicia Mansfield?" the detective asked the boy with little stick legs poking out of knee length shorts.

"She's my mom," the boy said in a tone like Bailey should have known, but still asked her how she knew.

"You look like her," the detective thought.

"God, I hope not!"

Bailey smiled a little and thanked him for the information so not to keep him much longer and make anyone worry if they were used to him being one place or another by a specific time.

Alicia Mansfield grew up a couple blocks away and sometimes crossed paths with Bailey on the last bit of the walk to school.

The homicide detective knew so little of what became of her schoolmates, it was kind of nice to

know one of them was still around and making a life
for herself in Lanester. It made the place, she should
have been able to think of as home, feel less alien.

Even knowing the streets, trees, and even the
behavior of the water running on the streets after a
rain wouldn't remedy the feeling that she no longer
knew this place. It had the air of walking into a
ghost-town… or maybe she was the ghost.

Across the street, at the Mahoney's, not a lot had
changed since Bailey still lived at home. So little
that she was confident the Mahoney's still occupied
the residence. There was an offhand chance that they
could have moved out or were wintering somewhere
warmer, but there was barely a chance her dad
wouldn't have told her about it.

While he hated them for as long as she knew,
once grandchildren started spending afternoons
there, the family was intolerable.

On a personal level, Bailey appreciated that they
always said "hi" to her, when she was a kid. Their
kids seemed happy and well adjusted. The grandkids
spoiled to near ruination. They seemed like decent
people. It was little wonder then that her old man
should despise them.

The homicide detective crossed the road and
followed the circular stepping stones to the front
door. When nothing sounded after the doorbell was
depressed, she knocked.

Mrs. Mahoney heard the firm tapping from the
kitchen and crossed the living room to answer. The
sound made her heartbeat quicken. Something about

its assertiveness without pounding, sounding polite while being loud enough to reasonably assume someone inside would hear it. It was the knocking of a cop, or just coincidently reminded the sixty-six-year-old of the one horrible night when she'd answered the door to find a patrol car in the drive and an officer at the door.

When the heavy interior door swung wide, the grandmother was perplexed by the strong feeling of familiarity in the sweetly smiling redhead on the other side of the screen. Noting blouse, slacks, and jacket as bearing the most basic sense of selectivity and broader characteristics of practicality—Mabel Mahoney's first thought was saleswoman or low ranking government personnel.

This was probably a census interview.

"Good morning, Mrs. Mahoney. I hope I didn't wake you."

Mabel grinned like the stranger should have known she'd been awake for hours.

"No, that's fine. The best way to start the day is watching the sunrise, I've always felt."

The detective smiled politely and nodded.

"My name is Bailey Jacobs—" the old woman's eyes widened "—would you mind if I ask you a couple quick questions regarding your neighbor..."

Stop being a cop.

Bailey sighed.

"Have you seen my dad?"

Mrs. Mahoney had been hoping Douglass was on vacation and, God-willing, a long one. No, she hadn't seen him. Hadn't heard him yelling in or outside of the house.

"Is he missing?" she asked the girl who everyone thought left town and didn't look back.

"It's been a month and a half since I heard anything from him," she told the neighbor. "The police haven't asked you about it?"

Mabel shook her head and told her that her hubby would have mentioned something if he'd been asked anything about it either.

Bailey looked at her feet.

Once, when she was almost eight, it was January, she'd stood on this doorstep, staring at her shoes, and asked Mr. Mahoney if she could wait inside, because school was let out early for bad weather, she'd forgot her key, and it didn't look like her dad was home.

"Have you noticed any cars or people you don't recognize on or near the property over the past two months?"

"No dear, I'm sorry," Mabel answered.

I'm sorry too...

Bailey thanked her and returned to her father's place. It was a little early for door to door Q and A's, so she was grateful the Mahoney's, at least the missus, was an early bird.

In her notepad were three columns of numbers and abbreviated street names.

"804," she drew a line through the number. By noon she planned to be through this residential list and through the business/acquaintance list by nightfall. Was there a right time to confront Missing

Persons about lying, about negligence, about how suspicious it looked?

The front bumper of her car was cold and damp with dew when the detective settled on the edge of it. The air was brisk and refreshing, barely whitening her breath as she drank the fresh air to sooth troubled thoughts and try to stay a guilty conscience from charging her with too many wrongdoings.

People are people, with faults and virtues as astronomically varied as snowflakes. Police are just people too. Operating as wards of the law without failure or faltering is a lot to ask from people with free will, experiences, opinions, and stimuli to encourage deviance from black and white laws when people see most situations in gray. The law isn't personal, but run by persons, therefore it can't be a perfect machine. So Bailey tried not to be too angry that, after almost two months, no one had even questioned the neighbor right across the street. And she struggled not to wonder if the message left on her father's phone wasn't the sum of effort to recover the only family she knew.

When the cell phone rang, she was surprised she wasn't startled, because she was so deep in thought.

"Hello, this is Bailey," she said into the line. She moved the phone far enough away so she could see the number and then held it close again so she wouldn't miss one word.

"This is Officer Jack Mackinnon of the Lanester Police Department. I don't suppose you're here yet?" said the male voice on the other end—even though she knew it wasn't Nate by the phone number—when he first started talking, she expected it to be her partner. When the phone rang, it usually was.

"I am. Go ahead."

"Well, your timing is perfect, because we need you and we need you now," his voice sounded strained and urgent, like the "Code Blue" message over a hospital intercom, in a pediatric ward.

Bailey's brow pinched and she looked back at her childhood home the way she'd regarded the ringing phone in her apartment she couldn't answer.

In trying to keep her priorities straight, she closed her eyes and made herself say:

"Where do I need to be?"

5

. . .

A WALK in the DARK

The sex was cruel and, at last, over. The unseen man lay spent, somewhere in the dark. The stink of his desire and release filled the teen's nose and added itself to the myriad of foul memories she would have carried with her into old age if she were not about to die young.

She was grateful for the silence now, because when he stopped panting and grunting he'd flung himself off her and went berserk like a tornado in darkness, breaking things, trashing the dark room— she would never see—and howling and growling and roaring like a beast. She was sure that he would bite her and rip her to shreds.

She was, unfortunately, dead right.

The majority of tools used to mutilate her were apparent and long departed—it was clear, at least to

Bailey, that they had gone with the killer—because they were attached to him.

Fists, feet, long, unkempt nails and—

"Filed teeth," she muttered to herself.

The small breasts, so defiled, appeared at first to be wearing a strapless bra of red lace and netting.

The face would forever, until possibly total decay, be fixed in a look of horror by the atrocities done to it, up to and after the victim's last breath.

Among the injuries by bodily parts were an array of slashes and stabbings. Obviously some portions of skin were clawed or chewed off, but the damage to others was too clean to have been the work of anything but a knife. The blade could be no longer than her middle finger and, oddly, played a bigger part in torture than in the injuries directly responsible for the girl's death. The killer was the tool of killing, the knife was his toy…an appendage of his sadism. An extension of himself.

Gluttony kills more than the sword, they say. Was he trying to prove that? The crime was greedy and selfish, and the mutilation resounded of voracious hunger.

Bailey was calm, but not unmoved.

The girl's family and friends would grieve for her—it was Bailey's job to catch the killer and she was hopeful. He left enough DNA for a watertight conviction. That made her grateful.

What bothered the detective more than anything were the *other things* the killer did to the victim—things that lay like blocks of concrete on Bailey's shoulders and added a cold weight to her chest.

She felt like she already knew the victim, like she'd already been to the crime scene and *that* made it hard to remain composed.

The detective looked at the skinless, eyeless face, and felt herself standing on the mud bed, could almost smell the salt water and the cold, wet rot of a little broken doll.

There was a place in her mind shaking its head in refusal and another that was nodding and readying itself to make good on a promise never forgotten made.

"I need someone to get a coroner's report and find out if we have DNA on record for the October sixteenth of ninety-five, murder of Leia Redding," she told the nearest lingering officer.

When he looked at her dumbly, she told him she needed to know by the time she got to the office.

"What's that about?" asked the officer, Mackinnon, who looked about twelve of his twenty-one years.

"I just need to know if we're dealing with the same person."

The young officer looked incredulously at the bloody scene. The coroner arrived for the body and shoved past him like he was an old coat hanging from the ceiling.

"I was one year old in ninety-five," he mumbled.

"I need you to clear those guys out of here if they're just gawping," she told Mackinnon when he finally moved to do what she already asked. "The only people I want in here are taking pictures and collecting evidence."

"Sure thing, detective," the young man agreed and hurried to tell the older cops to leave.

Sometimes when things happen in small towns the police know the people involved and it's hard to just stand around and wait to arrest someone for hurting people in your home town, but when people are milling around because an exciting, horrifying something has happened—it resonates apathy and entertainment. There are no two things that have less business in the company of a tragedy than these two.

Bailey could see the inappropriate interest written all over the faces of the officers who hadn't already cleared the area. The others were upstairs or out on the lawn trying to cope with what they just found—or already made themselves get back to work because this wasn't the only crime that needed their time.

This wasn't the right foot to start out on with the remaining others. Their resentment laid plainly on their smug and scowling faces. What bothered Bailey most was that Officer Mackinnon had to work with these guys every day, and hoped the ramifications of following her orders would be light or nonexistent.

Afterward, the young officer went to see about the file on the Redding case and Bailey was left to work without distractions other than the crime scene investigators who, being so used to working around them, were no more disturbing than shadows.

Check Polke phone records for that cell phone number, she wrote into the margin of her notepad.

She considered this a moment and added a sub-note: *It's going to be untraceable, pay as you go.*

"What do you make of the killer's sloppy work?" Curtis, a twenty-something forensic technician with deceptively naïve looking dark-brown eyes and an easy smile, threw at the new detective offhandedly.

"I don't think it's sloppy," she decided after some reflection. "None of this means anything if he's not in the system—I wouldn't count on him being in it either—it's purposeful, like a message saying, 'This is who I am.' It's… contrived in arrogance. At some point in his life he probably felt overlooked, maybe still. The message also says, 'Not anymore.' Or maybe, 'Not again.'"

"You said you think this might have happened to someone before?" the tech further pressed.

Bailey avoided meeting his eyes while drawing up a pointed reply.

"It did, but this might be someone else's—"

Upstairs there was suddenly loud talking and a number of people greeting someone and everyone, at once, seemed to be trying to tell the new arrival what happened. The man who came in spoke in a booming voice and walked heavily through the house and down the stairs into the room where, seconds before, a camera's clicking made the most noise.

"So where's this detective?" he asked loudly.

Bailey looked over her shoulder at the "suit" who stood grinning on the last step of the basement stairs. The guy was tan, with dark hair, and unreasonably blue eyes. He was looking at six people, five of whom had CSU jackets on and one was a woman in a white and blue striped blouse and tan slacks. One of the investigators grunted, but no one else felt like they needed to answer.

"So, what'd'ya got for me?" the "suit" said loudly, even on the concrete basement floor sounding heavy when he stepped off of it. Bailey guessed he was muscular under that dark blue suit and, because he looked slender, wanted people to know that he wasn't a lightweight.

He grinned shamelessly at her as he crossed the room, being stopped once by CSU to keep him from walking through a space they were photographing.

"So, you're the girl from Boston, huh?"

Bailey straightened to face the man, an inch or two shorter than her, she wasn't smiling.

"So, I'm Detective Michael Stull, I just drove up from Salem."

"Are you taking over?" Bailey wanted to know.

"Assisting," he answered. "Not that it happens a lot, but I'm assigned to most the homicides in Lanester—" the technician grunted, "What murders?" "—I'm a Rockport boy. Anyway, this is your ballgame."

Bailey blinked, waiting for him to say something that mattered and trying to plan what she'd have to do or say if he didn't soon.

"So, what'd'ya know about this chick?"

The female detective swallowed hard and, at first, seemed like she wasn't going to answer him. Even though she was looking right at him, she somehow fixed her clear, intelligent eyes into the fissure where people feel they are being looked into instead of at. The look said she *was* going to answer, but he better be listening, because she wasn't going to repeat herself.

"*Erin Polke* was fifteen-years-old. This is her parent's house. They've been away since last Friday to see family out-of-town. She was last seen alive one week ago, at ten o'clock last Friday after watching movies with two of her friends. We haven't been able to reach her parents, who are probably on their way home now, because they were due back tonight. This isn't a party. If you want to go catch up with the boys you like to work with, then you need to head outside, because I just had them sent away."

The enormous smile on Stull's face flickered only long enough to attribute Bailey's coolness to feminine insecurity. She looked all of twenty-five, to him, and assumed she felt she needed to prove herself. He thought that was cute, but typical.

"So, you know I'm a detective too, right? I just wanted to know what the deal was so we can get after this guy—you were first, I'll give you credit for that, but it isn't necessary to be rude."

Bailey's eyebrows raised slightly.

She'd purposely and perfectly kept any disgust or impatience out of her voice and just told him how it is. This brought to mind one of her dad's few less vulgar adages, "If you stick your finger in someone's nose you're gonna get snot."

He should count himself lucky.

"So, you get a look at the body before they bussed it away?"

The female detective's bright, glassy eyes widened momentarily as she took in the ramifications of such a hasty, foolish act, she could only hope would never happen.

Bailey nodded and turned back to her work—if he wanted to play catch up, he would have to do it without interrupting her.

"The victim was dehydrated and didn't appear to have eaten for a while—maybe the whole week. She looked 'deflated' and there were no signs of meals prepared or eaten down here or in the kitchen. The sinks were dry and the dishwasher still had the unwashed plates and cups from the pizza she and her friend ordered last Friday. There was still pepperoni on one of the plates and both the cups had tinted lip gloss on them. There was also food waste in the garbage inside or in the dumpster outside—though it had been sitting empty, presumably since it was picked up this Wednesday.

"The dryness of the fecal matter in the ice-cream pail in the corner suggests it has been a couple days since she's had a movement and while there is urine in the pail too, it's pretty stagnant, more so than the urine on herself and in the blankets.

"There are signs, however, that our perp used the bathroom upstairs. He also came and went from the property multiple times—"

"How do you know that?" Detective Stull interrupted.

"Because his boot prints make several different entry and exit paths, bringing in different sediment at differing levels of moisture. For example, I was told it rained once this week. There is a set of tracks that show his comings and goings that day, over tracks he made before that and under later tracks. One of the EMT's found the boot print in three locations in the yard. Twice in the bare spot between the driveway and the front door. You can tell it gets muddy when there's rain. There's a clear impression there as well as disturbances by the same boots when it was dry.

"We know it's the killer's tracks, because he walked through her blood on several different occasions."

Michael Stull looked over the blood spattered basement and tried to make sense of the madness—if no one had said otherwise he'd have presumed there had to be multiple victims.

"That's no smoking gun," he said, putting his hands on his sides. His jaw jutted out as he scoured the mess. "Give me some good news."

"Shoe prints convict people all the time," Bailey returned, a little surprised he didn't think of *that* as good news. "And, in this case, there are a few imperfections in the treads that will help to distinguish these between others of the same brand and style.

"We have no shortage of smoking guns, in fact, the average firing squad doesn't have as many as were left at this crime scene."

"How many gunmen are in a firing squad?" Curtis, the crime scene investigator, asked as he bowed to pick some hairs out of a seam in one of the basement's supporting beams.

"Umm, usually five, but sometimes as few as three," Bailey answered. "Can I get you to bring the guy with the camera over here? There's a pretty clear handprint right there."

"Sure. And that's Alex if you ever need to yell for him."

Bailey thanked Curtis and moved to the opposite side of the print so the photographer wouldn't have to work around her. She measured and documented it before Alex made it over.

"So, what were you saying about smoking guns?" said the detective with Rockport blood, but a Jersey mouth.

She wanted to tell Detective Stull she'd just send him a copy of the report when it was finished, but she wasn't sure how much she was going to have to work with him and, thinking about young Officer Mackinnon, decided to be tentative with dismissing him, no matter how much she wanted to.

"We have bite patterns, multiple hair samples, including public hairs, saliva, semen, fingerprints, shoeprints, footprints, handprints—" she gestured toward the almost perfectly unblemished print on the tan "river rock" concrete painted floor.

"Detective Jacobs, do you have a minute that I can show you something?" said the lower half of a body partially descended on the stairs.

The copper-haired woman made a quick note on a pad and excused herself without any indication she wanted Michael to follow, but he was already behind—he intended to be onboard when anything new came up.

One of the Lanester policemen was waiting on the stairs and when Bailey was close enough to follow, he started away. The forty-something officer looked anxious or impatient and she wasn't sure why until he led her back outside and saw how many people were milling around, apparently exactly where he didn't want people to be, because when he yelled at them to back off he used expletives she thought only her father would dare use in public.

He was still cursing, but under his breath, when she reached the patch of yard where he was waiting.

"It might be hard to tell now, but when we first got here I thought I saw something funny in the yard and then was pretty damn sure what it was when I went into the backyard, where the property touches the dirt alley where—" then in strong language he described the kind of people who walk on evidence "—took it upon themselves to wander like dumbass cattle around the property where a *fucking murder took place!*"

"What evidence?" Bailey encouraged him to just continue.

"I just got back from checking the victim's shoes and it looks like he walked her all around the yard. Her tracks and his tracks in tandem across the front yard and *all over* in the back."

"I like to roll that way too," Detective Stull butted in, missing all but some of the last sentence.

Then the middle-aged officer with red hair, now dulled by gray and white strands, that once blazed like hot metal, turned his disapproval on the still smiling Salem detective.

Bailey barely listened, as she moved away from the argument blooming behind her—it had, apparently, been a good idea not to tell Michael what he really needed to hear, because he didn't appreciate it coming from, what she heard him describe as, a "two-for-a-dollar beat-cop".

The angry older officer was absolutely right about what he thought he saw, not that Bailey doubted his instincts. Clearly, from the multitude of old and new tracks, the alley was a popular way for locals to get around. Unfortunately, the alley hadn't ever seen as much traffic at once as it had that day, and it was hard to make out the full route of what appeared to be an aimless journey.

"What do you make of it?"

The older cop was suddenly with her, she heard Stull talking loudly in the front yard and prayed this would be the last time she'd ever share a crime scene with him.

"I'm not sure..." she admitted, shaking her head as she squatted for a bug's eye view of the yard and the scrambled tracks.

Under the ugly smell of idling vehicles lay the clean smell of grass, earth, and rain. Down here, on their terms, the five-year homicide detective hoped for passive participation in the investigation.

Nature—by any terminology—in one school of thought, at least, begins neutral. When it is acted upon it is moved to react. Bailey, like most investigators, count on that because, more often than not, science can explain why the person, element, plant, and so on, reacted like it did.

There was an explanation to the aimless wandering—she just had to see and understand it. The good thing with police work is that it rarely falls on one person to come up with the reason.

"You caught mine, I didn't catch your name," Bailey said to the officer who'd wandered to look at some of the nearby impressions in the grass.

"John Winston. Do people always call you by your first name?"

"Mm-hmm."

"D—"

"Officer Winston," Bailey stood suddenly, panning her head from the alley and across the small house and tight yard, "Was she gagged?"

"Well, you saw the body—"

"Yes, but I'd like to know your opinion."

"Well," Winston began, "she wasn't, but it didn't look like she hadn't ever been. Maybe just sometimes."

The detective was nodding with her eyes closed, sorting through the info and filing it neatly into a scenario that would, at least temporarily, serve the situation.

"The firemen who first arrived reported that the neighbors who came over said they hadn't seen any vehicles, familiar or otherwise, in the driveway or the alley. So unless our killer was dropped off, he probably hoofed his way over and would have a hell of a time trying to transport the victim to a prepared location—or any other location.

"I think he covered her eyes and maybe even plugged her ears and walked her around and around this yard to disorient her before returning her to her own house and keeping her prisoner for a week in a 'strange' basement where he removed all the lights."

The officer shrugged, "What would be the point?"

Bailey regarded the neighboring houses, nearly all of them donning the silhouettes of their residents—looking horrified and confused at the commotion in the next yard. The detective's gaze landed on the older officer along with an answer:

"Because I could close a cupboard hard in that kitchen and the neighbors would hear it. *He couldn't move her,* because she would be missed—by friends and or parents checking up on their teenage daughter. I'm guessing we're going to find any number of dismissive and cheerful texted replies to calls that weren't answered. He probably made Erin think he *had* taken her somewhere, impressing the 'fact' that there was no one around so she needn't bother screaming. Why else wander around with her—for what, probably hours?"

"And probably hours when everyone else in the world would be sleeping," the officer thought.

"He forced his way into the house somewhere— we need to find out where– we know he didn't knock on the door, because when everyone else in the world is sleeping, it's that much quieter, and someone would have heard. The killer would have had to assume he was going to wake her up too. Will you find out if someone found signs of a forced entry?"

"Yeah," Officer Winston agreed and returned to talk shop with the cops who'd been handed their asses not too long before.

When Bailey looked at the house, it wasn't there, or she wasn't. Instead she saw Leia Redding sleeping soundly in the night and heard the sound of a window climbing its rubber lined tracks until it was open enough for a man to climb in. The detective smelled the odor of him waft in like a cloud of dust raising from the impact of his boots on the clean rose-pink carpet.

Dark with filth and shadow, the intruder stooped over the slumbering girl.

Bailey Jacobs may have been here in a thousand dreams—wondering what happened to that poor brutalized child—but she could not make herself remember nor accept the fact that this time *she was not sleeping.*

Helpless, voiceless, the woman watched the event unfold in half-speed.

Wake up, wake up!

I am *awake!*

When the blankets pulled back, it was no healthy sleeping child, but one horrifically mutilated...

In the hours when everyone else in the world is sleeping, it would be easy for a man to move a nine-year-old anywhere he wanted to go without much risk of being seen.

Most of the time when Bailey thought of the dead little girl, she is not silent or dead, but fighting against the man and crying to be saved. The vision left the homicide detective to wonder if a single cry was ever uttered and Leia Redding's only cry for help lay in the toothless, lipless cavern of a blood choked throat and twelve-year-old Bailey's ears.

The neighbors on the opposite side of the alley watched Officer Winston leave the woman standing alone in the backyard—she looked like she needed time to herself, concluding from her actions that whatever happened at the Polke's was horrible.

The hand that flew to the detective's mouth, arrived with enough speed that it hurt her lips and teeth when it connected with her face. There was a sound in her throat that would never reach her ears, and tears smarted in eyes that wouldn't shed them. Her left hand landed gently to help hold the face of a woman trying to drive out a vision whose visit is not unlike that of a demon or nightmare.

Before this murder, Bailey knew little more than the state the child was left in—she couldn't have imagined the agony the little girl knew before being dumped on a mudflat.

Don't worry. Don't worry. Don't worry.
It might not be the same man.
The homicide detective shuddered involuntarily.
You know it is.
Bailey moaned in frustration as she fought to keep the blanket from pulling back.

I'm going to help you this time.

She let out a breath, closed fists in both hands and lowered them beside her gently rounded hips. She felt like she would look up and be facing down the abomination who pulled back the blanket, again and again...

I'm going to help both of you.

She looked at the house stonily, even as the last tremors of fear died out.

How can you help someone already slain?

Bailey clamped her lips inside her teeth, setting her jaw with determination that mingled with disgust and anger—in a position suddenly to do what her twelve-year-old self was helpless to do or even understand—no one murdered is beyond all help.

She took a deep breath and let the cold air out across lips that felt swollen from her hand and pinning them between her teeth.

"How do you help someone already slain?"

You catch the killer.

There was enough proof to lock this monster up forever, if they ever got their hands on him.

He could be one of two things: brazen or stupid, to have left so much evidence at the scene.

Being either, he *would* make a mistake.

6

...

UNSETTLED

It was late when Bailey arrived at the Lanester Police Department. The strength of the sun was limited to underlining the dark rain clouds coming down from the Northeast. The air smelled of rain and was heavy. The humidity gave it a drinkable quality. Stepping out in it triggered sweat instantly, the kind that creeps down the topography of your flesh and demands blotting.

On the steps of the department's building, Bailey felt like an outsider. Since she was an adult she'd never went into a justice department of any kind without feeling like she was going to work. It had been more than ten years since she felt like a civilian and not a cop, but that's exactly how she felt in that moment. She felt stripped of power and purpose as she climbed toward the architecturally profound structure.

When she put her hand on the bar to enter, she felt like she might have made a mistake. She didn't know anyone or where to go. She sent people to bring information to a desk she'd never seen. The worst thing, perhaps, was that she would have to face people who didn't seem to be doing anything to try and find her father.

On the surface of these conflicting feelings was the still pounding heartbeat of the fallout from the victim's parent's arrival on the scene.

When someone suggested to Bailey that a local should inform the Polke's, the detective agreed and hoped the officer actually knew the family personally—from some of the officer's reactions, she thought maybe a few did.

The person who told them what horrors happened in their house while they were on vacation turned out to be one of the officers she'd dismissed from the scene. He jumped all over them before anyone had a chance to break the news with candor.

They were finishing up downstairs when Bailey heard the parents out on the front lawn, loudly demanding to know what happened and fearing the worst, because that's what people do when they see flashing lights, police cars, an ambulance, fire trucks, police tape, people sobbing.

No way could their version of the worst possible horror match the actual nightmare, because normal people's minds don't come up with things like this. The problem now lay with finding the mind that did.

And file a report against the owner of the mouth that told her parents, "Your daughter was sexually assaulted and tortured for a week before we found her vivisected."

For sake of getting off on the right foot, she hoped she wouldn't be the only one filing such a complaint, but on the other hand, could really care less. Her opinion of the Lanester Police Department could barely sink lower.

When the internal air of the police station washed over Bailey as the door swung wide, she was simultaneously struck by the scent of familiar cologne.

"Detective Stull," she nodded as she slipped past the man who didn't even pretend that moving out of the way was an option.

"So, it's going to be a long night," he mentioned, as he watched the attractive stranger pass by.

Bailey looked at him expectantly, his tone didn't suggest small talk and he didn't sound like he was stating the obvious, which he was, but there was something else, maybe obvious only to him, that Bailey was left out of.

"Have you spoke to the DA?" she asked.

"No time," he grinned hugely. "So, you go ahead and file the paperwork on the dead girl. She's all yours."

"Okay."

Detective Jacobs thought that was already decided.

"Don't you even want to know?" he pressed when she started down the foyer again.

She assumed, "Someone died."

He watched her enter the building through a second set of doors and proceed to the front desk.

Michael Stull wasn't grinning. While he could usually think and grin at the same time, in this instance he couldn't, because he couldn't decide what to think about the new detective.

All he knew was what the cops out in the yard were saying—she was a "big city hot shot" telling men, who'd been in the business for as long as she'd been alive, how to do their jobs. Detective Stull could have openly shrugged at this. More than once he got attitude when clearing a crime scene, but that's what you do when you're in charge.

When Bailey was led to her desk in the Detectives Division, she found it inundated with files and inter-office mail envelopes with forms she needed to fill out for life insurance and other job related paperwork.

None of her superiors were at the office or the first thing she would have done was report to them. She hadn't expected to work until the following Monday. The detective assumed she'd have to come in the next day and at least get the paperwork taken care of—something else she thought she'd have time to do before her job "officially" started.

The file she asked the young officer for was resting on the very zenith of the mountain—where it made sense to be, if there at all.

The expanding file was old and the paper was starting to develop the feel of soft fabric from being touched so often, at one time. After the case went cold, she wondered if any of the detectives, who so badly wanted it solved, had ever returned to it in hope that something would reveal itself and a possible identity of the killer. This has been known to happen.

Probably few of the people who worked Leia Redding's case were in service any more. If she didn't find the answers she needed in the file or evidence box she'd have to see what they remembered.

Which was probably a lot, Bailey imagined.

It wasn't a murder they were likely to forget—as she knew, all too well.

The crime scene photos were tucked in the back of Leia's file. Grateful, her immediate inclination was how unnecessary it was for her to view the scene again—that it was still clear in her mind, but a lot of people think that and are completely wrong. A lot of people talk themselves into entirely new realities and identities. If memories can become unclear or distorted, then a twelve-year-old discovering a mutilated corpse may naturally or intentionally transform her memory of the event.

Drawing up the first section of the file, the lead investigator's report, Bailey's hands trembled as she reopened a wound that, until then, remained raw and infected.

Silently her lips formed words as she processed the detailed minutiae, comparing it to her memories of the scene and filling in many of the blanks of her dated assumptions based on those memories.

Among the witness statements she found her own and could barely stand to read it.

As she poured through the case file, there were certainly things Bailey hadn't realized at the time.

There were ligature marks and also bite marks that were attributed to scavengers though, by their description—to say nothing of Erin Polke's injuries—she wondered if they were not the filed teeth of a *homosapien*.

The actual location where Leia Redding was murdered was never discovered and the fluids collected from her body were inconclusive after the prolonged exposure to salt water.

It would have been nice to be able to compare the DNA from both murders, just to rule out the slim possibility these were the work of two different men.

The handiwork, as far as the detective could tell, without reviewing the photographs, was identical. Only in horror movie sequels does a unique M.O. get exploited over and over again by different individuals who are either nut-ball copycats or apprentices to the original.

This was the same guy.

If DNA said differently she'd ask it to be retested. Maybe the idea that more than one person would be capable of doing what was done to these girls was too much for Bailey to accept. Though she was never in denial about any of the horrors she'd seen people do to each other before.

The list of leads was short—brief interviews that technically ended after only a few questions. Documents that supported the people's alibi's looked carefully drawn.

They were really serious about finding him, she acknowledged sadly. Sad for the family and friends, the investigating officers, and for Walter Douglass whose disappearance or death seemed insignificant.

She returned the file to the top of the stack and hand wrote the report on Erin Polke's murder, as she wasn't assigned a log-in for the computer. There are gains and drawbacks to almost everything, no matter how horrible, regardless of how wonderful. There really wasn't anything for witness statements to address—for that, her hands were grateful. The drawback, there really weren't any witnesses. What they got was a whole lot of neighbors who said they saw and heard nothing.

She pressed an adhesive note to the face of a file she'd assigned to evidence:

GET PHONE RECORDS

If she'd wagered money on the hunch that the only way people heard back from Erin Polke the last week was through texts—she'd have won.

It wasn't the first time she'd seen texts screw over a person needing help or helping a person screw someone over. People count on the sender being who and where they say they are.

The police station and the office in Boston used the same phones, so when the phone rang Detective Jacobs answered it instinctively and afterward, subconsciously motivated by the familiar experience, found herself operating on autopilot, though everything took significantly longer without knowing anyone's names or numbers.

Though unfair, Bailey wasn't expecting people here to be easy to work with, because she was afraid of facing the stigma that made growing up there challenging. Most of the officers, even though they inevitably knew her father, were too new to remember the daughter who lived with "The Wall", but had a different last name. If any of the older officers remembered her or realized, they kept it to themselves or didn't want to discuss it if they knew he was missing. She imagined they all did.

When Bailey finished the work she could, within her limitations, she made a copy of the "report", filled out a form regarding the parent's notification, and decided to call it a night, but not before leaving a note at the desk saying where she'd gone and that she'd be back early.

Her childhood home looked particularly empty on its unkempt lawn and dressed in slate gray siding like a giant tombstone.

For a hell of a lot longer than a month and a half had this house looked like no one lived there.

The darkness in the cramped, two bedroom building little bothered the woman, who in some ways felt significantly younger the very instant she crossed the threshold. She guessed that was a normal way for a person to react when they go home, or to even feel it's something like playing pretend when returning to their house.

Through the dense black shroud of a rain darkened night, her eyes first looked for any new calls on the machine. There were no calls to her cell phone either, regarding the missing persons case. Bailey never heard anything unless she called them herself and then she only heard the same thing, "Nothing yet."

"What did the neighbors say?" she'd asked.

Braced on the countertop, she let her head hang limp between her arched shoulders. Her jaw clenched when their reply resounded in her thoughts:

"We've talked to all the neighbors, Ms. Douglass, and unfortunately, no one has seen anything."

The detective found the light over the stove and switched it on so she could put her things down without disturbing the articles on the counter. It did occur to her that she was probably standing in a crime scene and that it might not be a good idea to linger too long without being able to properly look around. If someone was responsible for her father's disappearance, they might assume the house would stay empty for some time—after all, no one saw that daughter of Douglass's, but a few times a year. While, for the most part, Bailey dismissed any risk of the perpetrator returning as unlikely, the small part of her that said otherwise insisted that she check all the rooms before turning her attention to other things, or she might not have it when she needed it.

Next to her keys, phone, shield, gun, and watch, Bailey spread out real estate pages from the newspaper she grabbed on the way home.

The Boston Homicide Unit badge and I.D. glared at her from beside the worn holster of her service handgun. She clearly remembered the first time she ever had to take out the shield to identify herself as Detective Bailey Jacobs.

Few times had she ever felt so proud.

But, there was no point to keep them.

That was something the woman never imagined thinking, so she tried not to think of it at all.

She'd sat down to try and figure out where she was going to live, not to linger on an abandoned dream. After a little while she'd told herself that enough times to finally make herself start looking.

There were a few houses she liked that were completely out of her price range—a similar circumstance for anyone looking at a place to rent or buy—or probably *anything* a person could want, for that matter. With the equitable wage of a Massachusetts detective, there were a number of listings that were reasonable to look at, but was it reasonable to be looking at all?

If her dad showed up tomorrow she'd feel really stupid about leaving Boston.

Like how minimally she'd attached herself to life in the city, her actions were again telling her more than she was conscious of:

She wouldn't be looking at houses if she thought her father was okay or that it really was as simple as a trip to bet on cockfights in Albuquerque. She wouldn't have left her job if she thought that either.

Between the case today and what she just realized about herself, Bailey regretfully accepted she may have two killers to catch. One with the unexpected, but full and agreeable support of most her new colleagues. The other, it seemed, she'd have to catch all by herself.

"This one might be okay," she tried to say over her thoughts and leaned above the pen to better see the one-and-one-quarter by one-inch image of a small red waterfront home on the Annisquam River. She checked the listing on her phone and found the sprawling rocky shore, small, but open yard, long curving driveway, and ample trees behind the house gave it an illusion of privacy few homes on the water seem to have, because real estate is always at a premium.

While Bailey checked a few others, a sensible but sometimes intrusive voice warned her that liking the house might not be a good thing, because when she likes something, they both knew, she was seldom interested in trying anything else.

7

...

MISSING PERSONS

After raining all night, the morning air was temporarily purged of humidity. This would last only as long it took for the sun to reach its zenith, throwing eighty-six degrees of unseasonably angry rays across the small port city. As yet, the sun lay heavily half-risen on the eastern horizon, fanning beams of yellow and pink light against the cool shades of retreating night and washing out the last diligent stars. The heatwave, which was about to eat its sixth day, meteorologists predicted would be long gone, and probably missed, by the end of the week.

Bailey awakened after little more than resting her eyes and could not make herself sleep again, whether from restlessness, anxiousness, or the awkward duality of sleeping in a bed both familiar and not.

In the few moments of actual sleep, she dreamt again, or as usual, of Leia Redding and the blanket pulled back from her gruesomely mistreated face.

Only the arm that she saw pulling back the blanket wasn't a stranger's, but her father's…

…she woke up trembling and terrified.

At first, when the thirty-two-year-old detective left the house, she started walking to work, but realized suddenly that was not where she was going at all, or why. She found herself heading to the spot overlooking Mill Pond where she found Leia Redding and quickly went back to her car.

She'd only just sat down and drew her legs inside when her cell phone rang.

When the man on the other end of the line heard the phone picked up, he didn't wait for salutations before saying:

"We might have a problem."

He continued to tell Detective Jacobs about the call Stull responded to the night before. There was a body found under a guard rail on Atlantic Road and now another, similarly sliced and slashed, found this morning after abundant rain from the week before drove a nearby resident to finally check out a plugged culvert.

Both men had been dead for several days.

Something in the nervousness and urgency in the caller's voice bothered her—besides the fact that anyone could have answered her phone, including a child if she had one, who would have been subjected to the horrors the caller, regardless of how quickly, just described.

"There's something more?"

The man hesitated.

"Sunday morning there was a body found south of town that was all cut up too. At the time we thought it was probably Saturday night drinking and hot tempers, because he was found only a couple dozen yards from a fresh supply of low resistance. We thought the wounds were made with a broken bottle, though we never recovered one. We had the hospital looking for someone coming in looking like they got a little of that too."

"Is this Mackinnon?" she frowned at the familiar sounding, but as yet, unidentified caller.

"Yeah," the man said breathlessly.

"I need to go to the station. I feel really useless without being sat up. I don't even have a Lanester I.D. or access to my computer."

"Sorry for putting you on the spot yesterday," Mackinnon added, "Lieutenant Thomas said we had to roll the ball because the neighbors said the folks were coming home and we didn't know how long it would take Stull to come from Salem."

Bailey was glad she was there before Michael, but only told Mackinnon she was glad to be able to be there when they needed someone.

"Am I supposed to go to one of the scenes?" Bailey wanted to know.

"I'd rather you were here," Mackinnon said in a tone that suggested other people weren't that far away. "I just wanted to let you know that something really nasty is happening and you should know about it. Stull's partner arrived and he went to check out the body in the culvert. I didn't want you left in the dark, but you probably have your hands full with Erin's… murder."

He said the "m" word like it tasted bad.

As far as the Polke case went, it would involve a lot of typing this morning, she told him, but most of the next steps come from the assessments from the coroner, forensics units, and getting information back from labs and the phone company, for instance.

She asked how the family was doing.

MacKinnon told her the department sat them up in a hotel for two nights and then family—who was out of town on the same trip to visit relatives, but were able to stay longer because they didn't have a teenage daughter at home—would be back from their vacation and the Polke's would be able stay with them. For obvious reasons, her parents didn't want to be in that house.

After Bailey hung up and closed the car door, the badge and I.D. came off the wallet on the belt clip and went into her pocket. Doing so made the detective feel like a traitor.

The business of orientating herself at the Lanester office was an almost identical experience to that in the Boston unit. Pictures were taken. I.D. printed. A lot of meet and greet drive-by introductions with the scattered employees they happened to run into. There was a brief computer orientation and benefits enrollment to go over before Bailey was finally set free to do what she'd been doing well for half a decade.

Most of the detectives in the Detectives Division dealt with narcotics and ballistics. Bailey Jacobs was the only homicide detective on hand, because traditionally, the few murder investigations they had were covered by detectives from larger cities. It had been several years since Lanester had their own.

Auto thefts had been a big problem in the early part of the twenty-first century, thefts in general are a problem everywhere, and sometimes the number of rapes per capita was higher than the national average, but it had been more than ten years since anyone had been murdered in Lanester.

The fifty-eight police officers on duty were enough to handle almost anything without interference from the Sheriff's Department, who was glad to take on the bright young detective and honor the request to serve in her home town, and none too soon.

There was a note on her monitor to call the medical examiner, which she did, while organizing the piles of assorted documents and paperwork on her desk.

"Essex County Coroner's Office."

"This is Detective Bailey Jacobs of the Lanester Detectives Division. Is Doctor Shaughnessy available?"

She heard the receptionist tell him:

"…it's the detective."

"Hello?" she heard a kind sounding man answer in a voice aged by untold numbers of cigarettes.

"Hi. I got your message…"

"Good. Good," said the old man sitting in a cold room, soiled latex gloves inverted and bunched up in the hand holding the phone and donning a disposable sea-green smock lightly spattered with blood days past having warmth, or lending it to a body. "Because I've got your problem."

She let him know she was listening by saying nothing and he was well ready to continue with little prompting.

"I got the fax you sent over about the Redding case. You might be heartbroken about the DNA, but I can mend it with a little bad good news."

Bailey's heart lay quietly in her chest even while blood began to race through her limbs. Her chest felt cold—for a moment, utterly certain, he was going to say they discovered her father's body, but the truth was exactly as Shaughnessy said it would be.

"The similarities in these murders *could* be considered circumstantial, no matter how similar they appear, but I would be willing to testify that these crimes were committed with the same weapon. What would the odds be that the same knife would fall into another psychopath's hands who would use it the same way—unless they were possessed by the same demonic spirit trapped inside it? I shouldn't say that too loud or the bastard might plead insanity when you catch him."

"How can you be so sure?"

The coroner coughed wetly and cleared his throat. It sounded like some spit went down the wrong tube because he was just about to speak when the coughing started with a sharp little gag.

"Excuse me," he apologized and made a grinding sound in his throat to get rid of the lingering ticklish feeling.

"Are you okay?"

Doctor Shaughnessy nodded and took the brief intermission to throw away the gloves in his hand before it made his palm any sweatier.

"A lot of knives have three-and-a-half inch blades. We know that a three-and-a-half inch knife was responsible for the mutilation of both bodies that was not directly attributed to parts of a human being. We know this because of the depths of the wounds and impressions of where the handle stopped the blade from going any farther. This is basic stuff."

Bailey nodded.

"What makes this knife different than thousands, if not millions, of other knives is an imperfection near the tip of the unserrated blade. On both victims' left arms there are strange feather shaped injuries in addition to a significant amount of bruising in similar lateral bands. My theory is that while he was on top of them and biting their faces, he was straddling them, and while he was holding down their forearms he held this knife in his right hand. He uses the business side of his right fist, the knuckles, to keep her left arm to the ground, inadvertently cutting them when the blade in that fist was pressed down too. The imperfection is clear in every impression."

Maybe this knife was more than just a toy to the killer. It sounded more like an extension of himself, an accomplice, partner, vicarious second sex organ.

He heard the detective let out the air in her lungs and waited for her response.

"Will you send me a copy of your report when you send it out to the DA?"

He agreed he would.

"Thank you for checking that out for me. All your findings will be good for our case. I'm not thrilled that the Redding's will have to think about the killer showing up again, but hopefully we can catch the guy this time."

"I hope so too," the coroner tiredly agreed.

Thinking that the end of their conversation, the detective was about to thank him again and say goodbye.

"There's one other thing—bear in mind, it could be entirely coincidental."

"I'm listening," she told him, rather than wait for him to just know it.

"Keeping in mind how common a three-and-a-half-inch knife is, would it bother you to know that one was responsible for every wound on our bar fight victim?"

Bailey quickly returned, "No less than it bothers me that two people were found just a few hours ago slashed to ribbons."

The coroner was less quick to answer and, in fact, said nothing for almost ten seconds. Then all he said was:

"I imagine so."

*   *   *

When Bailey got off the phone she called the office for Detective Stull's number. Even though he wasn't the kind of person she would ever choose to work with, it was a choice few ever have, so it wasn't even a matter of sucking it up to share the developments with him. What bothered her most was whether or not he would use it or excuse it, because it came from her. If first impressions are everything, then it was better that they stay away from each other. At least, over the phone, she wouldn't have to see him grinning.

"Stull."

Borrowing Mackinnon's line as the perfect segue into the bad news, she informed him, "We might have a problem."

8

...

REPARATIONS

After the Polke girl's murder and three different slashing deaths conclusively linked to a three-and-one-half inch knife, though not necessarily the same one responsible for the deaths of the Erin and Leia, there was growing excitement in Lanester. To Bailey the energy bore an unnerving semblance to the energy before a storm. More similarly, she was hesitant to acknowledge, did it resemble the agitation of a herd or flock when a predator is sensed. Where there are dead, there are vultures. Reporters from all the local and several national news stations descended on a city whose citizens no longer felt safe and any privacy they had was quickly diminishing as well.

In the aftermath of these murders, the Sheriff's Department lent extra officers. Lanester's small police force and Deputy Division were suffering from extended hours away from family when they were surely wanted no place more than at home.

When those three weeks passed and, other than continued efforts to solve the four cases, no other bodies surfaced, they were equally surprised as they were grateful.

In Detective Stull's comfort with TV cameras and virtually all dealings with the press, Bailey found something to like about the stalky, arrogant, walking tooth-whitening commercial, and she was grateful that he actually conducted himself like a professional with reporters, if nowhere else.

One less worry between the murders and looking into her dad's disappearance.

Missing Persons was on the same floor as the detectives'. She regularly called to see if there were any developments in her father's case and they didn't even put enough thought into the report to remember who the caller was, because they never once associated Bailey with *her*, even though she stopped by once every few days to check the missing persons board, where anything about her father was conspicuously absent.

The paper boy was right about when her dad's newspaper subscription was cancelled and she found out, from calling the post office, that there was a four week mail hold, starting the week before she called home to check on him.

There hadn't been any calls from either his cell phone or home phone since the same time. She had tried calling his cell phone, thinking she might find it somewhere in the house or in his car, but unless it or the ringer was turned off, or the battery was dead, it was with him or had been when he went missing.

The rest of the neighbors admitted noticing "how quiet it was over there" and hadn't seen anyone take the car or snooping around, until she showed up.

The entire list of addresses was exhausted without any reward for the hours and footwork invested.

Her father's car surrendered no clues.

There was no activity on his credit card and his bills hadn't been paid, so Bailey took care of them just in case he came home, that he would still have utilities.

The unidentified phone number did belong to a pre-paid phone. According to the phone company, the calls to either her or her father were made from out of state. And, as yet, knew little more about it.

No one answered when she dialed it.

Bailey was leery about approaching people her father had a history of hatred or altercations with, should any of them be responsible it seemed reasonable to be concerned that Missing Persons might do just as much to find her as they had to find him.

She found it challenging to isolate any number of possible witnesses or informants who *didn't* have a history with her old man.

Who makes a whole town hate them?

Hate them enough that no one she spoke with had been contacted by the police about it before she came knocking on their door.

This, in no way, endeared Bailey to Lanester, Massachusetts.

They would find out how lucky they were that her personal feelings had no real effect on her work ethic, because very soon there would be little else between them and a guiltless butcher.

Far away from the chaos of reporters and strange civilians scouring the town for, as yet, undiscovered bodies like a madman's version of an Easter egg hunt, Bailey sat with her pants rolled up, soaking tired feet in the briny river. Her shoes and jacket lay on the rocky bank behind her. The items from her pockets and person, including her watch, were put away in their drawer in the kitchen without considering, at the time, leaving her coat behind too.

It had been two whole months since the Sunday evening when a concerned daughter called a father who should have appeared by now. He would never be gone this long without contacting her or showing up. She *knew* that. It was getting hard to keep peace with the officers in Missing Persons who all but dismissed her on the phone, but were attentive to the new detective. She knew that would only last as long as they thought she was a complete stranger.

It would only cause problems to point out what they were doing and she didn't think it would make them try any harder. Force and humiliation sounded like a good formula for retaliation.

The officer who over-excitedly proclaimed the brutal slaying of their only child, to the Polke's, was enjoying a month of unpaid leave. Detective Jacobs didn't have to worry about any fallout from the complaint she filed, because there were more than ten of them from officers, to say nothing of reports made by other persons on the scene.

It was a great comfort to the homicide detective to know the parents were out of town now and hidden from the media's prying eye.

For the moment, Bailey enjoyed a similar luxury—as lead investigator, the reporters were relentless for an inside view and suspicions about suspects and if she thought it would happen again. So much so that she started to tune out the phone ringing and was reluctant to even listen to messages.

The first three weeks on the job were a lot busier than she was expecting or hoping.

She wished there was a way to make her brain feel as nice as the unusually warm autumn waters made her feet.

Against the scent of the Annisquam and the breeze driving it against her, she felt something touch her back before catching the brief fragrance of a very familiar aftershave.

Her neck snapped around so hard something inside it felt pinched.

"Nate?"

Suddenly he was hugging and raising her inches from the large rounded stone where she sat.

They were both surprised when she hugged him back.

"How you doin' Bail?" he said over her shoulder.

Tears rose first in sensation and then into her throat and face where they died and were buried with a hundred thousand other tears she would not give to her father or the killer of Leia Redding.

"I'm fine," she sounded muffled against his shoulder, which smelled comfortable and, somehow, safe.

He let her go first, removed his shoes and tossed them onto the bank beside hers before sitting down on the most seat-like rock nearest her.

"You ever going to look good again, partner?"

She didn't know how to respond.

"No news on dad or just bad news?" he probed with extra effort in not sounding like a jerk.

"A little of both, I guess," she decided.

Nate nodded, a lot of cases are like that.

"I wanted to apologize for being an S.O.B. Took me too long to finally realize I couldn't do that on the phone."

"You didn't even have to apologize—"

"—Well, I know that!" he interrupted.

When Bailey looked at him to see if he was serious, she found the slightest smile on his naturally curving lips. Then he added, "But I really wanted to."

"You drove all the way from Boston to tell me you're sorry?"

He could tell she was feeling bad, if that were the case, so he was glad to tell her there was more to it.

"Not to tell you I'm sorry, but to show you," he leaned in and over a little so he was looking directly into her face. "Bailey, I've felt really low about the things I said to you and how I was after you put in for the transfer."

She shook her head, dismissing it.

"No really. I fucked up. You could have transferred and I would have still been able to know you, but I drove you off like I wanted nothing to do with you and that's just not true."

"I didn't see it like that, Nate," Bailey said seriously. "Even so, I appreciate what you're saying."

"Well, if you already feel better, fine, but don't deny me the chance to make myself feel better too."

Bailey smiled prettily at him, the sunset made her eyes look particularly sparkly and lent a false flush to her skin. Nate swallowed hard and resisted the urge to reach out and touch what once avoided being touched.

With the sun in her eyes, she saw no sign of the internal struggle that, had she been able to see, would have read strongly in his eyes.

"This is your place?"

"I—"

"—Oh my God—Bail, I almost said 'so' when I started to ask you!"

"So?" Bailey shrugged.

"*So*? Because that's what that dipshit detective says every time he opens his horse-toothed trap!"

"Really, Nate? You want to get excited about the word 'so'?" she wondered as he rose to help her stand safely before starting toward the grassy embankment together.

"Jesus-effing-Christ, you can't turn on the TV without seeing him carrying on about the killings up here. There's so much blah-blahing that *one word* starts to be the only one you can pick out!"

Bailey's smile broadened.

"You know, he talks about the cases like he doesn't know anything about them."

"The idea is probably that reporters won't know anything about them," she supposed. "We don't want the killer to change what he's doing because, right now, we'll be able to sort through any leads in no time."

Nate stopped to hand her, her shoes, "Have there been many?"

The detective shook her head, "No one who wasn't virtually eliminated in one or two phone calls. I think he's a local. So normal, so common, he's invisible. This guy is someone no one sees, like the Delivery Man killings up in PA. People around here notice when an out of town car drives up Main Street," she exaggerated to make a point.

"Do you have DNA?"

"Enough to fill a couple baby food jars," she barely overstated.

"And you guys really think these four—no, five—killings were the work of the same guy? I heard about that, by the way Bail, way to do your homework."

She shrugged as an answer without devotion to either.

Of course, he figured, she wouldn't commit to a 'yes' or 'no' unless she knew.

"That's not your car," Bailey remarked when she noticed the silver Chevy in the driveway.

Nate looked, just in case their happened to be a third car in the driveway and then explained how his windshield got broken when some little gangbanger decided to take a shot at the vehicle because he had a few questions for the kid's mother.

"I guess he was making a statement," he said lastly.

Nate's ex-partner wasn't impressed.

"Would you like some coffee?" Bailey offered when they reached the modest waterfront facing deck, which—though not the front door—appeared to be the preferred entrance.

"I've got a better idea," Nate countered, "if you're inviting me in."

"Are you a vampire that you need it spelled out more specifically than that?" she dryly returned.

Nate's eyes widened with surprise, "Sounds like you might have found a sense of humor up here."

"No… one just happened to drift up while I was soaking my feet. I thought I could use it for a little while before throwing it back," the reply came out with the stiffness of control, but in a more natural tone when she continued, "I'm just happy to see you."

"Not yet."

She watched him "detective run" around the side of the building and heard him unlock the rental car's doors. The detective run being the special way that men in suits, with nothing-close-to-tennis shoes on, tear up turf. On TV you can tell when they give the actors running shoes for chase scenes or not. It was a phenomena Bailey avoided by wearing nothing-close-to-dress shoes.

It only took him fifteen seconds to run there, do what he had to do, and come back. His rebellious

brown hair was lightly messed from hurrying—
though, truth be told, it could be fairly neat and
suddenly somewhat rumpled just standing in one
place.

The detective returned carrying a brown paper
grocery bag inside a plastic one with a logo on it
Bailey thought looked familiar. Rather than dwell on
this, her eyes focused on the moisture darkened
bottom of the brown bag and where the plastic bag
found it and clung tightly.

"That looks scary," she said as he passed her to
walk up the stairs onto the deck.

"Not to a man, Bail," he told her.

"You know I'm not a man, right?"

"Yeah," he returned with an inflection of
certainty, thinking that a mistake no one could really
make.

She opened the door and sat down her shoes and
coat while he tried to think of something smart to
say back.

"Those aren't the subs you were telling me
about?" Bailey worried as she looked at the grease
soaked bag.

It was little comfort when he shook his head,
because *something* was in there.

"I told you about a place that makes great
hoagies," he corrected, "but I didn't tell you how
good their fries are."

After they'd eaten, she was glad that she had
never been to that diner before, because the
sandwiches were as good as Nate boasted them.
Bailey thanked him and hoped he didn't feel so bad
about what happened anymore.

"That's not how I'm going to make it up to
you," he refused, shaking one finger at her like a

continuation of the sentence while he took a long drink from his soda can.

"What did you have in mind, Nate?"

He thought she sounded suspicious.

"I know it's not a lot of time, but I thought I'd take the weekend to try to help you figure some of this stuff out about your dad."

"Nate—"

"Don't tell me no, Bail. This is good karma to balance things out after what I said."

She was about to refuse his help, but that was stupid. There was a reason why she was grateful to have been assigned as his partner, Detective Nathaniel Treuer was someone she knew had a lot to teach her. Maybe there was something he could see that she couldn't.

"Okay."

Nate crumpled a paper towel in his hands after wiping his mouth and leaned back in the seat to start the investigation on her terms:

"Alright Bail…tell me what you know."

And when she had, he wanted to see the house.

Bailey was compelled to deny him entrance into her past, any more than she already had. When he saw her reluctance, he asked how a detective was supposed to solve a case without ever seeing where the crime happened—believing Bailey's instincts about where and when her father went missing.

"I asked around some more," Nate hesitantly ventured once they were in her car driving northeast into Lanester. "I heard that your dad was quite a cop in his hay day and an even finer detective. Why'd he become a P.I.?"

"Probably issues with authority, the system…"

"Not everybody remembers him as an ass—
though they remember him being an ass to other
people. He sounded like he was kinda rebellious, so
I suppose P.I. work would suit him, if he didn't go
legally out-of-bounds."

Bailey watched the road quietly, turning left
when they crossed one of only three bridges across
the Annisquam.

Her silence was answer enough.

"Being willful and intolerant can come along
with being bright and I heard he was sharp as a
Ginsu hypodermic."

"He is smart," she agreed.

Her stiff reply reminded Nate that none of this
was good for the case. Being a good cop, bull-
headed, and intelligent, just meant they were dealing
with somebody or bodies who bested that.

"Tomorrow we call gas stations within twenty,
thirty miles or so and ask if they seen anybody
matching his description in the station, at the pump,
or in the vehicle. I will give a pal of mine in the FBI
a call and see if he can't tell us if your dad did take
any flights and try to find the owner of your mystery
phone number. You are gonna call the Sheriff's
Department and file your missing person report up
there. If they happen to tell you to go to local law
enforcement first, tell 'um you already tried that and
they haven't even knocked on a door, okay?"

Bailey only nodded, because she was
apprehensive about doing that. Should someone in
the police department be involved then there was
nothing to like about the consequences of that, being
the man disappeared without a trace or trail and
Missing Persons was unwilling to help, to a degree
she thought suspicious even if someone there had a
beef with him. It seemed likely, to Bailey, that of all
the departments in Lanester, Missing Persons might

have the best reason to hold a grudge against her father, because when they couldn't do their job, he often went on the loved ones' payroll. They might think it was a fitting irony to have the mug of the diligent and, mostly successful in his efforts, gumshoe on a milk carton of his own.

She was reluctant to share her concerns with Nate, since the quickest way to make bad blood with another cop is to badmouth fellow officers—even though he wasn't all that concerned about her saying it to the state police. Maybe he wouldn't mind if she raised those suspicions, since these weren't Boston policemen, but she was not about to take the chance of destroying what only just started rebuilding.

As they were driving up Washington Street, Bailey could tell he was expecting it to be this house, or the next, or maybe that one—so she made sure not to even glance at him until they were both out of the car and standing on the driveway of the actual house. She was embarrassed.

"The last time you saw him, was your dad ailing any?" Nate asked as she led him across the lawn.

"He didn't appear to be," she answered instead of, "Not that I would know."

"You got keys for his car?"

Bailey shook her head. The keys were something else that spirited away with him and his cell phone.

"Were his shoes missing?" he asked as she unlocked the door and led her former partner into the place where she learned to both be small and "take no shit".

"Yes," she told him, another detail that reinforced the idea he was waiting for a cab or something and not *just* having breakfast. She never saw "The Wall" eat a meal with more or less on his feet than socks.

"Have you been through *everything*?"

Bailey nodded, looking grim as she recalled the chore of going through the clutter in his bedroom alone. The best thing about it was learning more about him. Like that he kept cash between the plates on the highest cabinet in the kitchen. That none of his family looked like her in the family album she found buried with his undershirts in one side of a drawer. The same drawer also contained a bottle of cognac and his tax returns from years when he actually filed them.

It would have been impossible to look through every scrap of paper in that mess, she told Nate, so she just glanced at most of it. He told her they needed to look at both sides of every piece and write down every name and number they found.

"If the needle in the haystack wasn't worth anything, people wouldn't bring it up so goddamn much," he told her as he moved in the direction he noticed she always gestured to when she was explaining what a mess it was.

"You got me, Bail. Use me."

9

...

PENNY for HER THOUGHTS

Nate woke up when he heard a phone ringing too distantly to be his own. He listened to the indecipherable sound of Bailey speaking to someone. While he lay across the long and flattened looking couch, with morning light filling the room in a way that should have been welcoming, he tried to absorb all the information about the missing man as he could without absorbing too many of the odors from the threadbare and stained sofa.

He was thinking about what life would have been like growing up in a house like this, regardless of what her father was like. There were dead mice and bugs under the junk in that bedroom and mouse holes in the walls. He was suspicious if the bathroom saw a cleaning since Bailey was living there. Even as he felt the weight and discomfort of a swelling bladder threatening to send him there, he couldn't imagine actually using it.

He didn't want to be rude when Bailey suggested they just sleep there and finish in the morning, but it was uncomfortable to be in that house.

Mountains of soiled, but not inexpensive, clothing were piled all over, contributing to the strangely oily and animal-like odor in the house. There was an unusual dichotomy between the household items inferring utter pennilessness and high-on-the-hog wealth.

The piles of pornography stuffed below the couch sat high on Treuer's personal list of things he wouldn't want to raise a kid around, but the Health Department or Social Services might very well have failed the dwelling, or those in it, without stepping inside the house.

There was no love here, not even a disgruntled asshole's love of himself—people who love themselves may not always be able to keep their homes perfect, or have everything they want, but anyone would have to admit there is a certain amount of utterly lacking give-a-damn involved when a person won't make an effort for themselves.

In this house there were no pictures on the walls, no memorabilia beyond what they found in the dad's room. Motel rooms do more to add personality to a space than her old man did. To Nate that meant one of two things:

One, the guy was really depressed, self-loathing, and hateful toward everyone in the world so he lived and treated himself like dirt.

Or two, this wasn't the guy's only place to live.

"Nate," Bailey stood at the kitchen counter, looking into the living room, "Did you sleep okay?"

"Sure," he lied. The couch smelled so strong of dirty human skin that he found it nearly impossible to even breathe. He wanted to ask who called, but she was about to tell him.

"That was Michael, Detective Stull, from Salem. He's on his way back because something happened to a woman south of town."

"Why didn't they call you?" Nate wondered.

Bailey shrugged, "I think they know his number by heart."

"Did he call just to rub it in?"

Nate's voice gave away a tinge of annoyance.

"No, someone asked him if they thought the evidence at the scene looked like it could be the same perp from the Polke murder. I already sent him a copy of my report, so he should have known the answer himself."

Her former partner raised both hands and shook his head as he tried to make sense of what she was telling him.

"If he was there, why did he need your report?"

Bailey explained that Stull was late and missed a lot of the progress, but withheld the fact that he was preoccupied catching up with the boys and seeing if, after four consecutive hours of talking without thinking or taking a break, it would affect his voice.

"So you gotta go?" Nate made a hissing sound as he sucked the air back in after saying "so", but the word was already out.

"He asked me if I'd like to 'check it out'…" her voice trailed off like she had no more interest hearing the offer a second time. Nate could tell she was bothered by the suggestion. Crime scenes aren't for spectating.

In Bailey's eyes Nate saw directionlessness, founded largely by the gravity of the issues preoccupying her, as she seemed to wander toward the window over the kitchen sink. It wasn't completely aimless, as it turned out, because she started making coffee.

Maybe she was just exhausted.

"You remember what you're supposed to do today?" he pushed the throw blanket he slept under onto the other side of the couch. He felt crawly, but tried to ignore it.

Her striking blue-green eyes flicked toward him, but she ignored the question, assuming it rhetorical.

Then he asked her, "Did you sleep okay?"

She didn't answer that either, because to answer truthfully would feel like complaining and if the way she felt inward had any effect on her outwardly, it was obvious anyway.

"How much time do you want to invest on that mess back there?" Bailey wondered. Having been through the whole house and finding so many papers without so much as pertinence to everyday life, she was feeling a little anxious and unproductive.

"The answer could be right in front of us. We don't want to miss anything," Nate suggested smartly, but it didn't feel very rewarding. "You been under the couch?"

A touch of scarlet dusted the highest parts of her cream colored cheeks, whether embarrassment or shame, indistinguishable. She nodded and said, "Yes."

"I was going to offer to do it so you wouldn't have to..." he excused. He hoped she wouldn't take it the wrong way. Porn really wasn't his thing, but it's hard for a guy to defend that when most people automatically assume if you're male you partake. She didn't seem suspicious that he might have only wanted to look at it himself.

"I turned over every leaf in this place except the jungle in there—though I toured it briefly. I even unscrewed all the vents and pulled up the registers to look inside and moved all the appliances—"

"And here I thought the mess was your dad's," he barely fought down the corner of his mouth from giving away how clever he felt.

Bailey didn't have the energy to feel the good nature in his comment. She'd been bombarded by nightmares and woke feeling drained and guilty. In the back of her mind she couldn't stop thinking about Stull's call and dreading the possibility they were going to find another victim. 'Only this house has no basement', Michael had joked, and that made her wonder if the Redding's had one or not.

"Have some coffee before we get into it again," Bailey suggested.

The perking noise was gaining a lot of energy.

Coffee sounded like a great idea, but he had to face the bathroom first. He excused himself and closed himself into the small space. If Bailey couldn't hear it, Nate would have run the exhaust fan for a while to see if that would help. No sprays, no air fresheners of any kind. He glanced at the wastebasket and saw it stuffed with toilet paper and facial tissue all closed in on themselves like little drawstring pouches. Through the thin, soft paper, he saw yellow-brown clumps crusting through every visible wad that were once great amounts of snot or phlegm. He quickly turned away, braced himself on the bathroom counter, and felt bile creep up his throat.

Looking between the sink and the soiled bowl, he had thoughts he tried not to be ashamed of having. The sink's height was almost perfect for...release.

In the end, the detective couldn't allow himself the easy out and, standing over the toilet, uneasily lowered his fly.

Sometimes Nate just didn't understand how women cope with all of life's catch-twenty-twos. He knew a lot of these, because his mother used them to make the males in the family feel bad. None of them, his three brothers, father, and himself included, ever knew if she was teasing or not.

When at wayside rests, public bathrooms or otherwise, and he was faced with the depravity of boredom, anonymity, and disrespect of its temporary occupants, he felt lucky standing there.

It turned out that Bailey's dad utilized the junk in his bedroom as a way to hide things. Nate and Bailey agreed that there was probably some secret order to it—once realized was already completely destroyed—that told her father exactly what was where.

In one area they found several wanted notices, statements by witnesses scrawled into the margins of magazine ads and takeout menus, for men with warrants Bailey remembered her father turning in. Nearby there were others she didn't remember and assumed they were on his "watch" list. They found bank receipts and account statements in other places. Missing people fliers in two different areas. There were several lost pet and item fliers too, which he kept, should he happen to come across either, but never actively searched for them. A lot of the printed papers were actually just digital photographs of the original wanted or missing posters, he'd just printed them off.

There were newspaper articles about random people that seemed to have no rhyme or reason. They wrote down all the names and pertinent information from the articles. None of the people sounded familiar to either of them, save maybe a few last names, which at the time meant nothing.

"No smoking gun in here, but at least it's done," Nate sighed where he kneeled, on the recently unseen floor, between stacks of sorted papers.

Every inch of him felt covered in some kind of film, grime, or crawling dust sized insect—a shower would have to happen before any work outside of the house was done. He asked if she'd mind him having one when they got back to her place, even though he felt bad touching her car in this condition. He wondered how she'd feel about him stripping down to his boxer briefs and undershirt, bearing the rest of his attire in a carefully tied plastic grocery bag.

"Were you paying for lodging last night?" she hoped not.

"Nah. I didn't make reservations because I didn't know what would happen."

Bailey considered this for a moment, her eyebrows slowly pushing toward the space between them.

"I'm sorry," she said.

"Nothing for *you* to be sorry about."

She didn't agree.

On the way back to her house, Bailey asked about the others in the Boston unit. At first, Nate was reluctant to get into it because he was afraid of making her feel bad or regretful, or think they all moved on without her. Business continued as usual, because it has to. Sometimes people just leave and more than one person had said, there were worse ways she could have gone.

Bailey decided it was a good time to tell him that she didn't want to start any problems between herself and the missing person's unit.

"I understand not rocking the boat, but you let those slackers keep on chipping away the hull, the whole thing will sink."

"I don't want trouble with them for poor police work if they are responsible for worse."

Nate understood what she was implying and was considering alternatives when her phone rang.

"Bailey," she answered and then was listening for some time, her eyes grimmer and grimmer without disturbing the calmness in her face. "Okay. I'll be right there."

She hung up and slipped the phone back in her pocket.

"It's him," she blurted in a tone almost identical to any number of witnesses at a line up. She didn't breathe or exhale as a balloon of tension swelled in her chest. She felt guilty. She felt despair. She felt like a bad daughter as she added, "They want me over there now."

Nate nodded, "Do you mind if I just work on this stuff at your place. You can drop me off if you're going south anyway and I will take care of everything we talked about."

Bailey took her eyes off the road long enough to throw him that penetrating look. He wasn't sure what she was trying to find, but she answered, "Thank you," so he was satisfied.

When Bailey dropped the other detective at her house, she told him where her spare key was and to keep it on him, rather than returning it, because she wouldn't put it in the same place twice had she ever used it.

It was weird to be left at a place he didn't know, to watch a person he felt privileged to suddenly know even a little about, drive off to chase a serial killer in Boringsville, Massachusetts.

He hoped she'd catch him too.

Boringsville is an okay position for a town to be in. It was never boring in Boston and he sorely missed hunting the bad guys with Bailey. He missed everything about her.

*   *   *

"He checks the windows and apparently watches her for some time at this one," Bailey pointed through the large picture window directly behind the sofa in the living room. "At midnight, she logs out of her website, receiving customers until…" she trailed off.

"There is a twenty minute slot of no activity before she logs off," Curtis, the crime scene tech she'd worked with at the Polke house, informed after rechecking his notes.

"She's alive, we know, at midnight when her psychic readings end. Your guys will be able to tell us if she hung out online after that."

Curtis nodded surely.

"Based on the humidity and temperature in the house, the blood would have taken some time to dry. Compared to the first officer's arrival and dryness of the fluids, we're probably looking at about one in the morning, if not only shorty after. The killer watches her from the window—" Bailey pointed into the room where a direct line of sight provides a perfect view of the computer screen "—he's waited this long, he's not going to make his move until the computer is off. He has just seen her taking phone calls and chatting with clients. At that time, IM may still be open, to say nothing of the webcam—when you check the computer see if you can bring up any video from last night to see if the window is in the shot."

The same technician, Curtis, was nodding even before she mentioned it. The look of triumph rode high in the technician's dark brown eyes and the color of his face. He was chomping at the bit.

"So, did you solve the murder yet?" Michael called from the open window of his black luxury car. He shut off the engine and "slipped some skin" with one of the officers before strolling across the yard, smiling hugely.

"You know there aren't any TV cameras here, right?" Bailey stepped aside to make room for the fingerprint gal to lift latents off the ledge and glass.

Stull's smile vanished for a barely registerable second.

"Maybe it's like this, my aunt has a coffee cup that says, "Act like you're wearing an invisible crown.""

Bailey bit her lip and stared hard at the grinning detective, when she let up she let out:

"Princes don't catch murderers, Stull. You're not up here because you're as dumb as you act."

The smile sunk into his face and left churning emotion in the vortex that drank it.

Curtis slipped away and went to tell another tech what was happening between the investigators.

"What I'm saying is, you can just talk to me. I think everyone will be just as impressed if you actually catch the killer, than just walking around making everyone think it's going to be easy," Bailey looked at him stonily.

She was grateful when he shrugged and said, "Okay. Okay." instead of throwing a big caveman fit about her being a bitch and that *this* murder was his, first. But he added indignantly, "So, if you're taking over the show, tell me what you want me to do."

Bailey's shoulders drooped and she tried not to let the sigh that happened come out audibly.

"I just want to catch him, Stull. If I'm stepping on your toes, just say so. If you want my assistance,

I'm here. If you don't want it, I can review the other cases. If you want me to do everything, just go back to Salem. Decide now. I'm not going to do this every time I see you."

Stull actually looked somewhat handsome, or revealed the handsome his jerk grin and arrogant mannerisms concealed. To be generous, he was like a short Javier Bardem. He, at least for the moment, was taking her seriously.

"So," the detective shrugged, "let's catch him."

Probably there were places, as yet unseen, that bore horrifying likeness to the bloody mess at the front entrance to the small, but modern home. Once the report came in that morning, an officer was sent to the house. He found the front door standing open and had to chase away a skunk who was checking out the carnage. There was little he could do about bugs with interest in blood, but listen to the incessant hum of their stiff, plasticy wings and watch the ants circle the drying pool with interest or laying unmoving when curiosity killed them.

There was some blood outside the residence and while there were unaccounted volumes, that could be anywhere between here and wherever the body was dumped if it was even shed at all. A lot of bleeding out happened in the small space where the front door met a hall going straight, a wide staircase with a landing to the left and the right where a small nook contained only a bench with storage baskets underneath. It had countless times said goodbye and hello to the woman who probably died there.

"So another one's all cut up? What's the point, or rather, what's the difference?" Michael shook his head in disgust, even as he smiled.

"Maybe h—" Bailey scanned the semi-private woodsy yard and was about to ask if anyone had talked to the neighbors yet, when something on the far side of the yard caught the least, but merciful, amount of light.

Detective Stull waited by the front door and watched the new detective's purposeful venture to the edge of the yard with curiosity, but no intention to follow. If it mattered, he would find out soon enough.

Bailey looked down at the thing and called Alex, the photographer, to come over right away.

The very instant he was close enough to see what needed documenting, she went back to the house and around to the back door.

"Did anyone ask the neighbors if they heard screaming?" she tried over the radio.

"Not a peep," a man returned. "One of her clients called this morning to report her missing because she never misses a session. Neighbors had no idea anything was wrong."

That was exactly what Bailey hoped they would say.

It was impossible to enter the house from the front without disturbing the technicians' work, so everyone came and went from the kitchen door. There were a few people in there discussing the scene when Bailey flew in, her eyes steady and deliberate like a bird of prey.

"Yes!" she gave the fridge a smack and was smiling big, for Bailey, when the other detective hurried in behind her.

"What the hell?"

"She's alive, or at least she didn't die here."

"No?" Stull grunted sarcastically.

"No."

Bailey stepped back from the fridge and pointed toward a picture. "There is a collar laying out front that's cut in two. A dog the killer probably dealt with after or during the attempt to subdue her."

In the photograph of a woman and spotted Great Dane, both were smiling contentedly.

"That's why there's more blood in the entry than they thought there should be, even if she was cut up like the others—most of the victims' blood supplies were probably drained before they were ever moved—there's too much blood, because it's a large dog's blood supply. A dog that probably outweighs its owner by thirty pounds—a difference of almost five pints of blood."

Stull was stammering something when Bailey left to the living room.

"He spent too long watching her. If he is responsible for those other killings, we know those were abrupt, because of the man who left the bar. When he was killed, the killer just decided to. This guy is patient."

She panned the room with her eyes and scanned it with every bit of instinct she'd procured in her five years as a detective, but understanding the details will only provide an analytical depiction of the events, a cold paradigm of what the woman really went through…

"Good evening <type, type, type> *Joshua*," the dark-haired woman said as she typed a message to the next paying customer logged in to chat privately with "Astrid", known to the IRS and all other legal documentation as Samantha Goode. She didn't really like to type, and preferred when people called the 900 number or wanted to video chat. The anonymous client almost always chose to chat— nothing strange on the phone bill and no having to face the person you're going to ask about what your husband will do if he finds out you're cheating.

"You…need…advice…and…the spirits have…been waiting…to help…you."

Joshua replied: IS THAT A JOKE OR R U SUPPOSED 2 START THAT WAY??

Sam smiled.

"Some people… expect…cheese… with their order."

Joshua sent a smiley face.

While she was making Joshua feel a little doubtful about his love life, encouraged him about his job, and worked out enough information to make one of those "freaky—how did they know!?" psychic comments about his brother's passing at an early age, her business phone line got active. A red light indicated a call and the ringer was turned off so video clients wouldn't hear the phone ring—though it was impossible to do a phone client and a video client at the same time.

"You have reached Astrid, the Salem Seer," she answered in her huskiest, most mystical voice. Her ex-husband Timothy, the Lanester Loser, always warned her she sounded a little "porn-ish".

She threw a sidelong look at the young and dopey picture of them by a concrete wall, with their names in a heart drawn with paint. He didn't know why she kept it, since they "aren't married" anymore, but the photo never failed to make her smile. Their hair alone was good for a daily laugh. Then, if she tried to think about what kind of pants they were probably wearing.

Ugh, she thought, sticking out her tongue.

"Would you like a Tarot reading, send me a palm pic, or an astrological prediction—all guaranteed to take up only thirty minutes. Or, would you like an open reading where you may ask questions and I give answers—a guaranteed maximum of two hours at the rates provided in the introductory message."

She looked at the clock and hoped they wouldn't be interested in the maximum time, because she was already tired and her eyes were starting to have a hard time focusing on the screen. It made her want to wear sunglasses when she worked.

The woman wanted to know how the palm pic worked.

To Joshua, who was ready to leave the chat, she wrote:

Have a cosmic evening, Josh. Remember, you went into your job with all the right ethics, but your give-a-damn should be reserved for the things in life that reciprocate.

It was 11:40, after a quick chat with a regular customer and "radio silence" after, Sam decided to jump over to eBay to see how the auctions she was watching, that were ending in the next couple days, were doing.

By midnight, there were no chimes to alert her to return to deal with customers, but she only guaranteed availability between certain hours and her time was up.

"Thank God," Sam said and quickly shut down her computer like something would come out of it if she didn't.

"Tard," she muttered to the large dog stretched out on the floor in front of the couch. "Must be nice, livin' the life." The dog, Leopold, looked toward her, but wasn't about to leave the nice warm spot it made.

She was herself stretching, her arms a "V" above her head and fingers spread like she was casting spells—the way she did as a child and pretending that was exactly what she *was* doing.

Suddenly the home phone rang and Samantha vibrated like she was electrocuted, instantly panting and held one hand over her pounding heart.

"Hello?"

"Is this Miss *Nex*?"

Her scalp prickled—the home phone number was unlisted.

"No…" she let the "nnnn" sound carry most of her answer.

"Oh," the man sounded confused. Obviously realizing the voice was wrong.

"Sorry, you must have dialed wrong," Samantha was relieved and even laughed at the beginning and end of her answer. "I don't know any Nex's."

The man apologized and said he hoped he didn't make the mistake again or he had copied the number wrong.

The very second after he hung up, the light on the business line came on.

She knew she shouldn't pick it up, even to tell a potential client it was after hours. They should know that, if they paid attention to the message and *definitely* when no one answered the phone, but she had to satisfy the bad feeling she was having, the way people walk out into the dark when they are sure something is waiting in it.

"You're a psychic," the same male voice seethed with quiet anger, like when someone is building up a scream, "So tell me what I'm going to do to you!"

Her mouth hung open and she spun on the unlit corners of the adjoining rooms.

Then she heard something she had never heard before and spun to face the dog who had never growled in its life. When Sam turned to face the direction Leopold was looking, she came face to face with her caller. Body and soul knew there was little hope in surviving what was going on behind his gleaming eyes.

A python strikes fast by nature, but the arm that cinched on her neck seemed inhumanly fast and locked like the bite of a wolf, with the precision of one who'd done it a thousand times before.

Sam fought at the arm, but could not penetrate the sleeves enough to harm him and there was no way to bite him when she could hardly even breathe.

The intruder looked between the hall and the slowly pursuing dog as he dragged her toward the front door.

The ferocity in the longtime and ridiculously friendly pet even frightened Samantha. There was some comfort in the fact that the man was wary of the beast who might be her only chance of escaping, but her fortune only lasted until a knife was pulled.

Then Samantha was trying to say, "Lie down boy", "Sit", "Stay", "No—bad dog!" and gestured madly when the commands only came out as wheezing.

Then she tried begging the man not to hurt Leopold.

"Please, please, please leave my dog alone! PLEASE!

"Please don't hurt him. Please don't hurt him!

"He's my *baby*! PLEASE—I'll do anything— just let him live!"

Only then she started crying, hitching, and grunting in desperation to reach the demon dragging her to unknown horrors. If the dog was spared, then in some way she could face whatever was going to happen to her because he literally was the closest to a child she and Timothy ever had. If something happened to Leopold, then it was all her fault, because the man was there for *her*. Clearly, he hadn't expected the dog.

With the hand holding the small knife, the intruder turned away to let them out into the pitch black night. Seeing the first opportunity to strike, without also hurting his human, Leopold lunged in on the part of man a beast most fears—his hand.

Surprisingly, the intruder didn't cry out, though he made a guttural sound infinitely distant from pleasure.

Sam was also surprised when he flung her aside, though she sensed he did so without hesitation, because he could easily catch her again. Or maybe the man was just so afraid of the one-hundred-and-sixty pound beast and forty-two bared teeth that, for the moment, she didn't matter.

On the ground, Samantha could barely move and realized how close she was to passing out. She was going nowhere fast, but thought she could maybe pull herself somewhere if Leopold could hold the man off long enough to reach a phone.

To do this, felt like abandoning her only child, a child who was, right then, fighting for both their lives while she lay uselessly beside the storage bench.

Blurred vision showed only a maelstrom of legs and movement. She needed to take the opportunity to get back to the phone and call for help because, while she was already at the door, there was no way she could get by them, get through it, and make it to a neighbor for help.

Her elbows bit the smooth bamboo flooring and inched her into a prone crawling position. She was regretting not having a nice, long shag carpet she could have easily gripped and pulled herself across. She was regretting not having a security system. She was regretting the divorce—wishing, wishing, wishing Timothy was there to make her feel safe, which he did.

He always did.

She wondered if she ever told him so.

Suddenly dog and man crashed against the stairs left of the door. It was apparent that the man purposely pulled the dog down with him.

It wasn't apparent to Leopold that this didn't mean he was winning.

Samantha saw that this put the intruder within easy reach of the knife he dropped when the first bite struck true. Even though it was almost seven feet away, she strained to reach it. She would have given her soul to get to it first.

Then Leopold was making other sounds she never heard him make. Angrier sounds, wet garbled sounds, high pitched whining sounds. There was also the sound of the man grunting with unchecked effort to cut, cut, cut, and kill the loyal and ridiculously friendly beast.

She heard the strange sound of flesh penetrated again and again and knew when it hit bone. The clink of the blade against teeth. Felt when it hit arteries. Heard it when the guts spilled out. Cutting. Cutting. Cutting.

"*Stop!*" she screamed as hard as she could, but did not hear it for the hands over her ears nor would she even if no effort at all had been made to muffle the savage sounds. Broken and exhausted, there were no words left in her, but there were more tears.

In the midst of this, the man stood up and now looked down on the small sobbing vessel of his growing bloodlust.

"There is a certain pleasure in weeping," he quoted to the crumpled and crying creature.

With one swift movement an arm hooked around her neck, this time loose enough for her to somewhat hold herself to him, which she instinctively did in her attempts to keep from choking and to fight him.

The ugly reeking butcher told her to get up and was mad when she had trouble standing. So he picked her up and walked her out into the yard where he abruptly threw her.

He took the dog by one back leg and both front paws in the other hand and carried him past her and toward the woods. She saw when one of the gaping slots in the side of Leopold's neck gave up the collar it stubbornly held, as if declaring the dog not be forgotten.

Samantha heard the heavy thump as her seven-year companion was tossed out like a dead mouse from a garage.

Then she heard the sound of the man returning—on a camping trip with Timothy they heard the heavy crunching and huffing sound of a bear wandering too near their tent—the sound of the stranger advancing was no less frightening than that. Suddenly he was standing over the small psychic, whose success was driven by her claim of being the ancestor of a Salem witch who escaped death by foresight. She didn't count on being that lucky—nothing in her life prepared her for this.

She wished she had the energy to drive her leg up between his legs, all the way up into his ribcage, but her strength was completely spent.

Seldom did she remember hating anyone, but the truth lay strangely within her that, should the opportunity arrive, she would kill him.

"*Forsan miseros meliora sequentur,*" he said to the woman sprawled on the recently mowed lawn.

She wanted to shake her head to show she didn't understand, but he didn't expect her to. Everything he did as much as said was for his own entertainment, as she would soon find out.

*　　　*　　　*

"So, you were right, Bailey," Michael sighed as he dropped the lab results on her desk. "It's not human."

"Hopefully this means we have some time to work with," she pushed her office chair away from her files to face the person she was talking to. "I have a hunch that our perp didn't just do his work in the Polke's basement because it was convenient, but because it more personally victimized her parents— like adding insult to injury. If he does operate like that, then we need to find out what places Goode frequents with friends, if they have any vacation spots in the immediate area that they go to. We need to find out who she's close to, if they have basements, sheds, anywhere he can work in private for a few days and then we need search warrants for all of them. When we talk to these people we need to tell them not to investigate these places themselves, but to wait for law enforcement to inspect the property."

"Sounds like a plan. So, did we get an address book?"

Bailey nodded and flipped through her notes for the name of the tech who was going through the computer and checking the phone records. She said he had it.

Glancing over the lab results, Bailey asked no one specific if the unknown DNA was going to match the killer, but Stull answered, "I suppose it will. We have a bona fide serial killer right here in Essex County."

Bailey stared at him, the blank look a hiatus from responding while she decided whether to say, "Yay" or "You say that like it's a good thing".

Fortunately, she didn't have to answer because she heard Nate's voice, the perfect excuse to get up.

He'd asked someone to point out her desk and was almost there when Bailey slipped past Michael.

Nate hugged her shoulder supportively and asked how things went while the other detective looked him over.

"Who the hell are you?" Stull wondered.

Bailey's eyes rolled toward her ex-partner, wishing Nate was from the DA's office or something. A person who may consequently educate the pretentious detective about acting without thinking first.

"Bailey's partner," he answered automatically, through a growing, one-sided smile. "And you're the 'so' guy."

"Partner?"

"From Boston," Bailey explained. "Speaking of partners, where's yours?"

Stull shrugged.

Bailey guessed "working" though not aloud.

"I meant to ask you," she sensed Nate was eager to see her and wanted to find out why, but had to ask Stull, "What took you so long to get to the scene today?"

"I was on lunch," Michael replied stiffly, smiling big with both sides of his mouth. "It was about one p.m. when you showed up."

Bailey nodded. That made sense…she guessed.

"You're not involving someone outside his jurisdiction on this case are you Detective Jacobs?"

"She doesn't have to justify herself to you," her former partner rebuked, "and my business here or anywhere is none of your business, understand?"

Nate inched forward, slowly separating Bailey from Stull. This was probably involuntary, at this point or from the point when the fourteen-year detective was assigned a twenty-seven-year-old partner on her first day as a detective. When the tension climbed, Treuer always wanted to put himself between it and her, even though she—like many female cops—had a way of smoothing out tense situations.

"Do you need to shut down or lock up any of your work, Bail? We need to talk."

"Yeah."

Either man moved aside to allow her access to her office space, where she logged out and assembled the spread out work into its coordinating slot in a file drawer.

"Thank you for bringing me the lab results. If you want to get started on the phone calls, I'll see if the lab can positively identify our perp as *this* perp and see if the techs found anything on her computer or from her callers."

"Sure. I can do that," Detective Stull agreed, the anger all but vanished, even if the neon smile hadn't.

"I'll call you in a little while," Bailey promised as Nate ushered her away and toward the exit.

He told her, "I thought I saw your car—I'm glad you're back. How was the scene?"

"Understandable, I think. This guy doesn't mind advertising who he is," she worried.

"If he's not in the system, he doesn't have any reason to care until he's caught," Nate pointed out, holding open the door that exited into the foyer. Then she held the door that went outside.

Bailey nodded once.

"How much do you have to work with that guy?"

She shrugged, "Not very much, more now, I suppose. There were three detectives at the Polke murder, but I have no idea what Stull's partner was doing and Stull himself arrived like Disco Stu. I have mostly worked on that while Stull and his partner dealt with the three similar murders. If it's one killer, it will be one case I suppose."

"He doesn't want to be a detective, he wants to be a star," Nate grumbled as they reached the parking lot.

It was late, almost ten at night, and both of them were hungry, so they agreed to eat first and talk on the way back to her place, leaving the rental car to be retrieved the next time she had to go into town.

"No such thing as a weekend off," Nate mused.

"That's one of the only things that's the same," Bailey confessed as she slipped behind the wheel.

"You don't like Lanester, do you Bailey?"

He watched her face tip down, momentarily sad, but long thoughtful while it otherwise appeared she was only separating her car keys from the others.

She almost said, "I hate it."

But chose to say nothing rather than struggle for a sentence to even remotely convey an earnest answer.

Nate, again, wanted to touch her face, but didn't let himself. He chose, instead, because he couldn't settle for less, to put one hand on her shoulder so she'd know it wasn't necessary to answer.

"You get to buy me lunch," he told her, "because I got through your whole list of to do's."

"That's fair," Bailey agreed and offered a trembling smile.

10

...

AWAKE CHAOS. SLEEP LIGHTLY.

Over dinner, Nate filled her in on the jack shit he learned calling gas stations and from that friend in the Bureau. Around Lanester, he said, people had a lot of opinions about her old man, Walter Douglass. Some of them liked to talk a blue streak, while others, who obviously thought more, said less. Some seemed defensive when he pressed for more information.

"All I could do then was laugh at them and say, 'The guy's been missing two months and you just told me you hate him and have motive,' what self-respecting cop wouldn't squeeze you for more info?"

"You weren't casual? You said you were a cop? Did you show your badge?" Bailey's eyebrows went up a notch every time she added another question.

Nate laughed and sipped his beer, "I'm not an amateur!"

"Let me guess. You didn't want to lie completely, because a lie comes out more honest when there is a little truth in it, so because you're doing this as a favor to me, you said you're a private investigator?" Bailey looked amused, he wasn't sure if she would be if he told her the truth.

To sugarcoat it, Nate began with a smile, "Actually, I told them I was with the FBI."

Without looking the least surprised, his former partner continued the previous topic.

"Anyone seem likely?"

"Honestly? Everybody, Bailey," he took a roll from the basket on the table and tore it open, focusing on that as he reiterated, "*Everybody.*"

With the silvery tines of a fork, she probed the remaining bits from the crab cakes. Nate almost detected a nod, but wasn't sure. He *was* sure, however, that his answer came as no surprise.

"There were any number of people who claimed he owed them money and others who said he was after them about debts to him. Almost all of the beef people had with your old man were about money or basically being a jerk—which I find interesting because nothing we've seen indicates the motive was to get money from him—besides the man himself, nothing of value was missing from the house. You said you recovered thousands of dollars in cash…unless the perp wasn't interested in the money anymore and just wanted *him* to pay," he hastily continued. "The ones who weren't talking were, to me, people who could very easily have things going on the side that your dad could have been a part of *or* could have P.I.'d himself into a mess. People with sporting shops, liquor stores or bars, and places on the harbor. You know how this works. Crime is hydrophilic."

"I thought you maybe had good news," Bailey laid down her fork and took an abbreviated sip from her water glass.

"Well, not so much good, but definitely thought-provoking."

"Why?"

"Your dad once tried to find Leia Redding's murderer," Nate leaned back in the plush cream-colored vinyl booth, looking satisfied with himself and the meal.

Bailey frowned and asked why he thought that.

So he rested his elbows on either side of his empty plate and told her, "Because the priest at the little church just down the block from your place said that was the only good thing he knew about him."

Bailey had been feeling really good about their chances of catching the killer, but it wasn't encouraging to learn it was a case even her father, a brilliant investigator, couldn't solve.

"It gets better than that."

"How?" Bailey managed to ask.

"Remember all those strange names we found when we were going through your dad's things?"

She did.

"Well, I did some looking and I found *all* of them."

Her slightly widened eyes probed, "And?"

"They're all missing people."

That wasn't too surprising to Bailey. Her father was a personal investigator. Most of his business involved finding something or someone, "A lot of families hire dad to look for missing people. He looks for people with bench warrants. He's been paid to find people who are hiding from people."

"Four of them, all went missing the same week, three months before Leia Redding was killed. When Leia was found, *that* week another five on the list had disappeared— though some people believe the remains may have been found, some of the bodies were never identified and a number of the families refused to accept any of the bodies could be whoever they were missing. Of the eight, three were positively identified, but were badly decomposed."

Bailey's upper lip parted from the lower to say something, but Nate wasn't finished.

"There was one more name on the list, Bail."

"Who?" she asked.

"Her name was Annie Kellogg.

"Three months before the Redding murder, her body was found by a lighthouse down the coast from Pigeon Cove and was almost impossible to identify, if not for the engraved locket her husband bought her for their fiftieth wedding anniversary. Again, critters were blamed for the disfigurement, including eating her fingers, toes, and eyes."

"Good God..."

"I know it."

Nate watched her process while he explained and saw her expression sink, until it could only be described as grave.

"Bailey," he began, leaning in on his elbows to continue, "I can stay pretty late tomorrow, just forty minutes and it won't mean nothing Monday morning if I lose a few z's, but my time is still limited and we have a lot of work to do. We need to talk to other county jurisdictions and see if, in the times between Annie, Leia, and Erin's deaths, if they had any similar incidents. We're going to build a profile for this maniac so every law enforcement officer in his feeding ground knows what to look for."

"He's getting impatient, too," Bailey told him. "If these other murders you found were his work too, then he's getting sloppy. We're finding bodies a lot faster than they were."

She thought of the little body lying on the mud flat and the small, dingy tennis shoes standing in the dirt beside it.

"He's also getting older," she added.

"Shall we get going?" Nate already slid to the outside of the booth.

Bailey left a tip and went to pay the bill, rather than wait for the waitress to check on them. Nate waited by the door, observing how differently she carried herself here than in Boston, where she sometimes came face to face with the worst kind of low life and held her own, but here he saw a savant and poised woman unable to meet the eyes of a seventeen-year-old hostess.

He also noticed that, while there was nothing lacking or spectacular about the service that a pretty hefty tip was waiting for their mediocre waitress.

Once she'd paid and joined him at the door Nate wanted to warn her about showing people fear, but decided she probably didn't need patronizing right now. He'd seen her fearless a hundred times when there was plenty to be afraid of. This was different. Bailey was different here. Or maybe the situation altered everything. She was the only homicide detective in Lanester. She was relatively new, even if she was a local girl. And, he hated to say it, but a lot of people think someone can't be beautiful and smart. In Bailey, the two characteristics were neck and neck for which brought her the most recognition.

A teenage girl had been sadistically slain and all eyes were on the new, young, female detective who was less a stranger than people thought. Keeping her head down might be a means to maintain that.

Back in her car, they were pulling out when Bailey got a call.

"So, Bailey," Nate heard when she answered. "I got officers in route to a list of likely residences and got all the people informed to take no matters into their own hands. A lot of people had ideas of places that were special to this chick, but as yet, nothing back from the boys checking those out."

"I don't want you to be redundant with people, but I need you to talk to all of them again. We're looking for places with particular meaning to the people close to her. Places where they'd go and think of her, if not their own homes. Not places where Sam would go for a good time, but where people would remember having or to have good times with Sam."

"What's the difference?"

"There might not be. Some people might have included those in their answers, but I just want to make sure we didn't just get a list of all of Sam's favorite places."

"So…what's the difference?"

Bailey cast a sidelong glance at Nate who leaned on the door, pinching the bridge of his nose.

"Leia Redding was just a little girl and liked whatever she happened to like—it doesn't matter—but her dad was a clam digger, professionally and recreationally. They lived on the river that fed the flat where she was found. I would have to look into it to know for sure, but I would put money on it now that she was left in a place her father liked to go or they liked to go together."

"So, don't you think that theory is a little flawed? I mean, the Polke chick was in her parents' house. It wasn't personal, it's where she happened to be when he nabbed her."

Bailey was shaking her head, but of course he couldn't see that, "He could have moved her, Michael. He just didn't want to."

"You don't think he just left because the parents would be home that night?"

"Yes and no," Bailey considered. "Yes, I think he knew the parents were coming home and that was the timeframe he had to work in and that's why he left—because he was done and done in time, not because he ran away. But, you're asking my opinion and I could be wrong. Keep playing devil's advocate and we'll ask each other all the right questions," a smile briefly graced her face.

Bailey never minded being challenged, Nate knew, and saw every question as a mini-pop quiz or as a lawyer poking holes in their case. It was a reminder that just because you're trained and have studied the law, that you're just a person who can't possibly think everything through, cannot always be right, and everyone makes mistakes—truths a lot of big-balled, seniored in, and rookie prodigies are oblivious to.

It wasn't comfortable to hear her working out a case with someone else. Nate didn't like feeling like a third wheel with Bailey and some jerk detective from Salem. She hadn't even asked if he'd been assigned a new partner—of course he had, and she probably knew that would happen or *had* to happen, right away, but the fact that she hadn't asked made him think it might bother her. That little made up for how bad he missed her or that he also, now knew, that she wasn't happy where she was.

Once the phone was returned to her pocket and the next steps with Stull were in place, it was time to discuss the steps they were going to take.

"You know this all has to come before your dad, right?" Nate wasn't sure if she could do that since she left one job to try to find him in the first place.

The look of calmness on Bailey's face was suddenly very hard and almost expressionless.

"You aren't really asking me that," the woman refused, flashing one very angry, very sad look at him.

"Look, I'd like to help you with this bastard before I have to go back. Samantha Goode has to take priority over what we've been working on."

Bailey's hand went to her mouth and her eyebrows pinched one small perfectly straight line between them, but almost as suddenly her hand fell away and with it the look of wounded disbelief.

"Is that what I've been doing?" she asked, regarding him coolly. "I don't give myself priority over anything—*that's* why I have to be here, because there would always be something happening, somewhere to be, interruptions, not enough time—I'm *still* doing my job. Even though it means putting my family on the waiting list—even though it's something I *need* to do, I always put the job first. I wasn't even supposed to be working this weekend—it shouldn't seem selfish that I might use some of that time on him, before he *does* become my job."

Nate said nothing, until he found the one thing that he could.

"I'm sorry, Bail," his whole body felt the pains of regret as he cursed himself silently for being so fucking stupid again.

She wanted to know if he really thought she was like that, but wasn't going to ask him any other way. If she chooses family over solving murders she fails morally and ethically, if she chooses career over family, she fails again. There was no reason she could think of, that she couldn't give herself equally to both—millions of people do every day—but the problem was that each seemed to demand more of Bailey's time and energy than there was to be had.

"Shit—BRAKE!" Nate cried.

The small white car's brake pads screamed.

Something dark and glistening suddenly crossed the shoulder and started into their lane.

When Bailey swerved to miss it, the headlights swung across the form, and in the hot white light, all that was dark and shining blazed red.

While Nate took a second to collect himself, Bailey turned on the hazard lights and let herself out of her seatbelt and into the night.

On the very edge of the headlight's illuminated path, a person with literally ribbons on bone, on hands and knees cowered from the braking vehicle even as they were racing against death to reach it. The coppery smell of blood and stomach fluids filled the area.

"You still keep a blanket in the trunk?" Nate sounded muffled, stooping in to open the glove compartment and pop open the back.

He vaguely heard her call back, "Yeah."

The wounded being, knowing little more than pain, found even the sound of the kneeling woman's phone being dialed unbearable to its pounding ears.

There was no way to humanely check their pulse, let alone the innumerable injuries. Bailey once saw a man stabbed sixty-four times who looked better than the poor creature Nate gingerly wrapped in a blanket. There was a gut churning semblance between the person and a sliced cylinder of cranberry sauce. The differences would almost completely vanish should canned cranberry sauce come with bones.

The sound of approaching sirens came fairly quick, but seemed to take an eternity to those waiting by the roadside.

Nate was looking down the deep ditch, eventually leading to a steeper descent into the river bottoms, the bridge laying before them breached. The detective's gut told him, maybe minutes before they came along so had a killer, one who in the dark did not dump his victim over the rail where the embankment is very steep. Probably the killer heard the body fall nearer than he expected it too, but didn't want to be messing around in the ditch, should someone come along who might think he was having car trouble.

Not that it matters anymore, Nate thought, as the EMT's raised the blanket shrouded body into the back of the bus. *Should all good things in life be rewarded on the effort put into attaining it.*

To Nate Treuer it was nothing but hope's cruel cycle.

Why people thought it was a good thing, he never knew. Hope is like a playing the lottery. It takes and takes and gives little or nothing in return. That pitiable creature fought pretty goddamn hard to live and had nothing to show for it. He or she would have suffered less to just lay where they dropped and bleed out than to crawl through grass, litter, gravel, and asphalt just to die anyway.

"So what does this shit mean?" Nate asked as one stop on a drive home degenerated into a crime scene. "You don't need to tell me that was your monster's handiwork. Why do you think he did this?"

There was only one reason Bailey could think of.

"I think it's all about self-control."

Nate and an officer overhearing both raised their eyebrows at this, but only Nate spoke, even though he did say what the cop was thinking, "This is random. It's savage. It's an exhibition of *complete* lack of control."

"Not if killing them helps him cope with his savagery. This would be the result of his efforts to control himself."

"I don't understand. If he's killing people he's not coping with his need to kill," Nate asked incredulously.

The officer behind them agreed and wanted to stay to hear the explanation, but needed to sign some papers for the crime scene techs who were suddenly swarming the place like elves. Nate put one hand on Bailey's shoulder and suggested they move a short distance away. He stood close to her then, so neither would have to talk above a whisper if they needed to.

"We know that the killer left the Polke's house on multiple occasions. I thought, maybe the guy has a job and can't be there all the time, but someone would have seen him. So we know he's going out at night and all of our cutting victims were last seen at night," Bailey looked steadily at the perpetually tired, but handsome detective standing across from her. "It sates his bloodlust so he doesn't kill his prisoner."

11

...

DOUBTS

A lamp in the kitchen fought no better against the darkness than the television in the living room, the only two lights in use, at the time. Brightness and color fluctuated as scenes of lighted squad cars and ambulances alternated between reporters and interviewees. On the couch, Bailey and Nate helplessly watched the press swarm on Lanester like piranha, when there's something dead or bleeding.

Fueled, not only, by the victim who died by the bridge, but on the other side of the small, vulture head-shaped, peninsula, the body of another woman was discovered. After almost a year since her demise, the sheriff's department was resistant to comment until she was identified and the family was contacted.

"One thing we do know," a reporter said earlier, "is what she has in common with the other slaughtered women—her fingers, toes, and teeth were all missing."

The press dubbed them the "Bad Penny Murders".

Footage of Detective Stull's earlier interview was played, but added that the detective assigned to lead the investigation was unavailable to comment.

If Bailey didn't recognize the number, she wasn't answering. Because she wasn't listed, she hoped the number of phone calls was just a coincidence. As yet, she hadn't shared one word with the press and hoped, by not answering, she wouldn't even have to say "hello" to them.

When she explained this to her captain, should someone try to reach her on their cell phone, he told her to just screen her messages and call people back—*only* if they were officially involved. He was mad because somebody had blabbed about the mutilations—not that people didn't know the victims died violently, but no one knew what the killer would do if his signature was made public. Would he change it? Would he try to exceed his previous efforts?

In addition, true and false connections were made between the victims. The media's sensational story was going to terrify people—if they weren't scared enough already. The sensation was doing as much hurting as it was horrifying. Among the alleged commonalities between the victims, that some reporters speculated to have instigated their untimely deaths, were prostitution, being "welfare bums", and that they'd all had abortions.

While Bailey's job was to know every detail about a crime, from understanding the victim's injuries to the recording and understanding weather's effect on a crime scene before, during, and after—there hadn't been a lot of time between Erin's death and Sam's disappearance to do a whole lot of sleuthing about their personal lives. Between Leia, Erin, Anne, and Sam, Bailey already knew there was no evidence or suspicions that any of the women had abortions or were prostitutes, and none of their economic situations were alike.

The press wasn't even aware of three of the four women, but did speculate that the, as yet, only missing Samantha Goode might be the Bad Penny Murderer's next victim.

What murders were they talking about then?

The assortment of mixed age, mixed gender, mixed social class, wrong place at the wrong time, victims were killed completely differently than the only victim the press even knew of with the injuries they described, Erin Polke.

"What a bunch of dumb bastards," Nate was scowling and irritable. He knew better than to watch the press filter its version of reality to the public, but when he was trying to find something to watch to help them unwind, he'd stumbled across a Special Report indirectly covering his ex-partner's case and, like always, couldn't pry himself away from a story with personal relevance. "Who do you think blabbed about Polke?"

Bailey shrugged. She was like a glacier sitting on the couch beside him. Her jaw was set so hard under an otherwise composed face, he wasn't sure if she could talk if she wanted to.

"It could be anybody," Bailey sullenly answered, "It was chaos. Clearing the scene was like trying to stop the bleeding when the head's gone. I was a stranger and didn't even have a badge yet. These were all Michael's buddies and he wasn't about to make them leave. The front lawn looked like a goddamn town picnic."

"Do *you* think these women have nothing in common?" Nate wondered.

Bailey was perfectly still, the answer immediately available, but not necessarily one she could say aloud:

"Not anymore."

Every so often, Bailey would leave the room to take a phone call and Nate would listen to the reporters and the network's crime experts' take on the killings—something else you shouldn't do if you actually know anything about the law or enjoy the rare gift of commonsense.

Though he started more or less tuning out the B.S., his eyes began to devour every screen.

One thing he was taught to do when first engaging a crime scene is to discretely photograph or videotape people, especially crowds, because you never know if one of them will be a key witness or suspect.

"Son of a bitch," he exhaled, bowing on the cushion until his stomach was almost flat against his lap. He scrambled for the remote and was disappointed at no Ti-Vo. He whipped out his phone and started recording the screen.

"Bailey!" he hollered.

If everything was as it appeared to be, in regards to the Kellogg, Redding, and Polke murders, then after the killer kidnapped someone, for approximately one week, he savagely killed people until killing the captive. The pattern suggested Sam Goode had only about five days to be saved. Nate didn't give a rat's ass who was on the phone.

She reentered the room, cupping one hand over the mouthpiece and was about to ask "what" when he urgently asked, "Who the hell is that guy? I *know* I saw that guy at your office, who is he?"

A slender shape crossed his peripheral as Bailey moved in closer.

"He was just there—they just keep repeating this crap, so hopefully they show him again before they go to their next story—forget it," Nate stopped recording and jumped to his feet to show Bailey the video.

"Can I call you back?" Bailey asked the person on the line. Either they were okay with it or she just hung up on them, because the phone went on the coffee table and she moved so she could better see.

When Nate paused the video and blew up the image, Bailey looked at it and asked why it mattered.

"I just want to know, because he was in one of Stull's clips, at the scene where the guy was in the culvert, and, right here," he pointed at the screen, "he's over in Plum Cove right now, milling with the other optical vampires."

"That's Mackinnon."

"Do you know anything about him?"

She didn't.

How could she?

Her first full day home and she's called to the scene of a long dormant serial killer—or so it had seemed. This followed by strange and brutal random murders in a town that hadn't seen a homicide in more than a decade.

Funny that they should get a homicide detective right then, some people said, just loud enough for her to hear when she was at the grocery a few weeks after arriving. She knew who the women were. They knew who she was too.

With only a few weeks reprieve, while trying to make sure every aspect of the Polke case was accounted for, documented, filed where and with who it needed to, witnesses interviewed, going door to door asking neighbors, getting to know who Erin was, what she did, why it happened, how, and what kind of man was responsible…

Then she had to start the same process for the other victims, who were "Bad Penny's" work too. The body in the culvert, by the bar, the Atlantic Road victim, and now this week, the poor creature who crawled out of the ditch into her headlights.

She also planned to recover Leia Redding's case file and evidence and reexamine it.

After what Nate discovered about Anne Kellogg, she was prepared to ask the district attorney to reopen both cases and those of the missing people. It would mean leaving Lanester, a lot, but she now served Essex County as a homicide detective, not just one town. It was only a matter of time, her captain warned her, before the recovery of this long dead victim fell on her plate too.

In Boston, Nate and her each had between six and nine cases at any given time, so very often as partners they were looking at a total caseload of twelve to eighteen murder investigations at one time. She wasn't overwhelmed yet, but there was a lot to do and the resources weren't as available, accessible, or familiar as they were in the city where she learned how to be a cop in the first place. And here, she didn't have a partner and she wasn't even sure where her authority lay. Stull had seniority on her and his partner on him, but she was called on the scene because it would take Michael and his partner a while to get there.

Her captain talked to her like it was her case and she was investigating them like they were, but she tread lightly, because she was afraid of stepping on anyone's toes if they were given the same impression.

It *was* hard to make time for eating and sleeping. What time she could shave from either of those to look into her father's disappearance she did.

Her sleep, in the meantime, played unwilling host to one relentless nightmare that, at one time, existed only in the nights of her childhood.

"I don't know him," she finally answered.

"You okay, Bail?" he worried at the dullness in her eyes that were once piercing.

He imagined the miller's daughter may have had such a look on her face when faced with the last and greatest sum of straw to spin into gold. If memory served him correctly, the father in that tale had a big mouth that also hurt his daughter a hell of a lot more than it hurt himself.

"I'm okay."

"You can't do anything much with this tonight, except talk a little, if you want to," he didn't think she'd want to. "You're not yourself. You seem… exhausted."

"I haven't had a lot of sleep," she remarked as if just realizing it.

"Tell me something," he began. She raised her eyes to his and for the first time he saw utter vulnerability in them. His chest hurt when he looked at her and, for a moment, forgot what he was going to say. "Do you really want to know what happened to your dad?"

"I need to know," she put flatly and a mile high wall of brick and mortar rose up between her answer and the helplessness he found in her.

"Okay."

"You can have the sofa if you don't want to try and find a hotel," she offered to break the silence thereafter.

He accepted with a nod. The couch was clean, new, and looked like it should sleep well. After the night before, he wouldn't complain if she made him sleep on the dashboard of his rental.

"I appreciate that," he said.

"I appreciate your help," she told him.

He expected this to be followed by, "But I need to ask you to never come here again."

"I haven't really helped," he sincerely declined.

Bailey hated these kind of "arguments". She wasn't going to list off all the things he'd said or done that proved helpful or revealing, to say nothing of the generosity of the act itself. The act of talking to a good man is sometimes more challenging than talking to a bad man and almost always more important, because you don't want to be the woman to ruin it.

In this case, as in any when she had doubts about her answer, she chose instead not to.

When Bailey went to retrieve bedding, Nate went to clean up in the bathroom. He was sporting an "I'm not supposed to be working" length of stubble and a wrinkled shirt opened several buttons down for comfort. From his small travel bag he removed a toothbrush and paste without looking, his eyes were busy in the mirror making sense of what was going on inside the pair looking back.

Even while brushing, he couldn't break the staring contest where, every minute, man or reflection was bombarded with another important question. Like asking if he really thought they could find Bailey's father. If she was going to catch this killer and what it would mean for her if she didn't, or did. Like what was going on in this small town, what was it doing to Bailey? How he was going to handle another week of that proxy he was working beside, when he still felt like his real partner was in the other room. Like what he was going to do with what he was feeling, if there was anything he could do.

He had to look away to rinse his mouth. When he raised his head he saw a miserable man looking back. Though outwardly, other than being slightly bedraggled, he looked like a man who had it all together, but his eyes betrayed him. People said he had an uncanny knack for reading people. He wasn't accustomed to turning that insight on himself.

After changing into sleep pants and a t-shirt, he left the bathroom and turned off the light. No décor. No flare. No accents that speak about what the homeowner likes or loves, or what she collects. No photographs or memorabilia. No knick-knacks, cups or magnets with quirky-isms. Walter Douglass might not be the only person they should have spent some time looking for.

He wanted to flat out ask the beautiful ghost taking the plastic off a new pillow, "What did this town do to you?"

Instead he stood awkwardly in the hallway until she was done and thanked her. He couldn't remember any woman ever making him feel at her mercy. Every play, he felt, was Bailey's if she had any intention to play at all. One false move and, he knew, the ghost would vanish forever.

"Bailey, I'm sorry for what I said in the car. Because, you know, I talked to the Sheriff's Department we can assume a real investigation is going to start—you won't have to make any tough decisions."

"And you didn't tell them how things have went here?"

Nate barely shook his head and said, "Nah…you know I listen to you, right?"

"I can't accept any mistakes," Bailey confessed tiredly. "He's—"

—the only family I have.

"I understand that," Nate's seaworthy accent somehow always made him sound sincere and so Bailey believed him and not wrongly. Regardless of saying a few things he regretted, he was trying harder than ever to understand her.

"Can I ask you something, Bailey," he asked after she said goodnight and started to walk away.

He heard, "hmm?" through her pressed lips.

"Are you planning on staying in Lanester after you find your dad and catch this murderer?"

For a long time she said nothing, but posed a question he would, this time, be the one not to answer:

"What if I don't?"

12

. . .

SLEEPLESS KNIGHTS

The long grass squeaked and creaked when circled by the little girl's small fists and squeezed hard so they might help her get down the embankment safely.

Most of the descent, she felt as if she were merely dangling between long mangled clumps of sawgrass and somehow finding other clusters to grab onto that were exactly an arm's reach closer to the smooth gray-brown bed of mud.

All at once she was flying backward through the air and just as suddenly found herself laying on the flat. A brief glimpse of her small dirty sneakered foot, before it too hit the ground, was the last hoorah of the fall.

After, when she looked around it was out of short bloody tunnels, doubling her vision. She was struck by the sour odor of rot. Instantly she realized who she was, at least now, and so who it was she was smelling.

She raised fingerless limbs before the deep red channels and stared at their paleness, their bloodlessness and the small bluish crab with a human mouth gnawing away at the stub. She tried to fling it away. It smiled, unfazed, and kept munching.

Dark, churning clouds gathered overhead, swirling like colorless cream in literally black coffee. The rain made bright red spots on the earth before it drank them. Her head rolled to the left, to the bridge at the end of the block. A black figure stood there.

She sensed the outrage of it being noticed and it rushed out of sight behind a building, but very certainly was heading her way. Its anger was enormous, shuddering, terrifying—like a minotaur with the force of a train behind its charge.

It would reach the rail above her any moment.

She saw the black shape flicker between the dull gray buildings.

She was suddenly aware of someone standing over her and expected to see her twelve-year-old self looking down.

When her head snapped back to see, she was draped with heavy fabric. Her heart slammed against her ribs, like a frog inside a fist. There was static in her brain, buzzing, humming, numbing fear—it would burst, it would pop, it would stop—if her heart didn't slow down soon.

She thought, *I don't want to die like those girls. Don't cut me up. Don't cut me!*
I don't want to live like those girl's died.

Madness was waiting, if she had to go through it. She was begging reality as much as the dream—I can't survive what he did to her. I can't survive what he's going to do!

She smelled the stink of uncleanliness, the musk of spent pleasure, and the odor of blood.

The cover pulled back—

She felt hands on her, holding her. She struggled against him, against the tangled blanket.

Suddenly the grip on her upper arms was tighter and shaking her.

Then she was looking up at Nate, whose eyes were round with alarm, his chest rising and falling quickly under his cotton t-shirt.

For a moment she was seeing him through the tunnels.

Bailey heard him ask if she was okay and tell her again and again she was dreaming, it was a bad dream. Just a bad dream.

"I'm okay."

Nate let go of her and sat down on the edge of the bed. Drenched in sweat and tears, she trembled with the chill of fever. Immediately her hands flew to her mouth and she doubled over to collect herself, staring out above her fingertips as the phantom of the nightmare played before her eyes.

"What was your dream about?" he asked, pushing aside the errant strands of hair clinging to her sweaty face.

"Leia Redding."

"It bothers you that the guy has a history," Nate assumed. "You don't have to take on the pressure of the years those cases weren't solved—that's someone else's burden. Do you feel guilty about that?"

"Yes," she readily admitted.

"Jesus Christ, why, Bailey? You can't do that."

"I don't choose how I feel, Nate," she defended, dropping her hands away so she could look at him. "It's not as simple as guilt, I feel bombarded…"

Nate sighed and laced his hands together in his lap.

"By all the victims? The pressure? With finding Samantha?"

"No. I can handle that," she looked right at him. "But I feel like I'm not allowed to not think about it.

Every time I close my eyes she's waiting for me, reminding me of unfinished business…"

He asked her why she thought it was Leia's death effecting her this way and not Erin's.

"Was it because she was so young?" he guessed.

The answer lay on the tip of her tongue and wanted badly to be heard, but she couldn't say to him, "Maybe it's because we both were."

Because the absolute truth was far simpler:

When you promise the dead you are guaranteed a haunting.

After convincing Nate she was alright, Bailey lay awake and without intent to try to sleep. One thing that always kept her awake was thinking about cases, not just *thinking* about them, but working on them in her head.

The best thing the case had going for it was the overwhelming amount of evidence. The worst thing was the complete and utter lack of suspects, as yet. A lot of people were questioned, but no one looked good for the part—this didn't mean that any of them wouldn't fit later on. You don't throw away a puzzle piece unless you know it doesn't fit. You can't know that until there aren't any spots to fill.

First thing Monday morning she was going to find out why Mackinnon happened to be where all the bodies were. Though she was ready to do it tomorrow, or that very instant, for that matter, she didn't want to do anything to alarm him.

She knew why he was at the Polke's, because he was the first officer at the scene. There was probably good reason for him to be at the scenes of any one of the slasher killings, because there aren't a lot of police officers and it isn't unreasonable that he shouldn't be one to respond.

The first argument that came to mind that made
Mackinnon an unlikely suspect was his age. As
Bailey recalled, he said he would have been two at
the time Leia was killed, so unless he was a copycat
the debate ends there.

In the small town of Lanester, it wasn't too far
of a reach to think Mackinnon could have been
looking through the cold case files and studied the
details of the crimes and was so moved that he
wanted to try it for himself. Less than that has
motivated other horrors, Bailey thought.

One thing that was nagging her about the bad
dreams she kept having was her father's sudden
inclusion as the killer. Was there something she was
missing, something she overlooked that her mind
was hanging onto that suggested her father's
involvement? Or was the dream just a cruel coupling
of the two biggest things on her mind.

She rolled on her side, a hot tear running across
the side of her nose and dripping onto the
pillowcase.

Whatever happened to you, dad, I hope it was
painless, but I need nothing to have happened. Let
nothing have happened. Please, God...

She made a fist in the hand beneath her cheek
and breathed hotly into the dampening pillow.

He loved her, she told herself, no matter how it
seemed. He could have left her in the hospital too,
but he didn't. Why? Instead of abandoning the child
he never claimed as his own, he took her in, hating
what her mother did—what he said no real mother
would do. Why would a mother leave her newborn
child? Probably the swatch of red hair glaring at the
dark-haired man who would, after, never recover
from the betrayal.

It made her feel like she was on his team—this
horrible thing they had in common. Probably he

sympathized with the baby, but more so with himself, because he *knew* what he lost. Though a flurry of profanities were required to describe the stranger who bore her, his rage was a measure of his grief. Bailey always knew that.

There were no grandparents, aunts, uncles, siblings, cousins, neighbors, nobody—nothing to expand her world. She could come into the house and feel what kind of mood he was in. She could feel him leave the house without seeing or hearing him.

And she gave the first month and a half of his disappearance to Lanester. That—she would never forgive herself for. If she was sleepless with guilt, she had every reason.

There was always the possibility he made himself disappear, she considered as she rolled onto her back. Perhaps saying he could suddenly go away, so many times, was meant to prepare her for the day when he would rid himself of the baggage. She was living in the city then, working as a detective with a master's degree and had a partner she seemed happy to work with, under a boss she respected.

He didn't care about the house and maybe he didn't care about the money or forgot it was there— though she couldn't imagine him forgetting anything—it doesn't mean he didn't. Leaving Boston might have been exactly what her dad wouldn't have wanted. He might have thought she'd be glad to be rid of him, if he ignored everything she'd ever done or said. He was smart enough to know she wouldn't leave it alone.

He had to know that.

She could have been rid of him when she left for college if that was what she wanted. No one *made* her go home.

Unless, Bailey sadly reflected, he knew he'd have to *make her* accept he was gone so she'd move on. Maybe he still had friends on the police force—maybe even in Missing Persons—who would help him make a clean break. "The Wall" was smart, too smart—so dubbing him a superb candidate to conduct any perfect crime—which was exactly what his disappearance looked like.

Then Bailey slept.

The first thing Nate did, after looking around to see if Bailey was awake, was go to her bedroom to check on her. He listened at the door first to make sure she wasn't dressing or moving around at all when he opened the door just a crack and found her sleeping like the dead.

It seemed sensible to assume it would take some time for her to get back to sleep, so he wondered whether or not it was a good idea to make coffee, should the noise or fragrance wake her. Because of a caffeine headache threatening to land somewhere between his left temple and left eye, he decided to take his chances.

The coffee machine only just started making grumpy bubbling sounds when a car pulled into the driveway. Nate stopped his search for cream, sugar, flavored syrup, whatever might enhance his liquid breakfast, to go check who it was.

When he saw the driver, the first thing Nate wondered was if Detective Stull had ever been invited there before.

Nate quietly slipped out of the sliding glass doors facing the river and went quietly down the stairs toward the driveway. He figured he would be too late to stop Michael from closing the car door very loud, but he hoped he would be wrong about

how loud he expected it to be. A man like Stull
walks heavy, talks loud, and makes every effort one
to draw attention to himself.

"Jesus Christ," Nate both exclaimed and
whispered, "Bailey's trying to sleep!"

The other detective was less than happy to see
Nate. He not so much as smiled and wasn't going to.
The swarthy local detective looked over the
underdressed stranger with contempt. The stranger
knew exactly why.

"Couldn't it wait until the sun's at least clocked-
in? It's Sunday for Christ's sake."

"That's why I'm here," Michael said. "I knew
she was supposed to have the weekend off."

"Do you like to be woke up early on your days
off?" Nate asked, folding his arms across his chest as
he leaned against the house.

"I haven't slept myself yet, so you can save the
rhetoric for someone who doesn't work the same
beat as you do. Yeah, I know she's tired. I didn't
know she was sleeping. I thought we'd talk about
the case and maybe figure out how each other works
if she and I are going to solve this together. My
partner just got assigned to a case back home. You
know, I actually don't need to explain any of this to
you."

A frown briefly creased Nate's brow and
vanished before an easy smile, "Bailey doesn't visit
with anyone but perps or witnesses."

Stull looked at the recently awakened man and
at the perfectly silent house before asking, "So, then
why are you here?"

"Because, I'm her husband—"

Surprise smacked Stull across the face.

"—Jesus! Why do you think? She told you I was
her partner—I came up to help Bailey with some
stuff this weekend and she put me up. You're going

to have to wait to see her, but I'd rather you waited another twenty-four hours because she doesn't need to think about that crap today."

"You think she won't?" Michael countered.

Nate wasn't sure if he was going to regret it or not, but he threw a retort at him to end the discussion, "I'm going to do my best to keep it off her mind."

Stull turned up his hands, dropped them at his sides and went to get back in his black Kia Cadenza. Only after the vehicle was backing out did Nate push off the siding and go back inside.

Bailey was sitting on the couch, but appeared to be sleeping somewhat slumped against the back cushion.

"Want some coffee, Bail?" Nate ventured in a low voice.

After clearly seeing a nod, he walked over to her and squatted so he could look up at her.

"Almost woke up?"

Another nod.

"Did I wake you?"

She shook her head and asked where he'd been.

He wanted to lie and say he'd just been out for some fresh air, but decided not to explain at all. She looked so tired she probably wouldn't notice. So he got up and went after the coffee.

"You have a really nice place here, Bailey," Nate said as he sat down a cup in front of her. "You grew up in Lanester, right?"

She nodded into her sip of coffee.

"You told that other detective that Leia Redding's dad was a clam digger. Did you ever do that?"

"Mm-mm."

"This spot out here looks better for fishing anyway."

"I didn't fish," Bailey told him.

"Next time I see my folks I'll borrow a couple rods and I'll show you how, when I can get back up here."

Bailey leaned away from her cup, balancing it between her knees with the light hold of both hands.

"You already taught me how to catch the only thing I need to. I never asked you, did I, about your partner before me?"

Nate looked over at her and thought he liked her tired, in a much different way than he liked her at her best. Bailey never asked him personal questions.

"Retired," Nate explained. "Then I had this young dipshit who, among other things, couldn't keep his cool. I told the captain he was going to get somebody killed and I didn't want it to be me. So the captain says, why don't you take the rookie? She's gonna be good, I can tell."

A familiar pinch happened between Bailey's eyebrows, like the wince or cringe that leads to tears, but she didn't look sad when she looked back at him.

"What became of the young guy?"

"You met him. Detective Stull?"

Nate smiled proudly at the look of surprise that came over her and then admired how the wideness of her eyes brought out the color in them.

"What really happened to him," she ignored.

"Got stupid investigating a drug related killing and became one."

Bailey suddenly knew who they were talking about and apologized.

Nate shrugged and didn't try to respond until he finished his drink of coffee and put the mug down, "You don't need to apologize. The real shame is that he never learned any better and it cost his kids and wife probably a good sixty years or more they should have had with him. I talked to his new partner—do you remember Smith giving me hell all the time?"

She did.

"Well that was because the kid got dumped on him. Anyway, I talked to Smith after the funeral and he said nothing he could say or do to correct the guy was working and finally had a heart to heart with him. The guy tells him that he'd found his own folks shot in the heads by a shotgun in their bed when he was five-years-old or so and being a homicide detective was all he ever wanted to do.

"Smith thought he almost got him talked into transferring to another department—figured the kid could probably do the job if, day in, day out, he wasn't still finding dead bodies."

"I think I heard about that," Bailey reflected.

"Can I ask you somethin'?"

Her gaze slowly met his.

"Did you know Leia Redding?"

"No," she answered, concentrating on a nick in her right thumb nail. "I knew there were Redding's in town, but the first time I heard of Leia was when she went missing."

"That must have been a big deal. Does the panic in Lanester remind you of how it was back then?"

"Yeah," she barely answered.

"Did you talk to your captain about setting up a curfew?"

She nodded emphatically, "Monday morning there's going to be a mob of bar owners and patrons who are going to show up at his office disgruntled."

"Hopefully, it won't be for very long," Nate offered. "I take it your computer guys drew a blank."

Bailey sighed long and tiredly, "The lamplight in the living room made it impossible to make him out even after enhancing the video. You could tell someone was there, or rather, something was by the window, but little more than that. When I called Detective Stull…he sounded relieved."

Nate asked if she knew why.

"My first thought?"

"Sure," her former partner agreed.

"He didn't want the techs to be the ones to catch the killer."

"Though they usually are," Detective Treuer remarked with a grin.

Bailey smiled thoughtfully. In a lot of ways, it was always true.

"Any more of this stuff you need to take care of right away," he asked her, "cuz I don't want this to eat up your whole day. You need to recharge."

"Right now everything is in the hands of our forensic team. I'm waiting to hear back about tire impressions and to see if the swabs done of the dog's mouth match the profile from the Polke murder. The coroner is inundated with victims, at the moment, but he's hopefully going to tell me if all these murders can be linked to the same guy. That is, going back over the records of those missing people and the bodies that might have been theirs. He's going to try and give it priority. In the meantime, Samantha Goode is not dead so it's not a case for homicide. If we find out the dog got a piece of our killer, then the case will be handed over to us, because that case is already ours—obviously working in tandem with other officers on her disappearance. Hopefully, in the next twenty-four hours, I'll hear something from one of the medical centers or clinics I called, that they had a man come in with dog bites. It's just a waiting game."

"Eh," Nate grunted, "We've all played that before."

Detective Treuer quickly determined that the solution for a long wait was several rented videos and a little junk food—for a couple reasons. If a movie is good or you're having a good time, then something is bound to interrupt it. And should the movies not be so great, but they were still amused, the time would pass more quickly, even if he didn't really want it too.

He was just getting up to dress when his pager went off. He muttered something and called back the number.

"Nate Treuer," he answered. "There is? Well that must have been his daughter. No she doesn't live in Boston anymore. Uh-huh. Well, you'll have to check with them. Hopefully they already did the work for you. Mm-hmm, I appreciate it. Okay. Bye."

Nate hung up. He noticed Bailey noticing he was just talking to someone about her and she wanted to know why, even if she didn't ask.

"That was the Sheriff's Department. They just wanted to let me know that they found a local missing person's report made out over a month ago. They're going to check the details with Lanester before jumping in."

He watched her face for a reaction.

"You know these guys are going to find out on their own that the folks here dropped the ball. Then you don't have to worry about telling anybody so yourself."

Bailey didn't seem relieved.

"What if they tell them that I'm his daughter?"

"They would already know that if they did their job."

Bailey looked away.

"Look, let's just forget about it. If something happens that you can do something about you'll deal with it, but you gotta just leave most this stuff… to come to you."

*   *   *

If not for the tablet, the space would have had no light. The glow faintly accented the small, dismal surroundings, but drove a fierce radiance against the person hunched over, viewing it, or rather, a video.

They were replaying last night's news and, since the broadcast began, he'd been making panting sounds like an ape.

They were talking about the victim found by the bridge.

"Detective Jacobs, as seen in the background, has not been available to comment, but sources tell us her sudden transfer to the Detective Division in Lanester suggests the police may have already been chasing the Bad Penny Killer for several months."

Between grunts the man said to the screen:

"Eram quod es, eris quod sum."

In the cramped space where Samantha lay, she spied for a good look at the man's face while also dreading the imprint it would leave on her memory. She had to have something to tell the police. In the self-defense class she went to in high school, more years ago than she'd ever admit, they did an exercise about identifying people and stressed the importance of it. Nothing else from the class came to mind, except that she kept trying to get Timothy to let her use some of the moves on him. If she remembered correctly, they actually got into a fight over it.

Suddenly the man's face swung toward her, but it was flattened by the filthy and threadbare t-shirt he'd pulled over his head. He made an "oh" sound, like "OH! *You're* going to be in trouble!" but the sound was relentless and he held it until he ran out of breath, which seemed an impossibly long time. It had to be about three minutes or more. When he made the sound, his head seemed to hang like he had a very long neck and it was broken, but somehow propped upright.

What she was seeing didn't even look human.

In the strange lighting and darkness, otherwise, any normal person's eyes would be playing tricks on them. So she couldn't tell if what she was seeing was real or a distortion of the mind. All she was sure of was that he didn't want to be seen and she didn't want to make him angry.

She didn't know how much more fury she'd survive.

13

...

SHE THAT WOULD MOVE the WORLD

Nate put off departing until there was no other choice. He did, after all, have other people he was responsible for and cases of his own to address.

At least, it seemed, that something was going to be done for her missing father, so he supposed he should feel like he accomplished something, but all Detective Treuer felt was confused. It seemed natural to discuss the case with her, because he still felt like her partner. Now he felt like he was abandoning her to deal with something that might be too big for even state police to handle. He wouldn't at all be surprised if the Feds took over soon. The more media attention the case developed, the more pressure there would be to wrap it up quickly—as if the local and state police wouldn't already be doing their best to do exactly that.

Bailey stood watching until the silver Chevy was out of sight and only then started across the police station's parking lot to her own car.

The dull sounding connection of her shoes to the blacktop brought home the fact that she was all by herself again.

Whether brightly or dimly lit, almost always does a parking lot feel dangerous at night. Though the detective's was one of only three vehicles in the lot and, therefore, the danger of "who's hiding behind the next vehicle" wasn't there—vulnerability was.

One of the first homicides she caught, in Boston, was a nightshift nurse who'd stopped at a twenty-four hour gas station for a few essential groceries. The parking lot was almost bare. When she walked back to her car, as shown clearly on the security camera, the son of a bitch, waiting around the side near the complimentary air pump, timed his attack so he would reach her exactly when she was opening her car door. He swoops in, pushes her in, sexually assaults her, and strangles her to death. He climbs out and runs off into the darkness.

If Bailey thought no one was watching her, she was wrong. She never discounted the possibility. She tried to never discount anything, but the reality of who was observing her was blissfully absent from consideration. They saw the woman and man part company and could barely contain themselves as she crossed the parking lot in almost perfect solitude.

Every detail about the detective was noted in the sidebar of the onlooker's conscious mind. About five-foot-nine, maybe five-ten. One-hundred and twenty pounds, give or take five pounds. Coppery, reddish hair, with a lot of gold in the alloy. Late twenties, early thirties. Pretty. And, as yet, illusive.

Even though her gait was steady and direct, it was really hard for Bailey to walk away from the projects waiting at her desk. What this translated to, in Bailey, was the people she was making wait until

Monday morning. The families and friends lying awake tonight wondering what's being done to help solve their loved ones' death or to find who they lost. It felt incredibly selfish to keep walking.

It felt so good working with Nate again that several times she forgot she wasn't *working* with him at all. When it started to get late she had to be the one to insist he think about leaving. She was worried about him being out on the road with all the last-call bar patrons or any impairment he might suffer from mere tiredness.

He wanted to know if it was alright, now, for him to keep in touch. Although she had been mad and disgusted by the stance he took about his work, she felt bad that, after this weekend, Nate still felt the need to ask before getting a hold of her again.

For the greater part of her life, Bailey wanted to be a detective, so everything from the moment she moved to Boston to the first morning she woke up as one, was about becoming one. Being a full-time police officer and student meant very little time for socializing, if she'd been interested. Between that and feeling like a pariah while growing up in Lanester, made her relationship with Nate the closest to a friendship she'd ever known, besides that she pretended having with her father.

Bailey realized she'd walked away from that relationship hastily and felt cruel and unappreciative. She wouldn't do that to him again.

As much as she wanted to go inside, like Nate, she recognized that at some point she was going to need to get home and sleep too. When she got in her car, locking the doors behind her, the station fell into sight. Even as she regarded it regretfully, the undeniable truth was, she'd be no good to anything or anyone without rest.

Tap! Tap! Tap!

The left side of the detective's body hit the car door hard as she recoiled from the sound at the passenger side window. In the dim light, Bailey vaguely made out a heavily made-up face smiling in at her under the arm laid across the window so she might better see within.

The woman tapped on the glass again. Suddenly there was a light in Bailey's face from the left side of the vehicle. It was impossible, at first, to make out its source, but as her eyes adjusted to the light she saw it suspended above a man's lower body, at shoulder level. A video camera. And the next time the woman tapped, it was with a microphone.

"Hi! Detective Jacobs? May we ask you a few questions before you call it a night?"

"Back away from the door," Bailey said to the camera man. It looked like he took a step closer.

"Would you mind, please, answering just a couple questions?" the reporter tapped on the glass again.

"Sir, please back away from the door," the detective engaged the man again. This time, with the reporter's prompting, the cameraman finally backed off and Bailey got out of the car to sacrifice a little time now and, hopefully, save a lot later.

The reporter rushed around the front of the vehicle. There was little sound, so there was also little surprise when Bailey saw the woman wasn't wearing any shoes.

The reporter looked familiar, but not "household name" familiar. That meant she had to be local. That probably meant Boston. Which almost had to mean she'd met this reporter before. Nate was better at dealing with the press. People liked to look at him and they liked to hear him talk about crimes. Nathaniel Treuer looked like a detective, at least in media terms. Handsome, intelligent, experienced, and, in a suit, really looked official without looking rich. Best of all, Nate delivered annoyance and impatience which wears well on a good looking officer who's also great at catching the bad guys.

As far as reporters go, Bailey lived by the wisdom of Shakespeare: "Have more than you show, speak less than you know."

"Can you please turn the light off, or away," the detective directed the man behind the blinding lumens. "I don't have a lot of time and can't guarantee that I can answer any of your questions."

"That's fair," said the reporter and gestured for the camera to swing back.

"Please," Bailey carefully touched the side of the camera and swung it the other direction. "Not on camera."

The reporter pouted and opened her mouth to protest—

"This isn't a negotiable. You have five minutes, no camera, no microphone, or no questions."

"I want to talk about the Bad Penny Murders," the reporter put bluntly. She looked about twenty-years old. She hadn't even grown large, unmoving hair yet. In fact, her short, light brown hair wasn't even made up, but pulled back in a ponytail. The inexpensive dress suit, the young lady wore, was probably "all-purpose professional" attire. The same suit, the detective guessed, that had been worn to any and every interview the girl had since she turned eighteen. The same black with gray pinstripes that suited weddings, funerals, family portraits, and "this-is-a-big-deal" moments on camera. Bailey had one kind of like it, but it was a pant suit, light gray with faint silvery white pinstripes. A few more washings and the poor girl wouldn't have pinstripes any more.

Bailey looked down at the microphone in the reporter's hand and read the channel. Boston local, she noted and raised her smart blue-green eyes to meet the somewhat small, and close set, brown eyes staring her down.

"What murders do you mean?" Bailey asked.

"The women and young girl found mutilated in Lanester and, now, in Plum Cove. All the murders have been attributed to the work of one deranged man, the Bad Penny Killer."

"By the press," Bailey reminded her.

"Is it not true that both the killer of the Polke girl and the, as yet, unidentified Plum Cove victim suffered the same grotesque tradition of murder?"

"You would have to contact someone at the coroner's office," the detective sounded regretful. "I don't know if the body recovered in Plum Cove was ever determined to be a homicide. In regards to the Polke case, it wouldn't be in the best interest of an open investigation to discuss specific details so, if you are getting any, you may want to reconsider your sources and how much attention they hope to receive from divulging information. People can and should expect that the very best in professionalism and integrity is being exhausted in the investigation of both cases and any sensationalism is most likely the far-fetched conclusion of someone without authorization to actual information."

"Okay, so what do you make of the unprecedented number of women who have been hacked to death inside your city limits?" the young reporter challenged. "Are these, or are these not, the work of one madman?"

"A trial ultimately determines whether a person is at fault or not, likewise I am not qualified to diagnose someone's sanity," Bailey calmly refused. "I only think it's fair to warn you that someone has been feeding you all misinformation. And in the interest of the public and the families who are grieving, unsubstantiated information about crimes and their victims is liable to cause any number of harms, including, but not limited to, the emotional distress and fear of a community and undue hardship to the families, especially when their loved one is publicly slandered."

"Such as?" the reporter almost got the microphone all the way up before snatching it back to her side.

Bailey kept her eyes on the reporter's face.

"People are looking for a commonality between deaths that might have nothing to do with one another. Some of these characteristics couldn't ever pertain to even half of the victims in question."

The reporter blinked hard, her small boring eyes drilling for more information, an explanation of the impossible claims, but she still had to ask for it.

When she did, Bailey answered:

"*Generally* speaking, a man can't have an abortion and neither can a virgin."

"One of the victims was male?" the reporter asked. She cast a sidelong glance at the husky cameraman who shrugged hugely.

"The details of these cases have been greatly exaggerated, unfortunately the press can only work with the information it's given. In this case, or rather, these cases, it has been misinformation. The duplicated mutilations described by the press, perhaps including your own network, simply do not exist between the victims in question and neither do the similarities, as a supposed motive for their untimely passing. What we may end up talking about, when our investigation is over, may be a bar fight, an unfortunate accident near a drain, a traffic accident, and whatever they find in Plum Cove," Bailey said apologetically and shrugged. "When the investigation is concluded you will certainly know the details, but at the moment we might only be talking about one homicide and, perhaps, two cases of manslaughter. I appreciate the work that you do and know the comfort you bring in keeping the public informed, but jumping to conclusions agitates the community and can compromise our position in the investigation."

"What about the Polke murder? I don't know who the source is, as it's not one of ours, but I understand them to be reliable," the reporter pressed.

"I assume that means the person is involved in criminal justice, so, just to reiterate, sometimes people who are not directly involved pretend that they are or exacerbate bits of information they might overhear from people who are. The truth is that Erin Polke *was* murdered and, no matter what means were responsible, it is a horrible thing to happen to someone, their family, friends, and a community. I really have to go. I hope I've helped and I apologize for being scarce. In the future, the captain of the Detectives Division can tell you just as much as I can. I'm sorry I can't be more helpful, but, I know you understand, I have a job to do."

"Sure, I understand," agreed the reporter who said her name was Holly Richards, if Bailey needed to reach her, and gave the detective a business card. Bailey apologized for not having one of her own to offer, being relatively new to the job.

Holly understood that too.

"I knew you would," Bailey smiled and waved goodbye as she got back in her vehicle and drove away.

For the first mile, Bailey kept her eye on the rearview mirror, just in case they decided to follow her home—where else could she be going at this hour?

Only after that mile did her pulse return to normal, regardless that she was outwardly calm. There are a lot of bad things she'd have rather dealt with than the press. It didn't matter at what hour.

Though unprepared, Detective Jacobs felt confident the answers she gave couldn't be abbreviated to validate the sensationalism running like diarrhea through the media. She actually hoped she might have just added a little Pepto. If they thought she was dumb enough to believe they weren't recording anything, then they'd be dumb enough not to expect deflective and conscientious responses.

"Thank you, Nate," she muttered with a final glance into the dark road behind her.

Detective Stull's Q and A's were something more akin to a monster chase scene in and out of a hall of doors. Definitely effective, but exhausting in an upbeat and entertaining kind of way. She wished he'd been there to deal with the impromptu interview from the police station stakeout. He would have had fun.

The next morning she was woke early by a phone call from the division's captain Kent Bell. It came as no surprise that there was a special report on MSBK channel four, a Boston news channel. He was at home and his wife pointed out the police station's parking lot directly behind this young reporter.

"My wife wants to know if MSBK is a college station."

"Does anyone still run Public Access Television?" Bailey guessed.

"You'd almost think so from the look of them. The video quality isn't that good," the captain went on to complain before telling her that he was happy with how she dealt with them.

Bailey thanked him.

"I know I've met this girl before. I'm going to ask some of the officers I know back there and see if she's a problem in practice or professionally."

"Well she seems to have taken your statement as gold."

That would be nice.

The captain continued, "Stull was thinking it might provoke this guy to react if we went ahead and made a public announcement that we acquired a clear image of the killer from the webcam."

"No—don't do that," she urged. "Provoke him? We might provoke him to go into hiding or to kill Samantha Goode. She might not be his only prisoner either. We don't even know, if the image was clear, if the face would even be visible. Want to make him laugh his ass off? Call a bluff like that when he knows he was wearing a black ski mask or something that night."

Captain Bell was heard clearing his voice some distance away from his mouthpiece.

"Good point," he replied after a few moments. "You know something, Bailey?"

"Hmm?"

"I've never had a murder. Not ever," he sounded tired and embarrassed. "I worked in ballistics before becoming captain of this division. Murder has always been someone else's problem. For the past however many years, that 'someone' has secretly included you. I'm grateful to have you on our team. I don't like seeing fear in Lanester."

Bailey waited for a few seconds before answering, "I don't either," because she felt like there was more he wanted to say.

"How long have you been captain?" she asked the silence that followed her reply.

"Eleven years."

"Are your roots in Lanester, Captain Bell?"

"Lanesville."

Bailey swallowed hard and mustered up the will to continue.

"Well, sir… I was born and raised here. What he has done is personal to me and—I will do everything I can to make this town so safe that my presence here will be questioned when you guys review your budgets."

The older man chuckled, "You catch this killer Bailey and we'll make sure there's always a place for you."

She couldn't say anything she was thinking. That sounded wasteful and purposeless, but how can you say so? If it was just flattery, it was a little embarrassing since investigating murders is what she's supposed to be doing.

The clock on the microwave read seven-twenty and she excused herself to get ready for work.

In the shower, she kept thinking about how she was going to approach Mackinnon. What she would say or ask when she did and trying to anticipate how he might react depending on the reason he was there.

She was squeezing conditioner into her left hand when she looked up and saw Leia Redding's mutilated face pressed against the rippled glass. Small fingerless hands smacked the glass in frustration before pressing her forehead to the sliding door. Cracks spread out from the dismembered nubs, and she let out a bawl like a slow and low storm siren.

Bailey gasped and almost slipped on the clear, bubbled, tub mat. Her long wet hair slapped across her face when she spun, staring down the shower doors, finding herself alone and lobster red in the, now cold, jets of water.

Even though she realized it was a dream, the sensation of someone else's presence in the house didn't go when the understanding came. While dressing hastily, and late, she was constantly looking over her shoulder or down at her legs, where she kept expecting something to be reaching for her.

At the car, she looked underneath from several feet away, before checking the backseat, and only then getting in.

Across the bridge, at the first road going left into Lanester, there's a only a short drive before you reach the largest cemetery in the city, though there are a few smaller historical graveyards scattered throughout the area. Every announcement for memorial services stated the Bad Penny Killer's victims would end up there, in the same hallowed ground as the poor bloated child she'd found lying on a mudflat twenty years ago.

The last time Bailey was there was the night before leaving for Boston. She didn't remember how or why she ended up at Oak Grove Cemetery. She'd taken the walk to clear her mind before taking those first steps to changing one's whole life. Usually such a walk would have taken her up and down the road behind their house.

Bailey heard the signal monitor in the dashboard clicking and turned it off. To get to the police station she had to go straight to the other side of town and not much else. When she didn't turn left, she had a gnawing feeling she hadn't done something she was supposed to. Like she'd forgotten to pick up a friend who needed a ride. The feeling was so strong that

she went over and over again what she could
possibly be forgetting to do.

There was nothing.

If it was Leia, or if it was just guilt, she'd
forgotten neither.

The detective felt foolish for even thinking that.
While she didn't believe in ghosts, one way or
another, her understanding was that, for such to
exist, they are supposed to be unsettled or have
unfinished business.

Why then, with so many supposedly haunted
places, do ghosts seem utterly incapable of doing
anything to help themselves?

Suddenly, a sleek black car cut out in front of
her. She remembered the first time she saw
Michael's car she thought the license plate read
GUDGUY, when it actually was GVD6UY and that
was the plate on the aggressively maneuvering
vehicle ahead of her, now far ahead of her.

When she pulled into the parking lot, Stull was
coming up the sidewalk, having parked farther back
in the lot, where there is shade. He was smiling,
even big in terms of his smiles, so when he waved
her over she was definitely curious what was up.

"Heard you quoted on the morning news."

"Oh…" was all she could say.

"So, keep an eye out for who's mad at you this
morning, because somebody's not going to like the
lead investigator eluding to the police they're a liar."

"Someone is."

As they were walking up the steps, Michael
leaned in and audibly smelled at her hair, having
said something about her shampoo. She leaned
away, staring at the dark, grinning, practical stranger
questioningly.

"So, do you usually go to work with a wet
head?"

"I was running late. Do you always drive like that when you are?" she wanted to know.

"I *do* drive all the way back and forth between here and Salem every day, you know. Sometimes it's hard to anticipate traffic—but, you're exactly who I was in a hurry to see."

"Why?"

It was his turn to stare.

"Because we're like partners now."

"No—" she said to both his answer and what he said in it. "—I meant why you were in a hurry."

"My girlfriend didn't want to get up, but I didn't really trust her alone in my house."

Bailey threw a frustrated scowl at him and hoped it felt like a slap, especially after she saw the way his smile changed. Of course, he knew exactly what she meant every time he answered.

"Do you like wasting time?" she reached to grab the door handle, but he threw himself in the way to open it first.

"Sometimes," he said earnestly—his way of apologizing for the way her wrist bent when he shoved past her and yanked on the handle, but also added an "Oops" if she hadn't caught the way he changed his tone.

Bailey got to the inside door before him and slipped through without waiting, then he was hurrying to catch up.

"Did your 'partner' tell you that mine got stuck on a double hommi over in Salem? So, you really are filling the part of partner for me now."

"How is he coping with his alcoholism?" she wondered, starting up the stairs.

Stull stood behind to let that one fully sink in and smiled boldly in conclusion. "No, that was his last partner. He switched to heroin when he got me."

A fleeting glance was the last thing he saw of her before the next flight of stairs took her out of view. Then he took the elevator.

When Detective Stull reached Bailey's desk, Curtis from forensics was there with a laptop showing her the footage from the webcam and what little good enhancing it did.

"This isn't useless," she consoled the technician. "Someone was there. The prints your team lifted from the window sill match the prints at the Polke house. It's not a slam dunk, but it's still a score."

Curtis looked only slightly inflated after being so disappointed.

"We should have had him," he grumbled, picking up his laptop.

"Hey," Bailey stopped him with a light touch to his wrist, "*should haves* are when mistakes are made. You did good work. It would have been nice to see a face there, but there wasn't. It's as simple as that."

"Okay," the purely average looking Joe finally agreed and said "good morning" to Detective Stull when he left.

"Everyone around here is either walking around with swollen balls or anxiety attacks," he remarked, as if neither comment applied to himself.

"Are you going to tell me the real reason you were in such a hurry this morning?" Bailey ignored. She switched on the computer and unlocked the top left drawer of her desk to take out a long and writing wrinkled legal pad.

"We checked out a summer cottage the Goode's liked to weekend at, when they were still married. Someone had been there fairly recently, within the past week or two, and left marks on a sand dirtied window where they tried to look through. The fingerprints and tire tracks match those found at Samantha's house."

"And inside?" Bailey asked with much interest.

"Nada. No entrance. But we know he considered it, so you're probably right."

"It will help narrow down his hiding spots," she hoped.

"There's more than that. The body over in Plum Cove? She was found in the crawl space under her own house. The husband had just won it in their divorce settlement, but it was their dream home. I don't know exactly how the negotiations went, but he gave up a lot not to give up the house. Then, when she went missing, he started to lose interest, and eventually put it up for sale because it was too painful. The new owners were having it inspected and the poor bastard found more than wood rot when he went under. The husband tried to say that the body must have been there before he and her bought it, but these folks, you know, they don't understand the rate of decomposition. They see skeleton and think hundreds of years, not a couple handfuls of months. So, anyway, my point is, that's a pretty personal death scene."

Little arguing there.

Bailey had a little new information of her own.

"We got a match on the tire tracks too. They belong to a vehicle that was reported stolen almost six months ago, east of Rockport. The plates must have been changed by now and our killer must drive a lot safer than you do," she told him.

He thought he'd impressed her and smiled accordingly.

"You won't be smiling after you run someone down," Bailey warned, without hiding her annoyance this time, since to do so obviously construed something unintended.

"Are you always this square?" he sounded annoyed too.

"Jesus Christ, there are laws for a reason," she stiffly reminded him. "We're not above them, we need to be examples of them, if anything, and more severely punished for breaking them, because it's our job to understand and enforce them. Do I think it's awesome that you were speeding down a street with very few pedestrian crossings, so people just cross wherever they want to thinking, for some reason, that people pushing a ton of metal down the road at thirty miles an hour might be watching for them?"

"You don't like action movies, do you?" Michael's smile broadened and her reaction had to go the way of the dodo, because, like the overhunting of the bird, there was a strong lack of give-a-damn.

Instead, she brought up an armful of files, sat them on the desk between them, and pulled a rolling stool out from underneath with the toe of her shoe.

"We need to get on the same page."

14

...

ANYTHING WHICH CAN BE COUNTED

It was raining, unnaturally dark for any afternoon outside of winter, as the black raincoat donned crime scene technicians scurried to contain a small section of the Catholic Elementary School's playground, under the careful guidance of a recently transferred homicide detective. Under her arm, in the shelter of an opaque white pocket raincoat, a plethora of hastily scribed notes captured the scene in perpetuity.

Among the essentials in her right hand pocket were any number of plastic bags, latex gloves, a couple pens, a notepad, and a half a dozen paper rulers.

One such ruler hung limply between her fingers, after unfolding it. The number of wounds was daunting. This, like each identical murder before it, would fill a page with measurements. Depth and length of wound. Widths. Number of punctures, cuts, abrasions, bruises... How did the victim die?

Under the plastic hood, the pelting rain sounded like bacon frying. Around her, people were yelling to be heard. Below her, something like a body lay like a deep red pile of shredded coleslaw. Across from her, Detective Stull had one hand over his mouth and was staring in disbelief at the atrocity. He'd asked her what she made of it.

"This is a female, age…probably early forties, give or take ten years depending on the rate she grayed. Lab will be able to tell us for certain. She…uh… She died from blood loss as a result of multiple lacerations. She appears to have been the traffic guard. It was approximately five-thirty p.m., as yet, the most recent time someone witnessed her alive. The attack took place in the back of a mini-van, possibly the victim's. She was drug roughly forty-five feet and pushed over the playground fence. Blood and tissue on either side of the fence suggest the killer used the woven metal surface as leverage to get her over. The body was discovered at six-twenty-one p.m.. It is six-forty-four p.m.," Bailey shifted the weight on her feet. "This is incredibly brazen. He just bitch-slapped us."

"I can't believe no one saw him! I really don't believe that at all," Michael said through his hand. "It's prime time! People are coming and going from work. People are going on dates, getting supper, going out. Someone fuckin' saw the creep. They might not have seen what happened, but somebody saw something."

"We're going to need to go door to door and ask people," the female detective looked over the other detective's shoulder when she saw Officer Mackinnon briefly through the commotion of police work.

Alex, from Curtis's forensic unit, stood ready with his camera when Bailey was ready with the ruler, but all of that was temporarily forgotten.

Mackinnon had Monday off and this morning he was scarce, unreachable. When Bailey saw him, just now, they made eye contact and she thought he looked more anxious when that happened. He hadn't been at the crime scene, and so shouldn't have been there now. Only those with the "need to know" privilege were allowed in the tape. The badge doesn't automatically give someone that, but these guys were definitely not used to sending each other away. Just because he was there didn't implicate him of anything, but the look on his face made her question what was up.

"Stull, I need you to do this," she handed him the ruler.

If it had been Nate, he would have known about Mackinnon and been able to help. He would have known about Anne Kellogg and the other murders and missing people. It was hard to trust him to do the right thing…to not make her sorry.

"What's up?" Michael saw the look on Bailey's face when she handed off the paper. He wanted to know everything she knew, for the second time looking totally serious.

"I need to catch Officer Mackinnon. It looks like he's going to leave."

"You haven't got to talk to him yet?" Detective Stull turned to look for the junior member of the force.

"No and I really need to."

"Well, you know it's okay," he assured her, while putting on his own pair of rubber gloves.

The entrance and exit to the playground was some distance away, but scaling the fence, for some reason, might look like she meant business and incite him to run, which was exactly what she was afraid he would do. Instead she waved to him and smiled without airs, to make him pause and wonder what she wanted—should he have heard Bailey had been looking for him yesterday.

Mackinnon hesitated, but kept going.

This, Bailey didn't like.

She hollered to the nearest officer on the other side of the fence, "Hey, can you stop that guy? I need to give him something!"

The agreeable, small town officer was all too glad to be helpful and trotted off to stay his fellow cop.

Bailey made for the playground gate in an urgent walk—the walk of someone who's catching their child for the lunch they forgot or who just saw an old friend on the other side of the street and needs to reach a crosswalk first. Other than noticing her, no one thought anything of someone moving at that gait—hopefully Mackinnon wouldn't either.

"Hey—hi!" she called ahead of her, pretending she was winded when she crossed the street where the friendly officer had stopped Mackinnon at his personal vehicle. "Thanks for delaying him," and to Mackinnon, "Thanks for waiting."

"You bet, Detective Jacobs," the officer said and left them. Mackinnon said nothing until he was back across the road.

"He said you had something for me?"

In the gloom, the taller officer looked down on him, no semblance of nonchalance remained, a stony look of intolerance taking its place.

"Some advice…" she said. "It looks bad when you run from a cop."

Mackinnon swallowed hard and avoided her piercing eyes. Though rain disguised the sweat breaking out on his face and neck, Bailey saw color both drain and raise from and to the appropriate places of stress and embarrassment. She knew he was sweating when he wiped at his forehead.

"What is this about?" he asked.

"Please don't play this game, Mackinnon. You know why I wanted to see you, because you know where I've seen you."

"Plum Cove?" his tone suggested a guess.

"Why?"

"I had a hunch, okay? I just needed to know for sure. When a body actually turned up, I just freaked."

Bailey asked where he got this hunch and he didn't want to say.

"Who are you protecting?"

"Myself!" he said too loudly and shrunk back against his car. Clearly anxious, flighty. Afraid.

"Why?" she encouraged.

"I can't talk about this here," he said.

"We need to talk about this now. I don't want to agree to meet somewhere and you no-show."

"I wouldn't do that."

She saw the lie written across his face.

"Do you know who the killer is?"

The shape of the young man's eyes pacing back and forth under the lids as he watched the ground told her he either wasn't sure or was thinking about lying.

"I have suspicions," he said earnestly. "It's just stuff I've noticed since you asked the DA to reopen the cases."

Bailey waited for an explanation. Actually, she was waiting for him to get the willpower to let it out.

"I moonlight as security at a club," he sounded young, his voice several degrees higher and trembling when he told her. "It's out of town. In Salem."

Bailey's eyes flicked in Detective Stull's direction and back to the young officer.

"It's an alternative club," he hesitated to divulge.

"A sex club?" was the first thing that came to mind, but he shook his head.

"Not that that doesn't happen all the time. There's not too much that doesn't happen there, but I need the job," he stressed. "My girlfriend and I got in trouble back in eleventh grade and our baby has needed all kinds of care, okay. I needed another job and they pay well for the patrons to feel safe when they make themselves so vulnerable."

"Vulnerable?"

"It's goth, industrial, bondage, fetish, vampire club," the twenty-something officer shrugged like they were all the same thing. "The only thing I really like is the live music and one of my favorite bands comes back pretty regularly. I know their songs pretty well, so when you got the Kellogg and Redding cases reopened I noticed some coincidences in their lyrics, song titles, stage names, things they say…"

Mackinnon shook involuntarily and tried to say the rest as fast as he could or maybe never, "They occasionally wear and sell these t-shirts that say, 'The rest of them shredded and one of 'em bedded'. They have songs called, Annie and the Other Holes, Leia's Red Riding Hood, among other songs with women's first names that I traced to five other missing women, though they can be coincidental. Last year they put out an album, though this one only appears in the line of a song, it goes, 'Lizzie Beth's sudden death, two feet of freedom above her breast.' They released the name of the Plum Creek woman discovered in the crawl space."

"Elizabeth Mercer," the detective knew.

"Last night they played a brand new song," Mackinnon finally looked up, "called, 'Sam I Am'."

"Who are they?"

"GCC—The Great Castration Caper—I don't think they're the killers, I think they're his fans."

"Who?"

Mackinnon swallowed hard and bit on his lip, like there were odds he might drop dead just by letting the name fall out of his mouth.

"He practically lives at the club. He's into everything. He takes a lot of responsibility for their songs, tells them stories, gives them poetry he wants to hear her sing. He's dangerous. A lot of the club members go there just to be near him and are freakishly competitive at that. Ninety-nine percent of the fights I break up have to do with him. He knows I'm a cop—he knows about my family!" the officer's voice broke. "Is he capable of this? Yes... I think so. How old would he have been when old Lady Kellogg was killed? About seventeen-years-old. Ever heard of Jesse Pomeroy? He was angelic compared to this freak."

"Tell me who. I'll take care of you, Mackinnon," she promised.

Thunder cracked directly overhead. The whole of the investigators cowered from the deafening boom.

Through the sound, she didn't hear the answer, but saw the young man's lips move.

She leaned in and Mackinnon brought his mouth close to her ear. Rain fell harder, the sound magnified by the plastic coats, agitated by the passing of vehicles, people trying to talk over the weather. A single tone, like a dead phone line, rose out of her mind and seemed to hang inside the foggy whitish hood. It almost sounded like there were mosquitos inside her ears while at the same time the stuffy-deafness of being submerged in water overcame her. Even so, the name came clearly to her ears:

"Fisher Cainen Meryl."

Bailey leaned back and searched the face made child-like with fear.

This was not a name unfamiliar to the former police officer. It belonged to a pompous, hedonistic, self-serving god of goths who lived in Salem, but occasionally indulged in the dark and alternative underbelly of Boston. He had followers, Manson-esque worshippers, in the numbers of Jonestown devotees and who would do just as much, but under less duress. He was seductive, persuasive, and deeply, deeply troubled.

"Listen to me, Mackinnon," Bailey put a hand on his stiff shoulder. "Anyone could have noticed the coincidences you did. There's no way anyone's going to know it was you. I'm not really worried about you telling anyone, but I really need you to not. We're going to arrange for you to have a leave of absence. Something convincing and unsuspicious. I'll arrange it with the captain. We'll get it worked out like you have a broken leg so you have to be laid up from both jobs. Maybe you'll take advantage of that and take your family to go visit some friends out of town, or out of state, if you have that."

"Not out of state, well probably, but no one I really know," he stammered.

"That's fine," she told him. "Now I need you to not go home, because your family needs to think you broke your leg too. Drive back to the station, I'll call the captain and explain things. Everything's going to be just fine."

"Do you have my cell number?" his voice barely squeaked out.

The female detective nodded and reminded him, "You called me my first day."

He nodded, remembering.

"I'm sorry for avoiding you. But the more pieces that fit, the less I wanted to put them together, until I just didn't want anything to do with it anymore."

Bailey stopped him when he started to get in the car.

"How was it that you happened to be in Plum Cove when Elizabeth Mercer was discovered?"

"I heard about it on the scanner. It doesn't take long to drive over there," he grunted. "Doesn't take long to get anywhere, around here. I probably wouldn't have went had I not overheard Fisher say things would get interesting over there soon."

Did he?

Her eyes narrowed thoughtfully, so thoughtfully there was only enough of her present to raise a few fingers "goodbye" to Mackinnon. Rapidly retrieving, sorting all the information that just fell into her mental "IN" box. After a moment or two of almost perfect stillness, she blinked away the rain gathered on her lashes and sighed hugely on the truth left glaring at her from the process.

Fisher was capable of this.

"Stull," she called as she approached the rain drenched detective. She was just putting away her phone after making the arrangements, or close to that, which she'd promised Mackinnon would protect him. Michael had moved on, the body was taken away, and he was standing off to one side of the area to finish his notes.

He looked up at her sullenly.

"We have to catch this guy soon—I don't want to have it hanging over my head—we don't catch this guy and Sam Goode ends up tar-tar or fillets."

"She won't," Bailey knew and then Stull remembered that's not how Penny would kill her.

"I don't want to feel responsible for that either."

"You won't be."

Stull was nodding, like he hoped he could believe that when the time came.

Then he threw a troubled gaze out over the crime scene, looking abandoned and lost.

"Death, I've done, Bailey," he stuck out his chin and turned the play packed grass with the point of one shoe. "I've done crimes of passion, vehicular manslaughter, boating accidents, black widows... This isn't murder. Cain murdered Abel out of fucking jealousy. I arrest Cain's all the time. This is something else. It makes me feel like I never investigated a murder before."

His blue eyes drifted over to meet her gaze.

"So, is this old news for you?"

In some ways...

"I've never had a serial killer," answered Bailey.

It made her realize that arriving earlier to the first crime scene would have done Stull, the investigation, and the victims a world of good— once the Salem Detective did arrive, Erin was already gone and so, maybe, to Michel, it was all just more blood and more blood, but without a body it didn't hit home. Which made her wonder where the hell he was when he and his partner were investigating the slashings.

If he was a creature of habit, she knew exactly where. Somewhere unhelpful.

"After we get this wrapped up, you and I need to take a drive to Salem," she took the clipboard he suddenly handed to her and glanced over his notes.

The idea seemed to cheer him up.

"Can I ask why?"

"A good lead," she said to the man slightly shorter than herself.

Stull told her he could live with that and went back to work with a little more energy.

Bailey couldn't wait to get the hell out of Lanester. Meryl had a way of always knowing when someone was looking for him and, as such, having a monopoly on the decision of appearing or not. No cop likes to play Thimblerig with a suspect.

While she hadn't any significant time on Lanester's police force, the mood when she walked into the building was noticeably different. The clerk at the front desk stared at Detective Jacobs like she'd never seen her before. One of the officers she met on the stairwell regarded her like she'd shown up in a Halloween costume. A number of investigators by the water cooler scattered when she reached the floor. While she had suspicions of why, the answer didn't come until she stood before her desktop and saw a Missing Persons report for her father taped to the screen. Had she reached out and taken it, she would have felt the warmth of its recent run on the photocopier, among almost a thousand others—one-fifth of these had been posted throughout the floor. The others were, in mass, finding homes in every business window and public bulletin.

Bailey stared at the flier, the first for her father's sake she'd seen. Rather than comfort she saw it glaring in spite.

"Are you offering a reward, Douglass?" an officer she didn't know asked when he went by.

At first Bailey didn't react, except that Missing Persons only called her Ms. Douglass, so she was conditioned, in some ways, of responding to it.

Finally, she reached out, pinching the edge of the sheet and slowly pulling up so the tape wouldn't split. She folded the tape over the top and lay the paper face down on her desk. Feeling sick, tremors of cold running through her arms and above her knees, Bailey left her desk and tried to walk casually to the Missing Person's office. Visibly successful, inside she felt herself moving awkward, like her feet had been replaced by small hooves.

She hadn't figured out what she was feeling by the time she entered, whether it was anger, nerves, or hurt, but when she saw the board canvases in copies of the notice, she decided she was mad.

The clerk, who had been really nice before, looked defiant when the detective approached.

"Before you say anything, I have something to say," Heather, the woman who'd been nice, informed her. "You call us wanting special treatment. Nagging us, calling, calling, calling. We're a small department and there's only so much we can do. When you don't get what you want, rather than talking to us—even though you stop by here all the goddamn time—you go over our heads and complain to the Sheriff's Department. I'm sorry to tell you, *Douglass,* you're nothing special."

"It's Jacobs."

"You're a Douglass to all of us," the clerk returned smugly.

"Well, that's fine, Heather. I'd sincerely prefer that," she started to leave.

"Hey *Bailey,*" called the woman at the desk. When she looked back, Heather told her, "Must be hard to have to hide from the limelight because everyone in Lanester knows how worthless you and your whole family is. A gaping whore, a fat-asshole, and an illegitimate bitch."

Old news, but never water off her back. She didn't respond any more than to leave Missing Persons. Nothing changes and nothing is different. She had to believe there was someone or something in Heather or anyone else in the world that privately and or openly torments them. You feel sick. You feel hurt. You feel like hurting them. But Bailey knew she was nothing special, no different, unspared, often unconsidered. As Fuller says, we are born crying, live complaining, and die disappointed.

Bailey was glad one cannot die *from* disappointment.

Detective Stull was waiting by the entrance to the detectives' work area. He'd seen the fliers, which meant only that someone finally got sick of "The Wall", but was not so unperceptive to not sense that they had something to do with the fluish pale under splotchy flush that wasn't so before they arrived.

"So, you just get sentenced to death?"

Her troubled eyes moved to him, but he wasn't sure if she saw him or not.

"That was a homicide detective joke," he explained.

"Sorry," she said, for not laughing.

He shrugged and laughed forcibly before dismissing the attempt, "It was a bad joke."

All she wanted was to get back to work. No sound, save the one time Stull cleared his throat, passed between them as they did up the paperwork. He felt tension in the air and noticed the more quiet than silence in the pretty detective. The stillness was like a vacuum. Like the air around the timid when they are about to be hurt.

When the report was complete and filed, Michael offered to drive them to Salem.

The sleek black luxury car still smelled new. Inside, with weather and pending darkness to lend nothing but lightning to brighten the black leather interior. It was like climbing into a hole.

"Is the bulb out?" she asked him.

"Yes and no," he said as he sat down behind the wheel. "I took it out so people can't see me when I'm getting in and out of the car. When I was a kid, this mother was waiting by the school for her son to come out of a late practice. She was doing crossword puzzles by the interior light. Didn't see the person approach her in the dark, they figured the light inside made it seem darker outside. Rolled down window for a little air circulation—boy finds mom stabbed thirty or forty times in the face."

"Is that a true or a Rockport urban legend?"

Stull shook his head and turned over the engine.

"True story. Indirectly, why I wanted to become a cop."

"Why indirectly?" Bailey wondered.

He threw her a huge white smile and was ready to tell her, "After the murder, my old man carried on twenty-four-seven about how shitty the cops were, how unsafe Rockport suddenly was, how things like this don't happen in America. It made me want to shut the old man up. I wanted to be an awesome cop, make Rockport safe, and disillusion myself about crime in America. Between the old man and COPS."

He flashed her another version of the same radiant smile, while otherwise paying good attention to the road.

"What made *you* want to be a cop?"

Bailey looked over at him and pulled at the shoulder safety strap, which suddenly felt like it was cutting into her neck.

"My father is a detective."

And I wanted to be everything he was, but do everything opposite.

"No kidding? Still?"

"He's a private detective now."

Stull remarked that a lot of fellas do that after they retire or can't do it anymore, "Like how ex-soldiers become security and bodyguards and shit."

"I suppose," she said.

"What did your mom do?" he asked the woman in the dark right side of the car.

She left us...

"It was just me and dad," she allowed.

The handsome detective looked at her again. The console played a soft glow across his rain wetted features and he wasn't smiling. He was just listening.

Sensing he was close to reaching a wall or crossing a line, he decided to make better use of, what suddenly felt like a short drive, to Salem.

"So, tell me who we're looking at."

First she wanted to know if he knew Fisher Cainen Meryl.

"Sure," he said, but not with much inflection.

"What do you think of him?"

"The guy knows stuff," Stull sighed out, like this was helplessly so. "Is he our lead? He's been helpful to me as an informant in the past. Sometimes people do shit and go brag to him about it. He's practically a sociopath, so he doesn't mind ratting anyone out and hasn't any kind of relationship with fear. Never met 'im."

Bailey searched for a safe way to progress.

"You admire him?"

Stull threw her a look that said the answer before it came out of his mouth, "The guy's scary, but he's useful to me sometimes."

"Does he ever ask you for anything in exchange?"

The answer was "yes", even though it never came out of his mouth.

"When's the last time you interacted with Fisher?"

The male detective threw his head back a little to think on it and told her it had been about seven months.

"The guy causes a lot of trouble for the boys in blue, but doesn't throw shit in my direction, very often."

She asked him about the band.

"Yeah, I know GCC. Hot chicks. Hot and *loud*."

"Do you listen to their music?"

Stull looked over at her through the dark.

"Not my style. It's loud, vulgar, and angry."

It was then that Bailey decided to tell him what Mackinnon told her.

Afterward Michael suddenly decided they needed to make a stop before hitting the club.

"Where?" Bailey wondered.

"Wally Purgis' Mixed Lot. It's a shop that sells a lot of prisms, incense, tobacco, clothes and cd's from local bands. I know they sell the Great Castration Caper there. Let's show up fashionably late to the club, Meryl is bound to be late to arrive and almost last to leave."

Bailey consented.

Only one shop was fully illuminated on the strip of street carrying dozens of small stores. To say it was "fully illuminated" was an overstatement, but it was also clearly open, not only for the bold sign declaring it, but the people coming and going and the light they let out with them.

Stull opened the door this time without doing Bailey any bodily harm. The smell that wafted out was dense with sandalwood and marijuana.

Standing out from the other patrons wasn't a concern of the detectives, but it seemed to concern some of the dwindling shoppers, who, when they scurried away, took the smell of dope with them.

"Cops?" asked, presumably, Wally, a gangly, scraggly, middle-aged man in capri shorts, a t-shirt with a half-dressed witch, and designer glasses.

Stull was about to answer when the guy behind the counter starts laughing his ass off and stops just as suddenly, pressing tears out of his eyes with his thumbs.

"Sorry, I always wanted to say that," he explained. "How can I help you officers tonight?"

"We were just looking for the cd's. Do you still sell local bands? My kid brother said I had to check out, *GCC*?" Stull said the name like he'd only heard it once.

The clerk looked disappointed and flicked his finger like there was a booger on it, "That's all over there."

"I'll just get them all," Bailey sorted through the rows until she'd picked out every different title, while Michael stood nearby, pretending to be interested in a few other bands.

"Bad Penny," she read the title of the last of the CD's. She turned them over discovered, "This is their first album."

Stull looked down, Bailey was looking at the date again on the band's fledgling album.

"What's the pic?" he asked and pointed to the image behind the track list. It was a black and white photo of sand with something written in it.

"Penny stole your thoughts. Nickel bought a thrill. Quarter of the month's gone by, plenty more time to kill," Bailey delivered flatly.

She'd seen enough.

When Bailey turned around she came face to face with a t-shirt glaring:

"The rest of them shredded and one of 'em bedded."

Stull put a hand on her shoulder and lead her toward the counter.

"You okay?" he asked.

She said she was fine.

How could she tell him that the first thing she saw was small toeless legs standing deep within the rack of clothes? How could she tell him how white and then bright the letters were when she read the line? That when they blurred, it almost looked like they read: THREE DAYS.

Stull insisted on paying for the cd's, since it was "his kid brother".

They divided the disks, once they returned to the car, and took out the booklets to hopefully find lyrics and did.

"Listen to this," Stull interrupted. "It's called, 'Delicious'. Listen to these lyrics."

The detective cleared his throat and, with flashlight against the small open booklet shared a sample of the first song:

"You beat me. You bleed, but what kills me is you'll never need me. All the things you make me swallow, all your bullshit, your come—ing around, your loose and dumb bitches—zip your britches. One thing delicious, keep it all for me to eat, my selfishly guarded treat. You beat me. You bleed. You beat…"

The detectives looked at each other. Bailey didn't know what to say. She was already put off by the song titles Mackinnon shared earlier. She didn't really expect to like what they had to say.

Bailey didn't any better enjoy what she had to read, but she could see where Mackinnon was coming from with lyrics like:

Bash me to the ground
Spill my teeth all around
Too scared to make a sound
… too scared to make a sound
You beat
Want to split your flesh
And make you eat the meat
Fill you with cowardice
A hands and knees retreat
Beg me, beg me not to kill
This power swap gives me a thrill
Beg me, beg me, come to my senses
Try to get me, let down my defenses
Drowning out a weaker age
Weigh it down with bricks
I take Charon as my lover
Fuck him in the River Styx
Accepting fate, let a new me emerge
Phoenix Goddess
Gather all I hate,
Leave the few I love to write their dirge.

Bailey pinched the bridge of her nose and waded through the next song and the next. Her hand cradling her forehead, her chin, her temple, her jaw. She shifted in her seat, which she was grateful was comfortable, glancing up every now and then to see how Stull was doing.

He looked engrossed. That was okay.

What wasn't okay was what the songs were telling her.

"Let's go, Michael," she urged him. "We need to talk to him if he really is responsible for these lyrics."

At the club, Samhain, there wasn't an overwhelming line at the door, but some. These were not the kind of people Stull thought of when he thought of Salem, but regarded them as the perpetuation of a stereotype and tragedy he'd rather abandoned the city.

They decided not to wait in line and flashed their badges for access without fuss.

They squeezed past any number of chalk-white androgynous creatures and into the head-pounding strobe-light lit madness and debauchery Mackinnon briefly described.

Bailey pointed out the five woman band on the high and deeply imbedded stage near the far back and left of the club. The stage was like a cave with hot flashing lights and headroom enough that the very tall frontwoman could flatten her hand against the ceiling while she sang:

"...is the worthless in you that lets all those men do what they do. At what point do you point and say, 'Disposable', 'Forgettable', 'Edible'? When did her cries not sound credible? At what point do you get to that point?"

Bodies pressed in around the detectives.

Bailey was conscious of every sensation, her gun, her pockets, and person. The setting wasn't comfortable, but she was calm and in her element. They were tracking down a lead. It felt good. It felt like they were finally getting somewhere.

There was a girl, standing out by just standing. She faced the stage, her slightly spread fingers lit gently upon her lips, fixed on the band—or rather the song—tears running black through chunky mascara. The girl, a cheap semblance of the high priced accessories and outfits donned by the writhing hedonists.

Bailey followed the enrapt gaze of the sorrowful girl and held the mournful sounding woman with her own eyes for a moment and her ears with her whole being.

"At what point did you wake up and think, 'Let's play God!'? When she falls...it's just a doll...no feelings at all..."

Stull's head whipped to the right when they passed particularly large breasts in a fishnet dress.

Bailey glanced at the stage and wondered how things looked from there. She wondered if she and Michael looked like a couple of gray sharks gliding through all that dark water.

The singer was looking at her.

Mousy black eyes closed the distance and locked on Bailey. Her voice that was before like a cello, raked savagely through the pounding bass and pain pinched her brow. She not once took her eyes from the woman detective. Bailey expected her to jump down, or backstage if there was one—the woman looked anxious, like she was watching a reoccurring nightmare playing out, and wondering if she was really awake.

"Disposable—though she lives—no life! She's just a sacrifice! Horrible—the nightmare she went through—but she still amounts to less than you!?"

"That's Fisher," Stull said loudly against her ear. He enjoyed being so close to Bailey. Here she couldn't restrict proximity the way she consciously or subconsciously did everywhere else. That close, his lips almost touched the proud curve of her jaw or where it meets her long creamy neck. If they were here together, instead of working, he thought he'd like that. He liked the arguing, that she was tough on him. Women came so easy for Michael, any resistance equated bitchiness he didn't have time for, but they had to keep working together.

As far as he was concerned, there was potential.

The density was like a mosh pit. It was hot and agitated. Coiling like snakes. Constricting on each other. Slithering against her. It was only appropriate that they should come to find a viper. She pierced the chaos and confusion, the patrons paid to participate in, and fixed her gaze on the familiar monster, reclining like Bacchus in his own private section of Hell and assured Michael:

"I know."

In this corner of the club, the crowd was strangely thin and, somehow, the light did not reach so far inside. The expansive corner booth had a wide, low coffee table, so Fisher sat almost completely exposed to anyone who wanted to see him and, likewise, anyone he wanted to see.

At once, the man's eyes moved from those vying for attention to the first thing he'd seen that night to interest him, the striking redhead with dangerously serious eyes and a mouth that, to him, looked made to fellate, but once he processed the familiar man and saw she was there to stay, his ice-blue eyes rolled up the male detective while a smile curled on a mouth that naturally tucked into a secretive sneer.

"Evening detective," the wintery man greeted his autumn equivalent. "To what do I owe this honor?"

Then he was done looking at Detective Stull and fixed on the waif.

"Let me guess," his dark makeup made more obvious what he wasn't hiding anyway, when he looked her up and down. His smile tucked deeper into his smooth, unblemished cheeks, raising lines like the curve of horns at the outsides of it. Bailey guessed groupies probably thought it sexy, because she thought he was doing something on purpose to exaggerate it. She remembered that smile too well to think of it as anything more than interesting, but mostly just belligerent.

"I don't think you want us to talk about this out here," Bailey encouraged.

One drawn eyebrow jumped with interest. The fine silver ring and bead on it announced themselves when a bit of errant light touched them in that moment, or they would otherwise lay unseen.

"Okay," he submitted and pushed off the seat and into the watchful gaze of dozens of his minions.

The pleather pants, zippered, belted, and buckled with long bands hanging for bondage, gathered neatly around his ample crotch when he sat and, standing, the uncovered zipper's curve gave the illusion or memory of the shape that recently filled it. A black wife-beater strained across his slender ash-white body. A white print of a celtic cross hung off center and wrapped around the side of the shirt. Just about as low as his long black tresses reached.

Like a turn of the millennium Dani Filth, but taller and without an English accent.

He was surreal and well knew it.

Beside the booth, where pulsing light couldn't reach, the darkness there and of the black velvet draped walls dissolved the slender incubus.

Stull watched Detective Jacobs find the place where he passed through and felt the expected falseness of the wall.

"Let me go first," he offered.

Bailey put her forearm out and blocked his chest when he tried to move past.

"I've got this," she assured him and slipped through the wall.

Turning on a flashlight would be both wise and predictable. There were red, wire covered bulbs at irregular intervals, enough that after a moment or two, she was sure she'd be able to see.

Fisher wanted to see if they'd follow him through the dark and would be far less helpful if he thought them unworthy of it.

Needing a light to help them down a hall state inspections had to declare safe pitted common sense against worry. However, state restrictions weren't dictating who else might be waiting in the almost unlit passage or what they were capable of.

Mackinnon would suspect Jacobs had followed up on the lead, but if both detectives suddenly disappeared without a word—his mouth would probably never open again.

"Missed me," Fisher had a smile in his voice when he called them from another room close by. The brief flare up of a match illuminated his ghostly features when he touched it to the cigarette pressed between his black shining lips. "Now you've got to kiss me."

They only just passed by the entrance to the room. The hot red ember of a drag of tobacco told them he'd either moved or handed it off to someone else in the room.

"It's too bad your life is so dull that the best thing you can do with it is waste time," Bailey said to the vile, but beautiful creature.

Only four of the sixteen baseball sized lights at the dressing table were turned on. In the darkness, Fisher had moved and was strung out across the arms of a red leather armchair, with one foot on the ground, like a vain little prince.

He dropped the cord with the small black rotating switch and returned that hand to his mouth, and so the cigarette with it. He was smiling at Bailey and squinting through the ribbons of smoke. It made him look amused. How else could he respond? A tantrum? Tears?

Bailey had noticed a minute green light near the floor when they entered and she quickly recognized the hardware of a laser motion sensor, much like the safety sensor on a garage door opener. When the light went out, he knew they'd passed by.

"I want to talk to you about the Great Castration Caper," she told him.

"Not interested," he returned, the smile put out like the cigarette crimped into the arm of the chair.

"Don't you want to know why?" Michael asked him.

Fisher looked up at the male detective, one thin eyebrow raised high and doubtfully.

"You guys finally putting two and two together?" he guessed, folding over himself like a straight razor to reach the scattered liquor bottles where makeup and brushes were typically found.

"You don't sound concerned," Bailey probed carefully.

"Why should I be?" he glared over his drink at Detective Stull.

"We hear you write a lot of their lyrics," he told Fisher.

"They finally got the Feds involved," the man turned on Bailey. "Flatulent Butt-loving Imbeciles."

"Finally?" she glanced his way, but was studying the room.

Rather than answer her, he answered Stull instead:

"Who said I write the lyrics?"

"We heard you said so," Bailey said.

"It would be helpful if people continued to think that," his pants creaked when he stretched.

"Why?"

Fisher looked at her, eyes busy with indecision.

"So if Bad Penny takes notice and has a problem, he might have it with me before Inori."

"The singer," Bailey told Michael before he asked. Then she said to Fisher, "Then the songs *are* about the murders."

"If you say so," he suddenly had a cigarette again and was lighting it.

"How did you know about Elizabeth Mercer before the police?" she pressed.

"You tell me," his eyes widened, the dark outline of the almost white contacts made his eyes look internally illuminated.

"I assume you'd rather I dealt with you than the band?" Bailey asked rhetorically. "I'm not going to piss around with you, Meryl, if I don't think I have to. You know what we need to hear to make us go away."

"I *assume* you don't mean a threat?" his eyes twinkled mirthfully.

"Not unless you want one returned."

Fisher looked over at Detective Stull and could see the impasse between backing up the woman agent or pressing his luck with him. He'd put money on Stull letting the agent take the chances, which might be the wisest stance to take, since Fisher didn't appreciate what he interpreted as a betrayal of trust. You only get to do that once.

"It's a little late to be interested," he finally said to the assumed FBI agent.

"I've always been interested," she answered in a tone that made the goth give her a second look.

"These crimes have been reported. There are records of all these dealings. Follow through? Not unless you make the grade, it seems," he said.

"I'm listening," Bailey lowered until her bottom touched her raised heels and folder her arms across her knees.

They looked at each other.

Fisher believed her.

"Elizabeth Mercer was the only person who went missing that week who wasn't found. When these broads show up they are so carefully placed—the others are spent and thrown away. They get found. The bitches are left where he wants them to be found. When the house went up for sale we knew the appraiser would find something. No one spends the kind of time on a house and yard and all the pointless, worthless frivolities of Dick and Jane couples like the Mercers, unless they were happy. Where else would Bad Penny keep her?"

"How did you know it was the crawlspace?" Bailey asked.

"Lucky guess," Fisher exhaled smoke through his answer.

Bailey waited for a better answer. At first he was going to wait until she asked, but he didn't want to spend the whole rotten night in a dressing room with a couple sleuths.

"If it was anywhere else she would have been found. You can tell the attic space is used by the draperies and shit through the glass. She wasn't going to be kept under a sink or in a closet. She wasn't going to fall out of the dryer one day when Mr. Mercer realized, without a woman, he might have to wash his own drawers."

Fair enough.

"When were you first aware of him?"

Fisher recalled the month after he lost his virginity, "I was twelve. I remember that my bitch was particularly pliable after, because there were all these missing people throughout ours and the neighboring towns. Six by the end of the week. Always six. One, to have some fun, but it takes six to get his fix."

"Always?" asked Bailey.

Fisher's smoky eyes closed and seemed all the brighter when they slowly reopened, with a slight drop in his jaw offering something of a nod.

"First, the broad. Then a single day, typically without losing anyone. Then one, one, one, and usually by the next day he needs two the night before his finale."

Stull looked doubtful.

"Look," the alternative, self-made god threw his hands apart helplessly, "you bitches with badges know not a lot of people go missing around here unless they're running from you. So when there are spells where you find more than average, you'll see what we've seen, but probably faster than it took us."

"Six?"

Fisher looked at her and agreed.

"Goddamn it," she kicked at the abused carpet. "How did you find out?"

The man leaned back, his lean waist stretched out across the space between the arms of the chair, "I listened to the band."

He looked down into the greenish-Caribbean waters captured in the agent's irises.

She wanted to know everything.

How it started?

How it got this far?

Why?

Why would *any* victims be ignored?

"I paid attention to the Caper because they're beautiful and there aren't a lot of asians around here. They stood out. Then I paid attention because I liked the music. Then I paid attention to what Inori was saying. Maybe she was abused and tortured herself. Maybe it was someone she knew. I've seen her cry until she couldn't sing through it. I thought I would capitalize one way or another. Sorrow makes a woman as agreeable as fear. That 'sexist' idea that woman want a hero—it's true. I tell some sobbing cunt that I'm going to solve all her problems and she becomes very compliant. I started to talk to Inori and discovered I couldn't tell her that, because she'd know it was a lie."

"Who was the victim?"

Fisher cleared his throat and shifted in the chair. The tall platforms of his buckle riddled boots made the length of leg hanging off the left side look exaggerated.

"A friend of hers. Used to strip down in Rhode Island after a history of selling it around Essex while drifting between the sofas of friends. When she was just 'missing' the police didn't do anything. They said she could have just moved on or moved in with someone Inori didn't know. There was no way to substantiate she was missing and didn't want to be. But when a body surfaced near their 'thinking place', Inori had a bad feeling it was her friend and went to identify her in the morgue."

Fisher took a long drag on the cigarette and then crushed it out, even though there was still an inch above the filter to burn. He hung a new one on his painted lips and started fresh, looking mad and frustrated in his brow and jaw.

"Was it her friend?" Michael asked when the silence following seemed to take up too much time.

"You know it was," the goth said grimly. "There weren't any tattoos. No dental records or fingerprints to compare, but she knew the girl all their lives. She pointed out scars she remembered, but there was no one to confirm them. If it was her, Inori was told, she'd probably just jumped into the wrong car. Those things happen. Whether they believed her or not, nothing was done. The friend was trash. People don't give particular consideration to the disposable or already thrown away."

"What was her name, Fisher?" Bailey asked him, notebook in hand.

"Kimberly Church," he said the name solemnly. "The missing people we linked to the week after her disappearance are: Josh Sutton, girlfriend and him went camping, she went to the bathroom and he was gone when she came back. Greg Linderman, a fisherman—drunk, poor, lowlife, hermit—whatever. Found the boat, didn't find him for two months. 'Boating accident' they said. We did the research, there's nothing in the water that would have done that to his body," his lip curled in disgust. "Olivia Hill disappeared from a laundromat. Left her purse, laundry, car, and a shoe behind. She was a single mom, lots of kids, lots of auditions to play daddy. They thought she was fellating guys while her towels were in the wash and probably offered the wrong guy."

Fisher turned in the chair so he was sitting, but slouched and widely spaced legs.

"Fifth victim was Josselyn Henry. People cared when she went missing. Twenty something nurse, clean record, good family. *Good teeth*," he hissed out disgustedly. "She was walking to a friend's house and never made it. Number six was Fred Tanner. A bartender from Chelsea. He was supposed to close up. He was never seen again, in any form, but his disappearance fits the bill."

Bailey stood and used the dressing table to help her write faster and clearer. When she was through, she looked over her shoulder at the seated man watching her.

"When did this happen?"

"December ninth through the night of the fifteenth. Fred was found the sixteenth. Five years ago this winter."

"I only have one more question for you, for now, Fisher," she put the notepad away.

He smiled up at her, his teeth as bright as his eyes in their brief and sarcastic show.

"Why does she write about the murders? Why does she write about the victims so vulgarly?"

"She's a little fucked up—" Fisher told her, then amended quickly, "—she writes about the victims the way they were treated by Bad Penny or society. It's outrage."

Bailey looked down. She was thinking of the theme she wrote about her dad. It wasn't flattering, but it was written purely out of affection and desperation to understand him.

"How many sequences of these victims have you and this *Inori* discovered in your 'detective' work?" Stull sounded a little sarcastic and it wasn't lost on the others in the room. Bailey turned to say something to him, but in white hot anger Fisher was quicker, reeling on the detective like a snake.

"If you want to call bullshit, then call it! I can back up every word I've said to you. We wouldn't be having this conversation if you cocksuckers had done your motherfucking jobs in the first place! You don't find people. You don't help the families. You sure as hell don't save anyone. You grade people like eggs!" Fisher rose out of the chair, a daunting six-foot-eight in the boots. "When Bad Penny captured his first, there was a witness to the abduction, but the police didn't act on it or keep record of it! Why? Because his first victim was a queer!"

Bailey put a hand on his shoulder to try and turn his attention back to her and as far from Michael's rhetoric as possible.

"When was that?"

It took Fisher a second to process that what she said wasn't going to make him angrier and then a second longer to compose himself.

"1967."

"Jesus," Bailey exhaled.

Stull rolled his eyes, but Fisher didn't see.

"Same six?"

Fisher nodded.

"But three days passed before anyone went missing. One the first day and four the day after the next day."

"Four in one day?" Bailey leaned against the wall, thoughtfully tapping the end of a pen against her lips.

"What do you make of it?" Stull asked her.

Fisher looked interested too.

Bailey shrugged.

"I guess I could stretch an explanation across it, if it was his first," she frowned deeply. "It makes more sense if it's his first."

Stull asked why.

"Because he wouldn't know it was going to be hard on him to wait," she reasoned. "He kidnaps the woman—"

"Man," Fisher interrupted.

"A man?" Bailey echoed.

"Well…." the goth considered a moment. "A youth. A male youth. He was sixteen."

"He only takes females," Stull said offhandedly.

"*No* he doesn't," Fisher turned on him. "He only started capturing women exclusively in 1988.There was one before that. In 1973, a woman in Atlantic City was found with the same… signature. She was a known prostitute—correction—she was a known *slut*. Seldom, as I understand it, did she ask for money. Once we found her murder, we were able to run missing people from that time in a search engine and got the corroborating hits," then Fisher returned his attention to Bailey. "What were you saying?"

Bailey cleared her throat, offering a second or two for Michael to say something back to Meryl, if he was going to.

"So…he kidnaps this boy and plans to spend a lot of time with him, but he doesn't know how hard it's going to be not to just kill him. There's something about these people the killer loathes so much that it agitates his bloodlust, or something he desires in them, that reaching the point when he actually takes their life is like having an orgasm. For him, he needs to take time to get the most out of the event. To just kill them, even though he already knows he's going to, is like premature ejaculation."

Bailey bit on the pen cap and nodded as reason came washing over her, "The first day he's alright, but the first time he goes off on someone it might even be a surprise to him. It 'just happens'. He's been erratic, panics, and lays low as long as he can. After a day of waiting for the police to catch up with him, he can't help himself—and hasn't learned to pace himself—"

"Killing more in a day than he ever has since," Fisher finished the thought.

Stull slumped against the densely graffitied and vandalized wall. It was his turn to curse.

"How many captives did you find?" he repeated his question.

The looming goth settled back onto the abused chair and addressed his reply to Detective Jacobs:

"Seventeen."

15

· · ·

A DISH BEST SERVED COLD

Outside, the sun beat hotly against the large brick building where Boston's Homicide detectives were mostly hard at work. Inside, diffused by semi-transparent blinds, the midmorning light played gently across the mostly unlit room—the sunlight delivering, not only enough light to work by, but a more pleasant illumination. What little comforts they could enjoy, they certainly tried to.

Amidst the bustle of couriers and officers were people taking and making phone calls, the buzz of fax machines, people running to printers, to court, to interviews, and to leave the office altogether, to do the worst, but arguably most important part of their job.

Nate Treuer found himself staring at the desktop's wallpaper. It was dark blue, no frills, but littered with files and applications. He was thinking about Bailey. And he was thinking about Samantha Goode and hoping his ex-partner and "so" guy would find her before she died horribly or, at least, before going through worse than she already had.

For absolutely lacking in the common sense to not leave any evidence, the Bad Penny Killer also seemed to know exactly what evidence to leave out, while not seeming at all concerned about being prosecuted later for the multitudes of incriminating exhibits left behind.

"Hey—wake up, handsome," a woman said behind him.

"Hmm?" he didn't blink or move.

Joanne, a brunette with a contrived smile and somewhat pointy nose, helped herself to the extra chair in his cubicle. She'd just joined dispatch and wasn't disappointed, as a lot of women weren't, when they found out he was single.

"Hey yourself," he tried to sound like he was in the moment, but he wasn't. Not even when he made himself look away from the screen, he didn't really see her.

"Where are you?" she laughed a little and waved a hand in front of him.

"Go blind, did you?" he returned.

Joanne smiled hard, scrunching her nose and holding the very edge of her tongue between her teeth.

He hated when people smile like that, but offered something of a smile in return anyway.

"Well, where are you?" she pressed.

"Thinkin'," he looked back at the cream and white colored icons, which seemed disordered, spread chaotically across the wallpaper.

"About?"

Nate looked over at her and *saw* her, this time immediately noticing she hadn't finished buttoning her top, which looked a size or two too small, and had hiked a modest length skirt to unprofessional heights. She noticed him notice, but whatever he was thinking, he kept it to himself.

She wouldn't have been flattered if she had been able to read his mind.

She was asking him about buying her lunch, since she understood he had no wife, kids, or girlfriend to use his big detective's salary on—he was trying to hear a conversation in the hall.

"How much would it cost to ship something that heavy?" someone asked right after he'd heard his new partner, Ronnie's, voice.

Nate logged out and excused himself just as Ronnie and another officer reached him. Nate could tell by his partner's walk that they'd just caught a call and by the tone of their voices, there was nothing usual about it.

When the other two detectives arrived, they also noticed Joanne's strategic wardrobe, but only one of the three appreciated it.

"Have a good time, Lewis," Nate patted the third man's shoulder when he moved past and Ronnie joined him.

"That wasn't obvious," Ronnie, happily married to a sweet as monk fruit, cheerful as jelly beans, Italian waitress.

"Jesus Christ," was Nate's way of agreeing. "This was actually okay compared to this one time a couple years ago—a bear attack wouldn't have felt as aggressive."

"What are you looking for?" Ronnie asked while handing Nate a thin file.

"I'm not that particular," he answered while reading the details of the single paged report within.

"I'd settle for single and intelligent—blame media for all these poor girls who're taught dumb is cute, cheating is okay, and slutty is cool."

"*I* think you're standards are pretty high," Ronnie contented. "You know exactly what you want."

Nate ignored him, except to think that there were definitely drawbacks to working with people who are trained to hear what people aren't saying.

What was there to say, anyway?

He was starting to understand why Bailey felt so trapped in Boston—forty miles is fine for a regular drive now and then, but in police work, with untold hours of overtime and being on-call, forty miles between you and the people or person you want to be with is just too damn far. It might as well have been four-hundred miles.

They stepped out into ninety-eight degree heat, which, for this time of year, should have been a comfortable sixty-five, at least. There was something different in the air, or maybe just in instinct, that gave Nate pause before pulling open the passenger side car door.

He felt something was about to happen. As he slid into the warm, fabric upholstered seat he really hoped it was the weather. His gut said otherwise and it took some internal struggling not to get out at the first stoplight, because he had a feeling he didn't want to be at this crime scene.

Within the hour after their departure, the department's natural air of busyness transformed into a horrible medley of shocked silence and urgent discussion when Ronnie made a phone call to the office.

16

. . .

THOSE WHO WAIT

Sitting in the dark, with no more than the light of the screen to stay it, might have been bad for her eyes, but Bailey always felt it did wonders for her concentration.

It was a little after one-thirty in the morning when Detective Stull dropped her off at the police station where her vehicle waited. As soon as she got home the only thing she could stand to do was work.

Fisher Cainen Meryl agreed to overnight mail copies of their findings to her at the police station. Meryl had innumerable resources when it came to people he could ask for favors or information about things happening *now,* but most of the victims he mentioned had to surface from the most basic of investigation— like search engines and multimedia databases at libraries. For the past three hours, Bailey was playing catch up to the facts he'd discussed using only sources available to Meryl.

The formula was simple. The motive and signature were unwavering between victims who were captives and those for coping.

There was very little in-depth information about any of the missing people or known victims, but little clues suggested she might be looking at victims of the same murderer, probably the same that helped Inori draw the same conclusions. Every possibility required research of their own—should the missing person be alive and well or passed away under other circumstances.

Every so often, Bailey would take a sip from the nearly full mug of coffee—it was already cold the first time she remembered it was there. Mostly she needed something to moisten her mouth. Her mouth went dry listening to what Fisher Cainen Meryl told her and nothing she was reading helped.

"Body missing fingers and toes," Bailey read below one of the links that came up from her search.

She clicked on it.

Something moved out of the corner of her eye.

Like a steel rod driven up beside her backbone—the detective sat up straight and chased the movement with rounded eyes.

She didn't see the article open on the screen, the one about a body found in Boston that morning.

Starting from just behind her right shoulder, her face turned quickly left until suddenly she saw a ghostly bluish face staring back at her from the sliding glass doors.

Whoomp. Whoomp. Whoomp.

Her heart lurched in her chest.

When she recognized the face as her own, lit by the computer screen, she let the held breath push out between her teeth, it made a sound like the steamy breath of a train.

When she tried to return to her work, the writing on the screen appeared too dark and the background too bright to look at, after staring into a pitch black room. She reached out and pulled the cord to turn on her desk lamp.

"Fuck!" she screamed at the filthy man leaning on the desk, inches from the light.

The chair turned over as she stood and the branching, wheeled legs, tripped her. The back of her head bounced against the hardwood floor and her right leg howled in a tangle around the base of the rolling office chair. Stunned, Bailey rose onto her elbows—once again, alone in the room.

After separating herself from the chair, the only thing to do was check the house for intruders. It was the best way to put off the truth—all of this was getting to her.

When Bailey was satisfied there was no one in the house she found herself out on the street, making good time. She was halfway down the block before she finished putting on her jacket.

Still pinched between her thumb and forefinger, the dangling house keys were finally allowed to slide around the ring and to join the others with a cold clinking hoorah. Bailey knew where she was going, but only as a passenger—something else was driving.

The dewy grass was sipped by the hem of her lounge pants, dampening and darkening them the length of fingertips on all sides of the leg. The wetness felt cold when it touched her leg.

Eventually Bailey reached the path that would take her the last length of the journey. The crushed rock made chewing sounds under her tennis shoes.

No one said anything as the detective passed by—even as hundreds of people were completely aware of her presence—she felt like they were staring at her.

Maybe they didn't say anything because she wasn't there to see them. Not this time.

They all knew that was a good thing—maybe *this* is why they said nothing—to just be left alone.

The truth is, most of them cherished *any* attention—just to be remembered was a coveted gesture. Except if *this* woman came to see one of them, something would have to be wrong. Naturally, anyone needing an officer's help would be grateful for any consideration toward their predicament. That was not the case.

Bailey Jacobs only came to see one person and only one waited for her—no one else had unresolved issues like that… not like *that*.

So maybe no one said anything to the detective because they could tell how important her business was.

In all likelihood, they *knew* all about it.

Probably the real reasons they said nothing to Bailey, but still knew exactly why she was there were the same—everyone was dead.

Having left the house compulsively, if not helplessly, Bailey obviously hadn't thought to bring a flashlight, but she didn't need one to find the grave.

There the earth was settled and slightly sunken. She remembered when it was still a slight bulge of exposed dirt with a greenish mist spreading across from the sprouting grass.

The detective looked through the dark with her hands and found the name with her fingertips and her voice:

"Leia."

A voice so faint, she couldn't tell if it was within or without her kept repeating: Saturday morning, you'll find Goode dead.

There was nothing she could do to silence it. Tearfully she traced the carefully sculpted shape of the child's headstone, many thought strangely absent of the lamb or angel motif commonly used in the death of little ones.

Lambs to the slaughter...

...the angel is in the grave.

The tombstone was cool and slippery from the same moisture that, crouching, wetted her knee and bottom of her jacket—her hand slid up it and clutched the top of the reddish brown stone that she loathsomely thought resembled the color of dried blood.

Even so, it made Bailey feel like she was putting a hand on the little girl's shoulder. A girl who should have turned thirty this year.

There she thought and asked a lot of things.

Did you know what you wanted to be when you grew up?

Bailey barely stopped the huge, choking sob that started in her chest, slapping a hand over her mouth. She looked up for strength. For guidance. For proof there is a Heaven where little butchered girls forget their sorrows and suffering. She needed a promise.

So often, she wanted to make her own promises.

"I'll do my best," she could promise.

What would that do, but reinforce the feeling she'd, as yet, done nothing at all?

She needed a slap in the face—she needed to always remember what was at stake—and to stay focused. *Always*.

For most of the walk back home Bailey was in a daze of precise thought and a fog of other worries.

She couldn't lump Leia's death among the others in the case. She couldn't feel the same way about it at all. If she could, how much easier this all would be to process! The promise of 'doing her best' was one made to every victim, every time. She'd made a promise built on a guarantee one time and, within the hour, learned a lesson that made her conscientious of even making promises to the living.

When she reached the end of one road, she turned right and was suddenly out of town.

The cool dewy morning air smelled and tasted clean, but the enjoyment was lost to the stretch of road before the bridge where some blood and crime scene tape remained. Bailey's eyes fixed on the dark brownish-red stains where muscle and bone ground across the pavement in a last ditch effort at rescue. The victim, though anyone's guess at the time, who turned out to be a teenage boy, was still breathing when Nate put the blanket around him. He was still breathing when Bailey laid her hand on his chest to feel for the rise and fall of life in it.

She remembered thinking how long it'd been since she'd touched a living victim.

Special care was taken when crossing the traces of him, not to step on the smallest drop of blood.

A light blue VW bug, coming from the opposite direction, slowed down a little when the driver saw her. The road belonged to them, it seemed, as they hadn't seen another sign of life, if you don't count deer or birds and the driver surely didn't. He didn't even count Bailey, for that matter, except that he recognized her from a brief clip on TV and, while there was no picture, he heard her say a lot of things about him.

If *she* was paying any attention to the news, he thought, she would be looking a lot worse than he saw. Maybe no one in Boston cared enough to inform her.

Bailey was rarely so deep in thought that she stopped paying attention to her surroundings. She made a point of remembering as much as she could about everyone she met, just in case. When she looked at the driver of the bug, she acknowledged a familiar face and put it in the "so noted" stack in her memory, having no reason to give it another thought.

Indirectly, she would be thinking about him once she got home, because someone was waiting for her on the deck. He was sitting on the steps, face in his hands, the posture of worry, of helplessness.

She approached him slowly, her feet feeling heavier and heavier with every step. Very soon, she thought, they will not move again and remembered this kind of dread like she was crossing the mudflat all over again, knowing just as she had then, there was no convincing herself this could be anything other than bad.

"Nate?" she said.

She sounded small and afraid, like when you're called into the other room by your parents and it sounds like you're in trouble and you know you did something wrong.

He looked up over his fingertips and flew off the deck to hug her. She let his arms envelope her. Felt his cheek against her temple, a hand on the back of her head, the other on the middle of her back.

"I'm so sorry, Bail," his fingers pressed harder.

"Why?" she pushed on him so she could see his face.

"*Why?*" Detective Treuer studied his former partner and helpless melted into horror. "You didn't get my messages?"

"When?" she went for her phone, but it was inside.

"Last night and this morning," he said.

"I didn't think to look," she leaned into her right fist.

When Bailey looked back at Nate he was gray and stricken.

This time she didn't ask why.

She didn't want to hear why.

She didn't want to know why.

The detective turned around and started for the front door.

"I went for a walk this morning," she mumbled, the first step she took to reach the door missed and she had to grab the rail or fall.

"Bailey," he moved to help her and was shrugged off.

She managed to reach the door and, after missing three times, got the key in the lock.

"You need to listen to me, Bail," he said, even though he didn't want to be the one to say any more.

When she got the door open, Bailey looked back at him, struggling with composure. If she'd realized she was doing as poorly at it as she was, she wouldn't have turned around.

"What?" she didn't mean to snap.

The shimmer of tears awoke on the rims of Nate's eyes as he closed the distance between himself and her.

"We identified your father," he began. The hardness in Bailey's face began to take. "I know it was your father."

Her face softened like he'd said he *wasn't* sure.

Detective Treuer studied her sleeplessly blanched face after the last words of bad news fell. She fixed her almost sea-blue eyes on his car, where it sat idling on the driveway. Its headlights wavered in the controlled tears that managed only to moisten her wide and almost almond shaped eyes. Her lips pressed together as much as if only sipping an invisible cup and she nodded mechanically. He wondered if she understood what he'd said and hoped she wouldn't ask him to repeat it.

"Thank you Nate," she muttered, the nod continuing faintly, like her jaw was on a spring.

"If you need anything I—"

The screen door balanced against her left hand cast a silver film between them as she slipped between it and the dark house behind her. "I appreciate it."

The white inner door swung shut, swallowing her like a nutcracker's teeth. All that remained of her presence was the yellow-orange porch light which was starting to attract moths.

She could feel him hover on the other side of the door like a shunned solicitor and prayed for him to just leave. If he left then she could breathe. When she could breathe then she could plan. She could start to make sense—but she didn't know where to begin.

Nate leaned his back beside the door, feeling Bailey's presence lingering behind the layers of aluminum and wood. His face was in his hands again and then clutching his disheveled hair.

"Bailey, you need to hear me out," he told her, even though he didn't know if it was a good time. But it might be better to kick her while she's down so she only has to get back up once.

"It was Bad Penny, Bail," he said through the wall.

"What?" she said, but so quietly even she couldn't hear it.

Tears stacked up in eyes rounded with disbelief. Her right hand went over her mouth. She felt like her heart stopped. No… that everything stopped. Deafness buzzed around her like white noise. It was getting hard to see. It was almost impossible to breathe.

Inside her was a scream too big to come out of her mouth. It got stuck trying.

How do you know?

"He was found in a crate addressed to your place in Boston. It was post marked the week you couldn't reach him. The inkjet label got wet and bled, so it was delayed. They were able to, eventually, figure out what apartment building it was supposed to go to, but the building manager told them to send it back. No return address. They were just about to send it to the Mail Recovery Center in Atlanta when they noticed a suspicious odor."

Nate looked over at the screen door, because he couldn't look at Bailey.

"The crate had previously been used by Reginald Betters from the Maelstrom Marina All-You-Can-Eat."

She closed her eyes, spilling the shining wall into three sets of hot wet tracks down her face. One found the trough of her lip and overflowed as the rose-pink flesh trembled. The taste of briny water found the tongue pressed behind clenched teeth. Another track breeched the seal of the hand, filled hinge of her lips and continued around the curve of her chin where she rubbed the sensation as much as the wetness away when it tickled her neck.

"Bailey?"

How do you know it was Bad Penny?

"I don't want to know," she whispered.

It was too horrible.

Visions of the dead played behind her closed eye lids.

She saw The Wall torn down.

No one deserves to die bad.

No one deserves to suffer.

Oh God—the idea of someone hurting him! The thought of him afraid.

WHAT DID HE DO TO YOU!?!

you really don't want to know…

Like air out of a helium balloon, Bailey began to sink until she was sitting, feet out in front of her, hand still at her mouth.

When she and Detective Stull were leaving the nightclub, she asked Fisher Cainen Meryl if he was responsible for the press calling the murderer the Bad Penny Killer, since he said the name like it were always so.

Inori, he explained without directly answering, had called the guy that offhandedly when they were researching the missing persons and subsequent bodies found in spurts over the past forty-eight years.

Fisher added:

"Bad Pennies have a way of turning up."

At that time it felt like a curse over Essex County.

Now, she wondered if it wasn't a warning.

Nate was facing the screen door, his hands pressed flat against it, his forehead resting against the mesh.

"Get the Feds involved, Bail. You need to back out of this case. It's too personal. I don't want to see you crash and burn. Come back to Boston with me tonight. They sent me over here to see if anyone remembers the guy who shipped the crate. It'll take me just a couple hours to follow-up. I'll call my mom, we'll figure out what happens next. You need to take care of yourself and your dad, right now. If you can't do both, then you just do what you have to for him. I will help you, if you let me."

"It's too personal," Bailey echoed almost silently.

Suddenly the door swung open. Bailey was wiping her face with one hand and opening the screen door with another.

"We were wrong," she almost tripped when she hurried past Nate.

"What do you mean?"

"Maybe they aren't random."

"Who?" he pressed, missing once when he tried to catch the sleeve of her light jacket.

"*Any* of them."

"Bailey…"

"Was my father cut up or was he…was he a captive?"

"Cut," the word was forced out his mouth. It was only half true, but the missing fingers and teeth may have been an unintentional result of the attack.

"That's the difference!"

"Bailey stop!" he yelled.

She looked at him blankly and fell silent.

"You don't have to solve this because a victim's your dad!"

"I'm not," she said tearfully. "This is for Leia."

"Bailey…"

"*Let me do this*!" she screamed.

"What if I don't think you can?" Nate challenged.

Bailey fell silent and staring at the Boston detective.

"I'd call it a bad bet," she said without conviction.

"I'd call it denial. I'd call it a distraction. Bailey—" he caught her elbow and moved near her "—you've conjured yourself some busy work so you don't have to deal with *now*."

"I'm not in denial," Bailey looked straight at him, "and I'm dealing with *now*. I don't have to compromise anything anymore—all my priorities are in one place."

"Then where are you running off to in lounge clothes? Are you gonna go arrest someone? What are you thinking?"

The woman looked at herself and her composure crumbled.

"Too much," she croaked, shaking her head, embarrassed, and disoriented.

"You push yourself too hard," he warned.

"Sam Goode dies in two days. I'll have to approach the murders like he's only one person. If he is, then he's been at it for almost fifty years and there are only so many ages this guy can be. This guy is local, Nate. I think I can find out who he is, but if I'm going to do it before Sam runs out of time, I'll need help."

"You have as much of it you want for as long as you need it," Nate consented.

"I'm sorry for getting upset."

"Your dad was murdered, Bail," Nate frowned.

"I just don't know where my head was."

"Overwhelmed," he suggested.

"I'm going to see if I can get more help," she murmured as she led him inside.

Nate didn't want that to mean Michael Stull, but assumed it probably did.

He followed her inside, noting the number of unchecked messages on the house phone. He also noted that, again, Leia Redding was standing out from the other victims. Bailey and her would have been only a couple years different in age and didn't live that far apart. Maybe, he wondered, if this hadn't been personal to Bailey decades before it involved her dad. That the two girls were childhood friends seemed likely. If Leia was as quiet and reserved as Bailey, she might have stood out to a predator—as they prefer to prey on the weakest in the herd.

Bailey was on the phone when Nate reached the living room. She was giving someone a list of things she wanted them to look for. The directions given tentatively, so she was obviously operating just shy of asking for a favor. It sounded like they were agreeing, but Bailey's careful delivery suggested the deal wasn't done until it was done, like Minesweeper.

She sighed heavily when she finally hung up the phone.

"You won't believe who I was talking to," she said to Nate. "That vicious, abusive sociopath who has an alibi for everything."

"Meryl," he didn't need to guess.

Bailey nodded.

"How did you end up dealing with him?"

"Thought him a likely suspect," she explained, "until hearing him out. I verified everything he told me when Stull and I went to interview him. He and another person have been trying to get the case attention for years—probably his reputation didn't help, but the same was apparently true for any number of victims. Meryl, by the way, was the one who told the press to call him the Bad Penny Killer."

"To help get attention?" Nate supposed. "I wonder if he also wasn't the one who said the murders were all linked by this and that, you know? So why do you need his help?"

"*Need* might be a strong word, but he could prove valuable in doing a little of the gopher work. While he doesn't have the information at his fingertips, like we do, he is a networker like no other. Nate…"

When he looked up, she was looking down.

"…I want to keep this to ourselves, just for twenty-four hours. If we've gotten nowhere after, then we go to the FBI. There has been a wealth of information people have been sitting on, and a lot of those butts belonged to cops."

"This serial killer has been active in Essex County for a long time," Nate agreed, but not without reminding her that times and people have changed. People's attitudes about class and character aren't the same as they were fifty years ago. He just didn't believe those kind of people were the majority anymore.

"Can we catch him in twenty-four hours?" Nate asked her.

Bailey blinked, her face calm and thoughtful, though the answer was obvious, "We have to."

17

...

A STUMBLE PREVENTS a FALL

Michael Stull stayed in Lanester after dropping Bailey off at her car, so when she called him to come out and help on the twenty-four hour push, he arrived in just under twenty minutes.

Immediately after his car pulled up, Curtis from the crime scene unit came bearing a heavy parcel from Salem and his consent to help.

Over in the notoriously witchy city, a goth underworld lord and a, meek in person, freak on the stage, artist and her band were pouring over the "to-do" list the female agent gave him.

"In 1967, Bad Penny kills William Connelly, a virtually closeted homosexual—it was only after his death was investigated that his alternative lifestyle was made public. The brutal nature of his death was widely viewed as something he provoked through overt propositions to a heterosexual. The five accompanying Connelly were Brian Johnson, Cole Thompson, Rusty Schneider, Brandon Grady, and Roger Fossand."

Curtis hastily recorded the details on a white poster board. Bailey made a point of having any number of these on hand to help organize her cases.

"1969, a two year tentative hiatus before killing Mitchell Walker—a student attending a private religious college."

She named the five sating victims and the captives in 1970, '72,'73, '75 and so forth along with the names and backgrounds of each victim.

Bailey looked at the charts and stumbled over her thoughts and took a second to rebuild them.

"We need to fill in the holes where neither Meryl or I were able to find the last victim or victims. We need to see the full portrait of this guy's work. Where every murder took place and compare them to the men in the Lanester area who are in the right age group. We'll look at their backgrounds, where they've lived before, what they did for a living. I think there's a pattern here. These kind of people are killing something in their victims, not just the actual person. There's something about them that makes him treat one different than another… something that made him look at the victim in the first place."

Curtis taped pictures of each victim by their section of the board and made boxes around the empty spaces where names needed yet to be listed to make the "six" pattern fit.

Bailey waited until they were busy making calls, searching their databases or online for info on victims or the list of Lanester men to be eliminated one by one, she took the opportunity to separate Nate from the group and ask him about something that came to her while she briefed them.

"What is it, Bail?" he wondered, having seen the verbal trip and knew, by the look on her face, that something had come to mind and broke up her mental train tracks.

Bailey leaned in so near he could feel the heat from the side of her head against his, and whispered, "Why was my father killed?"

Nate frowned and leaned back so he could see her face. Dead serious.

"What?"

It sounded accusing.

"Why did he kill my father?" she pressed, locking her gem bright eyes on his gray-green pair.

"I don't follow."

"Who was the captive, Nate? Who were the other slashing victims?"

Nate couldn't say, but wished he had an explanation.

"Maybe he's not the only victim that breaks the pattern," he suggested.

Bailey considered this, tipping her head down, brow inadvertently almost brushing his shoulder, "Maybe there's more to it than we thought. Maybe when he's waiting down a victim he gets impatient and needs to *do something about* the time between when he chooses the victim and knows enough about them to have things his way."

"We're going to need to look into that," Nate sounded committed, but was feeling the weight of the body count or maybe that, even as she was trying to explain it, Bailey didn't buy what she was selling.

"If it doesn't fit a pattern, we'll find out why."

Bailey nodded.

"Hey," he put his hands on both her shoulders and stooped a little so his eyes could meet the pair looking at the ground. "Go easy on yourself. If you're not up to being strong, give yourself the time and space you need. Don't make yourself do anything you'd cringe about any victim's family putting themselves through."

Sure...

Bailey looked up at him and he was a heartbeat away from putting his lips against hers when he remembered he couldn't. He wanted to tell her how he felt about her, if only so she didn't still feel like she lost the only person she had. He knew her dad was her whole world, even though he had a feeling that Leia Redding was a damn big part of it.

Why did he think "The Wall" was unique among the victims? Because Walter Douglass never stopped looking. If Bad Penny knew that and liked to send messages in blood, then the message might have been:

"This is what happens when you find me."

"Got one!" Curtis chimed in the other room.

The detectives returned before he'd fired off his explanation.

"Tony Gianno, the 1970 captive? His fifth slashing victim was probably Barnaby French, a known transient who occasionally worked the boat yards in Gloucester. Went missing the week after Gianno's disappearance, assumed he moved on. Tony lived about twenty miles from French's last known whereabouts."

"Unless we see any better auditions, write him up. Nate, can you get your friend in the bureau to verify that Mr. French isn't somewhere else?"

"Yeah," he agreed.

"So, I thought *you* were the one in the FBI, Jacobs?" Michael Stull teased from his spot on the floor near a plug-in where he alternated between paper and computer.

Nate grinned at her.

"You used my ruse?"

Bailey shook her head and shot Michael a look of mixed unappreciation and amusement, saying, "No. Meryl didn't remember me and thought I was someone I wasn't."

There weren't a lot of holes to be filled, but there were a lot that couldn't be confirmed because the bodies were never identified, if bodies surfaced at all. The coincidences of the disappearances were strong enough that the pattern would probably hold water, legally, but the coroner would do a lot of the water proofing.

What lay unspoken across the four of them was the fact that, unlike every other captive/murder combination before this, was that the Polke murder and Goode's disappearance were so close together. At least, not since Redding and Kellogg.

They were operating on a countdown and somewhere, sometime, Detectives Michael Stull and Bailey Jacobs were going to be needed when some other poor soul was caught in the wrong place at the wrong time by Bad Penny, as the holes in Sam Goode's five were not yet filled and her own time was running out.

"I think I might have another filler," Bailey sounded regretful as she turned to Curtis who jumped to update the boards. "The 1984 captive, Sean Casper."

Curtis moved down the panels and held a marker over the empty rectangle there.

"A woman named Mary Grossman was waiting at a Rockport middle school—" Michael looked up from his work to find the woman detective regarding him sadly "—she was stabbed in the face thirty-seven times. The guy two down on our list was reported missing in Rockport the next day."

Nate noticed the exchange and, for the first time, thought he might have caught a glimpse of a little human in the Salem detective who nodded and made no more of it than whatever the look between he and her said.

One thing they weren't uncovering, Detective Treuer was disappointed to find, was any victims, like Walter Douglass, who were clearly killed by Bad Penny, but were attached to no captive—at least that they knew of. Should there have been a captive at the time of Douglass' disappearance, would have meant three captives in less than four months! Nate was unwilling to accept that as a possibility until the twenty-four hours Bailey asked her over. If that was the game this monster was playing he wanted out and wanted his former partner out of it most of all. Nate had no problem chasing monsters, but if Bad Penny was going to take out six people every six weeks the public deserved more hands on deck than all of the Essex Sheriff's Department combined.

*　　　　　*　　　　　*

The police hadn't yet found the body of the little bitch from the fast food shithole, that or the press hadn't caught wind of it yet.

To say he was thrilled about the publicity would have been said in error, but to say he was amused was different. He didn't really understand why there was suddenly so much interest in the dead ones, except to lay a fair amount of the blame on Bailey Jacobs, who was supposed to be the lead investigator this time.

Operating like a god, and being none too discreet in his actions, in his mind's eye everyone had known about every dead one, every time, and either did nothing because they cared as little about the lives as he did or because his wrath itself was god-like. How stupid would they or anyone be to provoke it?

Essex County was his circle of hell, as far as the grimy man, hunched in shadows knew.

The streets left and right were empty, the lot with only a stray car or two, lighted windows with no silhouettes.

The crossing guard had put away his gear and left the elementary school whistling something annoyingly familiar, but too off to ever place.

Monty barely caught a glimpse of the person purged from the shadows between two parked cars before a fist was in front of his face, moving left to right, back and forth, like savagely underlining a sentence.

Pressure struck the old crossing guard before any pain. It felt like someone squeezing his neck tighter and tighter, when what was really happening was his neck being carved smaller and smaller.

He felt the asphalt under his head and the knife was going in and out of his thin chest, puncturing lungs with, as yet, undetected cancer, nicking ribs protecting a heart most people who knew him regarded as big.

Just before his soul jumped ship and life, as he knew it, was little else than excruciating pain, Monty caught a glimpse of his killer in the ugly orange light from the school's parking lot lamps and wondered why they would do this over something so little.

*   *   *

Across the room, at one corner of the couch, Bailey was making a lot of calls, writing furiously on a notepad, with a laptop open beside her. Nate stole a furtive glance at her after reaching one of the photocopied clippings Fisher sent, where he found her name somewhere entirely unexpected.

He stared at the words, swiftly processing the whole of this ordeal on the thirty-two-year-old detective determined to catch Bad Penny:

...body recovered after twelve-year-old, Bailey Jacobs, discovered it while walking home from school...

He took his work and moved to the middle of the couch.

"You look like you got onto something," he remarked.

"Maybe..." she frowned, never stopping or slowing the flow of writing.

She just opened her mouth when, simultaneously, three pagers went off in the room. Heads bowed like prayer was called.

"Damn," Bailey looked at the small screen and up at Stull just in time for him to raise his eyes to hers.

"Curtis?" she said to the investigator as she closed the notebook and laptop to get up.

"Coroner just sent his initial findings to our office," he explained.

"We got a call," she told him.

"I'll answer the body," Stull offered. "You retrieve the report so we'll have a head start on it when I get back."

Bailey didn't like that plan and it must have read in her face because then Stull was saying, "Don't worry. I took notes all three times I saw you working a scene. I think I can impress you."

He might have been talking to Bailey, but he threw the last sentence at Nate and smiled through it.

Detective Jacobs swallowed hard and finally consented because Michael deserved a chance and maybe a little trust, by now—and they didn't have time to wait until after, which could mean many, many hours, to go over Dr. Shaughnessy's report.

Curtis asked to ride along with Stull and Bailey wondered if Nate minded continuing on his own until she got back. Of course, he didn't.

"Stull," Bailey called to the darkly tanned, darkly dressed detective getting into the sleek black vehicle. "Page me right away if it's unrelated."

He nodded once.

The other detective had to leave first so she could get her car out. Since she had to wait a minute or two, she called the coroner, first thanking him profusely for the effort put into the report and then asked him, "In a nutshell, would you say this is one guy?"

"You get a suspect behind bars and some assistance for me and I'll promise you something more concrete, but for the time being I'd say it probably is and, with greater certainty, the exact same knife."

Bailey's knees felt watery as she slid behind the wheel of her small white car. He didn't hear her say, "Okay", and asked if she heard him, if she was alright.

"Yes, I'm fine. I heard you. Three and a half inches?"

She faintly heard an "Mm-hmm".

She thanked him for his time and wished him the good night he hoped the whole county would have. The night no longer belonged to anyone but Bad Penny. The community was gripped with fear. He doubted anyone would have a good night, especially Samantha.

Nate watched Bailey pull out of the driveway and tried to work on his own project as long as he could before lack of concentration forced the justification for looking into the notebook she left on top of the computer.

He devoured the rapidly recorded notes, his heart beginning to pound the way it always does when he feels close to collaring the bad guy.

"Jesus, Bailey, how on earth did…"

He looked over the pad and around the space illuminated by more than half a dozen lamps that suddenly looked at least ten watts brighter each. He shivered with the distinct feeling that only then was he entirely alone.

The cold wet feeling in Bailey's knees started working through her legs and arms, like she was slowly filling with water. She literally felt like something separate from herself slowly fused with her and the car felt like nine people were trying to ride in it, not one.

The expansive bridge across the Annisquam River appeared around the next curve bearing left. Foreboding, it lay like a long black dragon across the deeply cut river route, where certain death lay to any motorist who breached the low concrete wall.

The bloodless, white form of a girl lay immediately on the road before her.

"No!" Bailey cried, and braked so hard the end swung to one side like she meant to block traffic.

Highway 127 lay dark and empty.

She idled for the seconds it took to be sure she was alone on the road. When she looked far down through the trees to her left, the moonlight struck the curve of something smooth almost perfectly lost in the darkness, or maybe even the day.

She knew that about two hundred yards down that slope was an unmaintained access road that began about four miles back and several turns away.

The white car was turned around and parked, straddling the ditch, where you'd almost have to be up to the road to see it, if approaching from the ditch on the opposite side.

Detective Jacobs immediately turned the ringer off her phone and pager and slunk into the woods faintly touched by the moon.

About a hundred feet in, her scalp prickled, and she realized where she was heading. Dropping to one knee and shoving the phone into her blouse to try and block as much light as possible, she sent a text to Nate:

DON'T CALL BK. RINGR OFF. CALL BKUP 2 ANISQM BRIDGE & RD BLK@ACCESS RD@JCT11.
I FOUND HIM.

She drove the phone into her slacks, where the light of an incoming call would face her hip, and armed her Beretta.

The thing gleaming on that narrow, overgrown road, below her would likely turn out to be the stolen car. Finding out for certain was for another time. Every single second now belonged to Goode.

Soft soled shoes make stealth on hard surfaces easy, but she wasn't confident in her ability to move silently through forests. She counted on Bad Penny having the same problem, but probably not taking the kind of care to make up for it as she was.

As Bailey approached, she was figuring out how much space, or how little, she was about to deal with—the width of a road against the angle of the slope under the bridge.

Pulse resounded in her head slow and deep, even as she felt her heart quickly pounding in her chest.

The open mouth under the bridge yawned blackly over the cold dark waters flowing dangerously far beneath it. Baily approached almost parallel to the road, where no one looking out from that place could see her.

Ten yards.

Eight.

She suddenly felt like she was crossing the mud flat. Leia lay out there, only she couldn't see the little girl yet, but the child was alive and calling for help.

Bailey silently answered her.

I will, I promise. I promise....I promised.

She didn't feel the hot tear track down her face as she got close enough to hear the way air sounds different where trolls wait passersby.

In the distance, sirens approached.

Ignore them. Ignore them.

And then the vehicles slowed down, starting somewhere out over the end of the bridge.

Oh God...

Bailey ducked under, raising flashlight and gun against the monster residing there, but the monster was coming out.

He struck her, the flashlight fell and rolled almost ten feet before resting, but not even death could have pried the gun from her hand, even as he fought to control the armed limb.

Never before had she been stabbed, but she knew she had when she felt something punch her in the side. She grabbed the offending wrist with her left hand more committedly than the right bearing the gun.

This close, she smelt the stink of him. The foul sour reek of death on him. Blood and semen. The breath…

Bailey drove a knee between his legs and he grunted, not with pain, but pleasure.

She felt the blade miss and open a long shallow gill on her side before finding purchase in the meat under her ribs.

"*Aeternum vale*," he growled inhumanly.

"I hope so," Bailey returned, biting just below the sound of his voice. She felt the Adam's apple retreat as her teeth sunk into his neck.

He reeled back, the weight of him knocking Bailey off her feet. She saw a black shape send the flashlight down the dangerously near embankment and was falling after when a hand caught her wrist and stopped her, in fact yanking her back hard, just to make sure she would not fall too.

In the distance she heard officer's getting out of their vehicles, door closing, saw their lights running across trees.

She could smell Nate beside her, clean and familiar. She knew the hand that stayed her, but did not register the relief until she found his fragrance in the barely moonlit night.

"Send somebody after him," Bailey directed, reeling away from the other detective to reach the mouth of darkness.

"Wait," Nate took out a flashlight and hurried after her. He watched Bailey slip under the bridge and by the light of her cell phone find the shivering, brutalized semblance of the fortune teller.

Then she was asking for a blanket and calling for an ambulance. Nate told her there was one up on the bridge.

"Get somebody after him," she urged and Nate went.

"Samantha," Bailey approached from the direction she was facing. The light from the phone was too bright and the desecrated woman recoiled.

"Sorry, sorry," she held the glow over the ground. "I'm a police officer. You're going to be just fine, don't worry."

To say Bad Penny wasn't going to hurt her anymore would be a lie that might last the rest of Sam Goode's life, if there was nothing the support of family, friends, and a good therapist couldn't resolve.

Bailey wasn't used to knowing the body laying out at a crime scene could hear her, could answer back, she struggled for what to say.

She got down on her hands and knees in the small space, tears gathered at the sight of Goode, now falling freely. She untied the captive and held one hand in hers, overcome by the feel of all five fingers closing on her hand and said in a tearful whisper:

"I'm going to help you... I promise."

Far below the women, the sign of officers searching the embankment was marked only by the beams and brilliant faces of flashlights. An officer arrived with a blanket and, after someone from ballistics made sure there were no traps under the bridge, gave the go ahead for CSU and the paramedics to swoop in.

Sitting beside her, Bailey watched the preliminary check-up before evacuating the victim from the site and took a moment for herself to breathe and digest.

"You okay, Detective Jacobs?" John Winston asked her as he went under the bridge from the opposite side.

She nodded her head and tried not to think what she was thinking about how it would feel to be chopped up.

How long would it take to die?

Is there a Heaven?

Not now. Not now. Not now.

She remembered the way her dad looked at her when the school held a Mother-Daughter Picnic. The way his head snapped away and he'd whisked his thumbs across his eyes, the way they were still shining when he looked at her. The way she didn't care because it was someone she never had to miss. Dad is all there was. Dad was all she needed.

NOT NOW.

"Bailey?" Officer Winston probed as he came closer.

Tomorrow. Tomorrow. The job's not done.

"Take that tablet to be checked out right away!" someone was yelling to one of the forensic investigators.

Bailey scooted out of the narrow space, at the very corner where the bridge married to the road, so she could at least walk stooped over.

"Thank you, John, I'm fine," she answered.

Men were coming in with a couple spotlights to scatter the darkness from the makeshift lair.

Bailey hesitated to regard the graffiti discoloring almost half the French gray concrete:

Timothy LUVS Samantha

: scrawled inside a white heart.

She could almost see the couple smiling, happy, having publicly announced a feeling that, at the moment, they felt was as permanent as the writing. She had remembered the picture on Goode's desk when she was getting close to the bridge and felt a cold tremble seeing it now. It read like a plea to find the missing woman.

"We have a positive ID on that stolen car," she heard someone nearby saying as she emerged into the cool night air without the stench of urine, excrement, and blood. Without the resonating aura of danger and the environment's memory of pain to weigh the air, invoking primal instincts of fear. She felt like she'd just belly crawled out from under the Boogeyman's bed.

Someone said "Good job" to her as she started through what seemed like dozens of people, to get back to the road.

Suddenly Nate was by her side, saying something about the officers working down the slope.

"Did they find her?" Bailey asked him.

"Samantha?" Detective Treuer returned, even though he felt like she really meant Leia.

"Bad Penny," she answered blearily, grabbing at the nearest tree to keep from falling. Nate caught her elbow to balance her, but losing balance didn't seem like the biggest problem, just standing at all looked barely manageable.

"Are you hurt, Bail?" he asked her as she put her weight on the tree.

She nodded into her arm.

"Well, where are you going?" he sounded alarmed.

Her chin jerked up toward the flashing lights above them.

"Where are you hurt?" he asked, turning his flashlight on her and quickly finding the blackish-red stain growing on her left side. The flashlight glinted off the riveting in the short black handle sticking out of her side.

"Sweet Jesus, hun," he breathlessly told her. "You got the goddamn knife!"

She looked down at the thing with the chipped blade, the thing that butchered Leia Redding, and recently voided "The Wall" of life. It was the source of almost every cry. The accomplice to half a century of twisted works. The toy. The appendage. The witness and, soon, the snitch.

If objects have memories…

Nate was yelling something, but it sounded like there was water in her ears. She felt like she was falling away from him, down into the deep red cavern of a gouged out eye. He was far away.

A pair of fingerless hands pressed on either side of the unassuming black handle. Deep black hollows, with bits of flapping skin of what were once eyelids, studied the tool or the wound indistinctly.

"Now that you know, what are you going to do about it?" Leia Redding asked, without lips or teeth.

I'm going to help you.

Somehow, somewhere in the cruel disfigured mess of the little girl's face, registered a smile and added:

"Cogi qui potest nescit mori."

18

. . .

WOODEN NICKELS

"She who can be forced has not learned how to die."

Bailey opened her eyes and found herself lying under a single lighted sconce, the width of the hospital bed where she lay, the rest of the room was dark.

Nate sitting in a chair beside the bed.

"What?" she murmured.

"It's what you've been saying," he forced a smile to try and lighten the mood, but ineffectively.

"How long?"

"That you've been out? About three hours."

"The knife?"

"Safe and sound and impounded into evidence," he assured her.

"I want to see it," Bailey told him.

Nate was premeditating the best way to win an argument about her staying right where she was.

"How bad am I hurt?"

"You know doctors would rather tell you how close you were to worse than tell you how you are," he deflected.

"Nate…"

"You're gonna be okay," he confided, but it came out like he just had to tell her she wouldn't make it and turned away just long enough to collect himself.

"They didn't find Bad Penny?"

Nate shook his head, she was nodding before he was finished.

"I want to see the knife," she asserted.

"You don't seem worried," he pointed while she assessed how to release herself from the tubes and cables attached to her.

"I'm not," she looked right at him.

"You wanna tell me why?"

"Yes," she said.

Detective Jacobs pressed the nurse call button, in the meantime dropping the arm on the right side of the bed and sitting up. It hurt to move, and folding herself into a right angle pressed the recently sutured wounds.

"Just give me one moment with that knife, Nate, *please*."

"Bailey?" she heard Michael say on the other side of the curtain.

"Stull, I need you to help me get this off me or get me a nurse."

The Salem detective was quick to enter the space enclosed in tall, ugly curtains to free her.

"What are you doin'?" Nate jumped up.

"Helping."

"Are you a doctor? No. If it was good for her to leave they'd release her."

"You're right Nate," she told him, "but I have to do this."

Michael Stull regarded the detective coldly.

Nate wanted to tell him not to fucking look at him like that, but this wasn't the time or place to raise voices or tempers.

"We'll talk while you take me there," she said to Nate. "I need one of you to do a little research while the other drives. After tonight I won't push this," she promised her former partner. "Let me do this."

He studied her face and tried to find any sign of lacking sincerity in her request, but came up empty.

"Okay, but you promised."

Bailey understood.

"So, what did you mean by 'not knowing how to die'?" Detective Stull asked her once they were on the road.

In the back, Bailey leaned against the door, wrapped in a hospital blanket and donning her bloody clothes. She shrugged.

"How is Samantha Goode?" she asked instead.

"She's going to be just fine, Bail," Nate assured her from shotgun. "Fear, exposure, and trauma were her worst enemies. The wounds, as yet, were superficial."

"And the call?" Bailey asked Stull.

Michael looked at Nate who was facing the road.

"Don't worry about it," he told her.

Then Nate looked at him.

As if that doesn't say all she needs to know.

Bailey was looking over at the back of Stull's head and turned her gaze to the white line racing beside them.

"Sss—What did you want me to check?" Nate barely stopped himself from the despicable "so".

"I want you to run a social security number for me," she said and recited the numbers when he was ready. "You should be looking at a Robert Graham."

The person filling page after page in her notebook…

After a couple minutes, as they pulled up to the Police Station, Nate had hung up the phone and held it in the hand laying still on his lap.

"It's not his SSN," he was thinking about what she said out by the bridge.

Bailey was getting out of the car, leaving the blanket balled up on the seat. Their eyes met when she stepped off the pavement onto the curb and she'd looked back.

Stull was coming around the front while Nate got out. She wasn't waiting for either of them to help her and was halfway there by the time they started up the concrete.

"He stole someone's identity?" Stull assumed, he and Nate walking in tandem up a sidewalk Detective Treuer thought suddenly seemed incredibly narrow and answered:

"Nah, he changed his."

Bailey had her fair share of experience working with witnesses in a lineup, but this was the first time Bailey every felt like she was wearing their shoes— nervous, uncertain, wondering what happens if they're wrong, what happens if they're right, and fearful of coming face to face with the one in that row who is guilty.

She looked at the knife from across the slate gray evidence holding room. It lay within an evidence bag—categorically unique amongst its peers—the most important difference being, without it, none of the others would exist.

If it hadn't been this knife it would have been another.

There was nothing special about it, really. A kitchen paring knife—this happened to be a Vüsthov, three and one-half inch, triple riveted, black handled paring knife—but the kind you'd find in any home.

Nearly this entire time, they knew what kind of weapon they were looking for, but it was different to see it before her—she could touch it, if she wanted to.

A world of blame lay in her flat, thinking eyes. It had killed so many. Just looking at it was almost silently interrogating a killer she had in some ways never seen, while also knowing exactly who they should be looking for.

Deviant, diabolical, psychotic, homicidal—as unseeming on the killer as the second nature given to the innocent knife.

They were looking for the kind of man you'd find in any home.

"How did you know?" Nate whispered a few steps behind her.

"Mrs. Connelly told me that Bobby Graham was Billy's only friend. In the tiny article about the funeral, I found his name and called her to ask about him. So I thought it was ironic when I read that a Robert Graham was questioned about Mitchell Walker's disappearance two years later, apparently because there was some kind of altercation between the two of them shortly before."

"And then you just started looking into Graham," Nate reasoned and Bailey affirmed immediately thereafter.

"It has the chip?" she not once averted her gaze from the small knife.

Nate nodded, but out of sight standing behind her. She didn't ask again, because she knew what the answer was.

"Do you need more time?" he wondered.

She shook her head, but still didn't look away.

"Do you still think you were right, you know, about all the murders being personal?"

Bailey looked over her shoulder at the handsome, and worried looking detective with sloppy brown hair.

"Tell me on the way," he reached out for her and she let herself be led by the hand on the small of her back.

Michael Stull waited in the next room, to give her whatever privacy he felt she needed. Nate was afraid to turn his back and find her collapsed somewhere.

"So, how you feeling?" Stull asked when the two emerged from the storage room he hadn't thought of as creepy before that night.

"I'm alright."

"Are we going to catch him?"

Her chin barely moved to affirm, but added a "yes" to ensure the message wasn't lost.

While the three crossed the yard to the parking lot, Curtis finally finished his duties where the crossing guard was killed and, with flowers in a mug, and a silvery helium balloon wishing a speedy recovery, slumped miserably into the chair where Michael Stull sat only an hour earlier, and worried about the woman detective laid up on the other side of the tall ugly curtains.

"What's the common thread, Bailey?" Nate pressed as soon as all three were inside the dark vehicle.

"There's a common thread?" Stull swung around in the seat so he could easily look in the direction of either detective, though mostly hidden in the unlit interior, except for the places where the light from the lamp posts found them.

"I'm sure there is, but I didn't have time to call everyone and some of the people I contacted just weren't sure—it didn't help that I had to ask about a couple possible names…"

"You said they were all personal," Nate prompted.

Bailey was nodding in the back seat, "I'm sorry, I was getting close but I didn't have a chance to throw my theory at you guys before we got called away."

Detective Treuer, having briefly looked at Bailey's notes before getting her text, had a pretty good idea where this story was going to end, what he didn't understand was why she was so sure she knew who the killer was.

"Robert Graham, I think, was maybe experimenting with homosexuality when he realized that his good friend, William Connelly, was gay. I suspect that Robert, who Mrs. Connelly described to me as being socially awkward and a little odd, might have come on strong, thinking William would *have to* want what he was offering. When he didn't, it might be that Robert wanted him anyway and found a way. However, I think it more likely, that William Connelly had no idea Bobby Graham was interested in him and the relationship was illusory."

"So, Graham decided to take what he wanted?" Stull guessed.

"I think so."

"Why?" Michael threw back.

Bailey was drawing the heavy knit hospital blanket around her shoulders when she explained, "Because that's what he's done ever since. Every interaction means a lot more to him that other people, positive or negative. His second captive, Mitchell Walker, was a handsome, intelligent and morally sound young man—as it was expressed to me. He was desirable, seriously dated a few girls, but was sought after by many. I think Graham wanted him too."

"And the victims he slashed up in between?" Nate Treuer asked.

"The guy we pulled out of the culvert grew up on the far west side of Riverview, where Robert Graham spend much of his childhood. I called what family I could find and a few of his close friends— one related to me that the victim, Pat Cooke, bullied Graham pretty ruthlessly. Greg Linderman was notorious for intolerance and very likely said horrible things to Graham or any other person who came off as homosexual, which I'm thinking, Graham certainly did."

Bailey stopped to take a breath and give her aching side a moment.

"I was informed that the victim by the bar had made a remark to him a few days before you caught the case, Stull. Fred Tanner apparently rejected Graham's advances maybe crassly, but probably just to make sure there was no confusion. This apparently pissed him off pretty bad.

"Jealousy is as strong a motivation as Graham's rage. Elizabeth Mercer married an old love interest of Robert's."

"Reciprocated??" Stull grunted in surprise.

"Apparently so," Bailey answered, "because Annie Kellogg, Mr. Mercer's stepmom didn't approve and drove the couple apart. Leia Redding's parents were a popular power couple, high school sweethearts, prom royalty, who married and had a perfect daughter and perfect lives…"

"Until a Bad Penny turned up," Nate added softly.

"Mary Grossman had confronted Graham about being a jerk to people the day before he caught her waiting unsuspectingly in her car.

"Pretty women, like Josselyn Henry, Olivia Hill, and Erin Polke were his competition. Kimberly Church, Diana Rosewood, and Donna Reedus—who were generally regarded as 'easy'—were the ladies actually getting what Graham wanted and getting it wherever they could. Bobby very likely took it as a personal attack, like they were flaunting it in his face."

"I read a lot of those reports and testimonies. I didn't see Robert Graham even once. You make me feel like I should have," Nate sounded doubtful.

"What name came up when you ran the SSN?" Bailey asked knowingly, while she found the most comfortable way to slump against the door.

Nate hesitated, then clarity widened his smoky gray eyes, "John Mercer reciprocated because he thought he was involved with a woman."

Stull looked between them, confusion and horror written across his face.

"So, Robert Graham is a woman?" he gawked.

"I suspect he started crossdressing when he left home. He attended the same prestigious catholic college as Mitchell Walker, but as Ellen Benedix."

"But not legally," Nate pointed.

"Apparently not, but I wasn't sure. I didn't get a chance to run a SSN to see what Graham's turned up."

"You *know* the name that came up was not Robert Graham or Ellen Benedix," Detective Treuer accused. "How?"

Bailey affirmed with several short bobs of her head, "Because I just shared zero space with her and I knew exactly who she was. All doubt went away when she threw that Latin bullshit at me."

"Why?" Stull wondered.

Detective Jacobs looked over at him, her face calm and certain.

"Because I had a teacher once who did that to me all the time—who reeked of roses and cigarettes."

Then she looked over at her former partner and added, "She hated me for a paper I wrote about my dad, where he went missing after making enemies with the real life buffet owner of the Maelstrom All-You-Can-Eat, Reginald Betters, but I gave everything fake names."

"Why did she hate you for that?" Nate, swallowed hard and yearned to see through the dark and glean more hints of what she felt than the accent from towering lamps outside.

Bailey put a hand over her mouth, anticipating sorrow, shame, regret that did not come...

...*because I'm going to finish this.*

"I found Leia Redding on my way home," she explained, "and the principal wouldn't let her fail me or really grade anything I did for the rest of that term..."

"...because of what you went through," Nate finished.

In the half dark, where she sat, it barely registered that Bailey raised her eyes to him.

She didn't say yes, or not, or affirm in any other way than saying nothing at all, which said everything.

Stull turned back in his seat, so he was facing the wheel again. This was her home town, her innocence, her every reason why—Michael felt like a real asshole suddenly, but was lost for a way to undo the things he'd said and done.

The man sitting across from him, though unknown to Stull, had his fair share of times saying and doing the wrong things himself—as we all do—but the look on his face said that understanding had taken the place of all those things. Nate and Bailey were on the same page.

"So, who is she?" he wanted the name so bad his gut hurt.

"Barbara Seles."

"You'd think people would notice the filed teeth," Nate pointed.

"I always thought she had dentures, but it must be caps," Bailey considered.

"So, can it be okay, just this once to hit a girl?" Stull smiled hugely at the other two detectives.

"Take me back to the hospital," she suggested, "and you boys can go pick her up."

"How do you think we're supposed to find her?" Michael questioned.

"Go to her house," Bailey offered with a shrug.

Nate pulled on his seatbelt, smiling to himself as Detective Stull pulled out of the spot and headed back toward the street.

"You really think she's that stupid?" he challenged.

"Kinda stupid, but kinda cocky," Nate replied.

Bailey added, "We've found semen and fingerprints, handprints, footprints, his blood, teeth marks enough to convict him at least a couple thousand times. She probably went right home, a long stroll at a normal pulse."

Stull met her eyes in the rearview mirror while she continued, "He's reckless because no one is looking for a woman."

They let Bailey out at the visitor entrance, but didn't leave until the second set of sliding glass doors separated her from them.

"How fast can you get an arrest warrant?" Nate wondered.

"A heartbeat," Stull said.

"You gonna call for backup? You know, I'm out of my jurisdiction, you're going to have to bust her ass yourself."

"Then you're my backup," Michael told him.

"I don't think it works that way," Nate challenged.

"So, you mean to tell me, you're out of Boston, up in some other county and you see someone in trouble, you don't help because your badge doesn't mean the same thing somewhere else."

Nate regarded him uncertainly.

"But only a sucky cop is gonna get in trouble with a junior high teacher," he finally answered.

Detective Stull laughed shortly and smiled enormously, "I never had a teacher I *didn't* get in trouble with. Sounds like me and Bailey have something in common."

The other detective looked over at him and then out his window—Stull took that as conceding a loss.

Stull made a few phone calls and told Nate to watch the street signs, just in case his memory of the side streets was off. It wasn't.

Barbara Seles lived in a small, uninteresting home, with the tallest privacy fences either man had ever seen. The windows, they could tell by the dense white backs facing them, were blackout curtains. There was even one over the three small diamond windows set into the bright red front door.

"So, you've got my back?" Stull asked the detective from Boston when they pulled up in front of a house three doors down.

Nate looked over at him through the pitch darkness Stull found between streetlights.

"I'll be right behind you, if you call for backup *now*," he told him firmly.

After a minute and a half of hesitation Michael finally agreed and made the call—Nate made sure to listen hard that all the right things were being said on both ends of the line.

"Okay, wimp, make sure you got your handcuffs ready," Detective Stull directed and then, chuckled to himself and his afterthought. "Though every real man already should."

"We get out of this car and I'm gonna need you to be a whole lot quieter and infinitely smarter, *capiche*?"

"And I'm gonna need you to relax," Stull suggested, still smiling and together emerged from the loyally dark interior of the vehicle into the last few hours of night.

Bailey let the clerk at registration know she was back and took the elevator past the second floor, where her room lay, and up to third where a private room—ordinarily reserved for mothers who'd lost their child—was giving Sam Goode a lot of peace, quiet, and privacy. The OB/Pediatric floor has highest security, when news of her rescue hit the press, they would be overrun by news teams again and there would be nothing to dissuade them, this time. At least it would be good news.

She went to the nurse's station and asked if Goode was awake, but she'd been sleeping hard, she was told, almost since they brought her in. She apparently had no illusions about her environment or if she was really safe or not.

One of the nurse's led Bailey through a secure door and to a recessed hall where the reserved room had a little distance from the sound of babies crying or really any sound at all.

She wasn't surprised to find the room fairly lighted, since the only way for Bad Penny to control Sam Goode was to keep her in the dark, literally.

There had been a hood, sleep mask, ear plugs and noise blocking headphones tucked just under the bridge above and to the right of the woman some people knew as Astrid.

Bailey took special care to cross the floor silently, doffing her shoes by the door and padding to the recliner near the bed and crawled slowly into it. The hole procedure left her tired and winded, even though Nate said she would be alright, it made her feel like there was something wrong with her left lung, too spent, too overwhelmed to attribute her exhaustion to all the blood she lost.

The detective watched Goode. A living, breathing, woman who was going to see, hold, hug and speak to friends and family soon.

It's been such a long time, the homicide detective was thinking again.

Then she was looking at a naked, brutalized child, laying stiffly atop a neatly made bed.

Bailey raised up on one elbow to better see and did not feel she was dreaming.

The blackhole-eyed, lipless, defiled face with full, cute cheeks, but little remaining skin, turned suddenly toward Bailey.

The right side of the small head dropped limply against the plush pillow where it rested, only now it was pink and warm, a small roundish nose, and pretty squinting eyes appeared above an almost red-lipped smile made of both baby and adult teeth.

Samantha woke to the sound of crying, the copper-haired woman tried to stifle.

It was obvious to Goode that the woman in the blanket had no sense of her and did nothing to interrupt what, from the look of her, needed to happen.

Several of the houses on that particular block enjoyed the whimsy of solar lights, color changing flowers, crackled glass bulbs on stakes, animals bearing lanterns, and stringed solar lights along their walkways. Quite a few others left their porch lights on, so to say Barbara Seles' place stood out was a gross understatement.

Other than a broken section of light from a post ten feet beyond the privacy fence, the lot before detectives Treuer and Stull lay in almost peerless dark compared to most places in a town, any town.

What sealed the deal at Graham's property was the dense row of giant arborvitae more than twice the height of the gapless fence. Where the yard met sidewalk, this anti-snoop wall continued for about eight feet on both sides. Then the fence disappeared and smaller spruce bushes gave the illusion of stately landscaping rather than malevolent blinders.

Neither wanted to enter any portion of light cast from the nearby streetlight, just in case Bad Penny was peering out one of those dark windows, but Michel Stull pointed out a few dark spots on the light gray cement path. They didn't dare take a closer look.

Had the light they were both cursing, as they approached the lot, been a few feet further away or the spots old and dry, the radiance could not have penetrated the fluid and shown the two how red it was.

In the distance from all around them, they heard the hum of nearing vehicles. Stull and Treuer were halfway across the yard when they first heard them, one by one, stop some distance away to narrow her chances of escaping.

Should Seles escape knowing she was about to be arrested, the chameleon would certainly change, but only her identity.

Bad Penny would never change his habits.

"So, how should we do this?" Stull asked in a whisper.

"Do you mind if I get the ball rolling?"

Michael felt the other detective smiling in the dark.

"Be my guest," he replied, mostly because he wanted to know what the plan was.

Nate went up to the door and knocked.

Stull rolled flat against the wall closest to the left corner and yanked out his gun.

After no answer, Treuer knocked again with more urgency.

"Ma'am," he called to the silent house. "I'm sorry to disturb you, but my car—" which sounded like "caw" with Nate's accent "—got a flat over there. I saw you go by and hoped you could help without my having to disturb your neighbors at this hour."

The door opened and a washed, robed, and very tall woman appeared, wild eyed and heaving with her whole being, like a bull about to charge. That it was a man standing there, in part or whole, was about eighty percent apparent to Nate. Densely packed wrinkles, androgynous jaw line, and no feminizing or masculinizing maintenance helped make the distinction more difficult.

Nate smiled, looking grateful and apologetic.

"I'm so sorry, ma'am," he gushed. "My cousin lives just a couple blocks further, but I didn't feel safe walking that far with that killer around," he hesitated and then blurted, "Geez, I bet that scared the crud out of you—I'm *so* sorry! I wasn't thinking about how whoever answering the door would feel. I guess we're all scared."

"You're from out of town?" the gravely, masculine voice probed.

"Uh-huh. Yeah. I don't suppose you have an air pump? The wheels bad, but if I can inflate it I should be able to make it a few blocks since I made it all the way here knowing it was a goner," Nate tried to sound scattered and awkward.

Seles thought it was cute, but the rest of him incredibly attractive. She felt a rush of blood into the organ between her legs and disguised the outward symptoms with the modest gathering of her rose patterned fuzzy white robe.

One hand made sure her business was covered, the other gathered the top of the robe under a bandaged throat.

His long fingered, boney hands looked powerful and monstrous, not at all helped by the fact that the nails of these hands were so crudely washed that blood gathered in the wrinkles, around and under the nails, and stained the fingertips like betadine.

Confident his cleavage was safe from prying eyes, Barbara raised one hand near the top of the door frame and leaned on it with one non-existent hip jutting out.

The rail thin, industrially built, bone and sinew monster glanced swiftly at the hand on the frame and flicked his eyes back to Nate's almost too quickly to notice.

It wasn't lost on Bad Penny the state of his hands any more than it was lost on Nate.

In the split second of shared realization the two men saw what the other knew.

Nate raised his gun.

Bad Penny dropped his hand.

A broad flat blade drove between them—cord pulled tight in Barbara's great knobby fist.

The detective cried out, simultaneously firing. Then both gun and Nate dropped to the ground.

Stull ran to the doorway while Barbara fled, moving far more quietly than the second man on the deck who she hadn't even been aware of.

"Gaw-damn-it!" Nate groaned, rocking on his knees with his arms folded across his chest.

"Treuer!" Michael exclaimed at the blade embedded in the floor and the blood droplets forming below the Boston detective.

"Go after him!" Nate yelled and Stull leapt over the blade and into the poorly lit house of Bad Penny.

Detective Treuer expected to look down and see nothing left of his arms after his elbows. What he was left with was nine fingers and five of them owned bloody voids with glossy white caps, where their second knuckles were shaved off.

Paint blenders don't shake like his hands were and the cold coming of shock threatened to overcome, like a tidal wave raising its deadly mass above him.

Pick up your gun, he told himself, because he knew he could. He didn't feel like he could. Nate didn't even feel like his hands were getting reception from his brain.

He rose up and leaned over the dully shining black handgun.

Shaking. Shaking. Shaking.

"Jesus, please!" he groaned angrily. Feeling really cold. Really, really shaky.

He was thinking about the trap and thinking about the other detective running through the nest of a calculating psychopath.

One bloody hand went out to the gun and lay flat on the handle. The other moved to pinch the bits of tissue and bone lying near the embedded blade. Nate stared at the finger, completely deaf from the sound of a heart beating in his ears. When he touched it, he almost felt like he felt it more from the side of the finger than from the hand picking it up.

Even though he knew how, in practice, Nate had never shot left-handed before.

The finger dropped into his pocket.

"Come on," he urged the bloody, dripping hands as they closed on the gun and he unfolded from the ground until he was leaning, at almost full height, in the door frame.

You were just scared, this is nothing that's going to kill you, he told the part of his nature that didn't accept the risks of law enforcement—the part that almost never dared to have a voice. Some officers are great at keeping it shut up until the first time they face death. This wasn't Nate's first dance with the Reaper, but it was hard to tell himself he wasn't as bad off as he thought he had to be.

Once halfway down the first hall, Stull entered stealth mode under the full internal alarm of realizing he'd utterly abandoned it for a little bit and Bad Penny knew he was coming.

The house smelled strongly of potpourri, rose pedals, an old lady smell that mingled with the heavy, oily odor of unfiltered cigarettes.

Silence of the Lambs had him expecting the odor of rot, formaldehyde, and that of being occupied by some unwashed beast.

At the same moment Nate was trying to reach the Lanester police to tell them that Bad Penny could be fleeing or Stull might be in danger, Michael had reached an open doorway where the air inside smelled of cat piss and mold.

He reached in, slapped the light on and jumped into the doorframe, gun raised.

The fluorescent tube above the sink blinked and partially illuminated. The room filled with a cool, eerie glow. The drip-dripping of a recently used shower resounded through the small space. Piled beneath the tub were any number of soiled and bloodied articles of clothing.

The sink too was spotted with blood. It looked like this was where Bad Penny dealt with the bite. None of them thought he'd be dumb enough show up at a hospital, no matter how much they hoped he would be confident enough in his safety to give them a break. *This* was the break, Stull realized, and there was no room for fucking this one up.

If he never, never, never, did anything right in the rest of his days of service, he wanted to do everything right today. In the back of his mind a little voice piped up to say what it thought about Stull possibly screwing up every case after this— Michael ignored it. He'd bargain again if he had to. He was only worried about now.

Stull crept over to the tub, half expecting the freak laying naked and hiding. Penny would turn his head around backward and, with a pipe, plunge holes into where the detective's eyes should be. POP!

There was nothing but an ugly residue.

Behind the door, the towel cabinet, nothing.

He felt sick at the thought of going back out into the hall. Washboard abs, enviable biceps, thighs like a roman gladiator, and a lot of police training did nothing to raise his confidence dealing with a monster. Bad people—yes. Horrible, awful, senseless criminal acts—all the time. Most the time those people had a reason, even if it was a bad one.

Stull took a deep breath and stepped out of the room.

The hall seemed particularly narrow and, all of a sudden, seemed to have a lot of doors near its end.

He switched on a light, grossly mounted near the middle of the hall, where it couldn't be turned on or off from either end.

Three small faux candle sconces lent enough light for someone needing to go from one room to the bathroom to do it without killing themselves, but not a lot more.

"Toiletries," he muttered, closing the first door past the bathroom on a stockpile of toilet paper, feminine pads, cotton balls, and the like.

Vacuum, mop...

Behind him, in the unlit bathroom, the double doors beneath the sink opened slowly.

"Fuck," Michael said flatly as he flipped on a light over stairs to the basement. He didn't want there to be a basement.

"Later," he told himself. Clear one floor at a time.

To Stull's right he could clearly see the entrance to the kitchen. Across from that would probably be a coat closet, because the back door was right there.

The detective didn't see or sense the heaving, silhouette enter the hall.

Michael pushed the basement door closed with a small click, a line of yellow light pushing through the gap under the door, but he was looking ahead of him.

Three yards from the back door, he finally made out what he was both afraid and relieved to find—the chain lock draped between the frame and the door.

You're still in the house.

WHAM!

His body collided with the left wall and he dropped to the linoleum floor.

He recoiled when something large and dark fell heavily against the ground beside him.

The vacuum.

Looking over his shoulder, a hand was coming down on him, Stull reached for his gun, laying within arms' reach. A whitish cord slipped over the hand and the detective immediately knew the sound of a flex cuff when it shortened on his wrist.

Stull let Bad Penny take the hand and all the force he could move with it, hitting Barbara somewhere in the chest. The momentum turning the officer just enough to reach the gun, when he was kicked in the head.

"AH. AH. AHH! AHHHH!!" the monster grunted over him, like a goat with no tongue.

He went for Stull's left hand, which held the gun. The boney fist struck like a snake and seemed to come together like a 3D puzzle bracelet, into a form or position that made those fingers feel like manacle not man.

Drool ran over the murder's lips and into Stull's mouth as Barbara gritted her teeth with effort. The detective was bigger than this thing. Stronger. Bigger and stronger by a longshot, but not tonight. Not with a heart-bursting amount of adrenaline removing all inhibition, all pain.

Bad Penny was trying to force the officer's hands together while Stull tried to get the business end of the gun to face her.

An erection slipped out of the struggle loosened robe. It was heavily scarred, but less than the testicles angrily swaying beneath it, having never been able to put himself through the kind of pain required to dispose of, what Barbara considered the last of his masculinity.

The detective's right hand had to go over the left, so the unfilled loop of the cuff could go over the end of the gun, thus over the hand clutching it.

Bad Penny started panting, thrusting his hips back and forth, like he was having sex. Stull's knees were outside of the killer's legs and, as far as Penny was concerned, not even pumping had to wait until he got inside the swarthy creature laid out before him. He imagined coming off all over him.

A morbid smile curled across the retired teacher's cracked and flaking lips.

One long horrible tone came out of Barbara's mouth as the end of the cuff finally made it over the gun. He felt like Stull just entered her and got down on his knees between the intruder's legs, holding the groan without yet needing a breath, testicles drifting across the grounded man's crotch.

Horrified, Michael twisted on his side and drove his knee into Robert Graham's kidney.

The hard grunt and impact spilled a section of bridgework onto the floor. In the low lighting, Stull caught a glimpse of the monster his victims had seen in every second in his company.

Stull's blood ran cold.

She paid no more attention to restraint, being there was nothing they couldn't enjoy as much dead, as alive.

Even as Detective Stull heard the sound of vehicles driving fast and then braking hard, he felt like death would happen before anyone or anything would arrive to help him.

The back door crashed in.

An officer spilled through on momentum.

The sound of a tent flap zipping, flash of heavy blue-gray metal, from neck to mid-bicep the body divided.

Barbara climaxed as she stared panting at the pieces of falling man and growled, slobbering, snapping, as the body danced violently like a bit of bacon fat on a scalding, oily, griddle.

In slow motion, Bad Penny lifted off of him, hovered like a hummingbird, a look of surprise reading madly across her blazing eyes.

Then she was flung away in a wide arch, driving her face first into the wall on the other side of the bloodied man whose oozing hands wrung painfully into the puffy robe.

Stull jumped to his feet, pulling his left hand free from the uncinched cuff and pulled the empty line tight so it couldn't be used against him later.

Nate easily grabbed Graham's left hand.

The other contended with a missing forefinger and all the joys that brought to overpowering the jerking, boney wrist.

Michael hurried to help.

Her right wrist broke free.

Treuer cried out involuntarily.

Seles twisted, squalling like a baby in the detective's grimacing face, filed teeth bared against the sconce light.

Stull grabbed Bad Penny's flailing right wrist with one hand and moved the other on her throat to distance the snapping maw from Nate.

It bore down on the hand coming near it.

The row of triangular yellow-brown points closed over the thumb of the reaching hand. Even as the teeth sunk in, the tongue busily raced around the thumb and sucked it.

"Christ!" Stull yelped.

A dully gleaming shape on a wounded hand divided the arms like a thread through the eye of a button. The muzzle pushed deep behind the killer's mandible.

"Bite harder and you'll pull your last breath through a hole in the back of your head," Nate told her.

Stull yanked his hand free the second the bite let up and went for the handcuffs on his belt.

Detective Treuer cast a sidelong glance at the familiar officer laying at the back door. There was another cop there now, looking lost, weeping, staring at a dismembered friend. How long he'd been there, neither detective knew. Probably the cop didn't know either.

Nate swallowed and looked down just long enough to regather himself, literally only three or four seconds, but all of it was suddenly very hard to digest. It was never easy, if at all possible, to accept what was happening beside them.

"You're under arrest," Nate said breathlessly. "You have the right to remain silent and refuse to answer questions. Do you understand?"

The half-naked man writhed, the robe remained by virtue of the hands holding the wrists inside the sleeves and nothing else.

"I'll take that as a yes," Stull grunted.

"Do you understand that right, Robert?" Nate pressed the wild eyed butcher.

The officers in the hall stared horrified at the person who taught some of their children and even some of them.

"I'm not stupid," said Graham effeminately.

"Is that a yes?" the detective said impatiently. "Are you not smart enough to realize this is a yes no question?"

"I understand my rights," she spat.

"Then you know that anything you do say may be used against you in a court of law?"

Bad Penny scowled deeply at the detective with the pain blanched face, hating him. Hating his pleasant voice, his handsomeness, the doubtless way he carried himself—knowing exactly what he was and not giving a single thought to how Barbara felt when men like him looked right through her. Or... when they didn't, like right now. This attractive stranger gave her no less than his full attention, but was looking at her like she was a monster.

Stull closed the handcuffs below Barbara's powerful hands and finally felt like he could let his guard down, if only a little.

"Can one of you guys take her, read her rights and make sure none of them are violated," Nate half-begged the nearest officers and added appreciatively, "Thanks for getting here so goddamn fast. A little bit longer and we would have needed it."

He looked at the back doorway. The body was covered, the weeping officer was out in the backyard with another cop who seemed to be dealing with it.

"You radio your guys have them on full alert for traps. I don't really believe there are only two in the house," Nate warned the officer who stepped forward to take her.

"So, how bad is it?"

Nate nodded repeatedly, "Need to go see about getting my finger put back on. Sooner than later."

"I'll drive," Stull offered, smiling hugely.

The Boston detective smiled a little too. He was thinking about the ER physicians putting the bone tips back on his knuckles like the little plastic caps you hammer in over screws after assembling some furniture.

Michael helped Nate into the passenger seat and did the seatbelt for him too. When the door closed he looked out at the nice, normal, American neighborhood lit up like a disco with red and blue lights. Normal people huddled in their doorways or windows wondering how they'll feel about home sweet home by morning light.

"So, don't bleed too much on my car, Treuer," Stull asked him as he turned over the engine.

Nate nodded.

Then Stull warned, "Don't die in it either."

The other detective looked at him and smiled. Michael was smiling back.

"Tell me why I didn't let him kill you," Nate replied.

19

...

A PENNY SAVED, A PENNY EARNED

"What did you say?"

"I'm sorry about your dog," answered the woman in the chair.

Samantha rolled onto her back, face prickling with tears.

"He was a good dog," the woman in the bed told her.

Bailey nodded, knowingly, and felt horrible for Sam. In the dog alone Sam's loss was infinitely worse than that of many other tragedies. It was the loss of her only child. Best friend. Partner. Protector. Confidant. Playmate. Roommate.

Losing a good pet is like losing at least one wonderful thing from every person that you love— someone wrote that in a card they'd all signed for a K-9 officer back in Boston.

"What was his name?"

Samantha raised the back of her bed so she didn't have to try so hard to see the woman curled up under a blanket, looking cold, in the big recliner.

"Leopold," she answered, smiling thoughtfully. "It seemed so funny on him as a puppy with his oversized feet, long gangly legs and smallish square head. We thought it would be distinguished when he was grown, instead he made it sound like a lazy dog's name."

Bailey smiled a little too. Great Danes *are* silly looking puppies. She raised her glassy blue-green eyes to the recuperating survivor of a living nightmare.

"You're going to be okay," she told the woman in the hospital bed.

Goode snorted loudly before a short and somewhat serene laugh.

"I knew that from the first time I saw you."

The woman with hair the colors of rust and gold returned, "I thought I blinded you."

Sam Goode laughed again, having apparently blocked out that part.

"When do I get to know who you are?" Samantha asked the woman, after her laughter died down to a sigh.

"Anytime," she told her. "I'm Bailey."

"You aren't just a good Samaritan, are you Bailey?"

The women looked at each other for a long time, because the detective didn't know how to answer.

Finally, she drew a shallow breath and replied, "I guess that depends on why people in my business do what they do."

20

...

BETTER SORRY THAN SAFE

On the broad patient room windowsill, Detective Jacobs enjoyed a view that did not include the vast number of news vans, curiosity seekers, well-wishers, and the servicemen trying to control all of them.

By that morning, few people hadn't heard of Bad Penny's capture and that Samantha Goode had been recovered without any life threatening injuries.

While no one told the detective that Stull had apprehended the killer, she hadn't been concerned about him succeeding. She hadn't been worried at all, until early that morning, when she returned to her room and found a mess of flowers and a shattered mug beside an overturned chair. A small silvery balloon pressed against the ceiling, its message silenced against the water-stained tile. There were droplets of blood leading out or into the room, but their path had been erased by a mop or a rag, shortly before she returned—she could still smell the solution.

Neither detective answered their phones and, exhausted, Bailey could think of little more to do than rest and hope one or both men would appear soon. Between her third and fourth tries to reach them by phone, she fell asleep.

Now, sitting beside the window, she stared blurrily through the cold glass. The heatwave appeared to be broken, and winter was growing its teeth.

There was no doubt in her mind that Bad Penny, Robert Graham, or Barbara Seles should spend the rest of their life in prison. If the detective was a betting woman, she would win that bet.

Bailey was vaguely aware of her fingertips shifting against her left cheek, where her hand wrapped gently, shakily, across her pressed lips.

Somewhere, lying cold, cruelly slain, with no one else thinking of him, was her father—no matter what he claimed or denied. How many years of experience and schooling were required before she was qualified to pursue justice for the dead? How many dead had she seen and meticulously served? How many times had she been the messenger of devastating news?

More times than she cared to remember.

Yet she had no idea what happens after the messenger leaves. Who do you call? What do you do? How do you know you're doing what the person wants? Can a spirit suffer unrest if they are buried when they want to be cremated? Was there a will that would tell her what he wanted—if only just this once! What happens now?

"What happens now?" her breath felt hot against her cupped hand.

Would he want a funeral? Were those old "acquaintances" friends? Would they come? People should know these things! She didn't feel like she even knew how to be a person.

She was sitting on a window sill, but felt like the whole world fell out from under her.

No father. No family. No anything.

A strange feeling of emptiness came over her at the thought of Bad Penny's capture. It felt like running, running, running, and then being thirsty— famished—when you find a glass of water, you guzzle it down and realize it was what you were trying to get to the whole time.

The promise was kept.

Bailey hadn't realized how much power it had over her, until the power was gone.

There was relief, but little joy in how this left her. She felt emotionally beaten, as if, for having taken so long to fulfill the promise, she was not allowed or deserving any reward. Though who feels they should be rewarded for doing what they said they would do? Bailey would have settled for feeling settled.

As she punched the number to Nate's cell phone, she wondered if he was somewhere phones weren't allowed. The first place she thought of was the ICU. She went cold as she slid off the sill and was worried by how severely her hands trembled.

When Bailey came around her partially closed curtain, she found a housekeeper just discovered the mess. The short woman in brown scrubs was squatted by the spilled flowers, drawing up a small, soaked teddy bear from the pool of water. It was still partially tied to a piece of the mug's handle.

"Is this yours?" the housekeeper held the tan, dripping bear up for the patient to see.

"I don't know," Bailey managed through chattering teeth.

"Is this your blood?"

The detective shook her head as her eyes fell to the dried droplets.

"Can I find out if anyone was taken from my room last night?" the patient said through the hand pressed lightly over her mouth.

The housekeeper frowned helplessly and suggested that she check at the desk. She told the patient that all she knew was late last night—because of all this business—her boss thought he should be "on the scene" and one of the night housekeepers had told her that he'd got bitched out by a guy with a badge.

"The housekeeper that saw it cleans the rooms on the other side of the fire doors. Maybe this is my boss's blood."

Bailey looked at the blood and then up at the woman cleaning it.

"Why would you think that?"

The woman pushed an errant strand of golden brown hair off her sweaty forehead as she regarded the remaining spots.

"I was just hoping," the woman shrugged and left the room for a garbage bag. The detective followed.

"Did the night housekeeper say what he looked like?"

The cleaner was unrolling a dark brown bag, while she considered the question and if she had an answer. Finally she shrugged, again, and offered apologetically, "Only that he had the bluest eyes she'd ever seen."

After thanking the housekeeper, Bailey hurried to the nearest nurse's station to ask if Michael Stull was admitted.

"I can't give out patient information," the ward secretary, Trisha, told her without looking.

"Can you tell me if he is *not* a patient?"

"Yes."

Bailey leaned on the counter, her knees felt unreliable. She tried to take in her surroundings, remembering faces, reading names, looked at the clock—no typing.

"And?" the detective pressed, almost crossing her fingers hopefully.

"*And*?" the ward secretary looked confused.

"Is he here?"

"I didn't check," said Trisha.

"Why not?" Bailey's voice rose.

"You didn't ask," the woman behind the desk told her.

"Well I am now."

Trisha stared at her, eyebrows raised expectantly.

Then the detective recognized the woman she was talking to, obviously later than it took Trisha—who as a child liked to tease Bailey for being motherless—probably already knew Bailey was on the floor.

The woman must have seen the recognition cross the pretty detective's blanched face, because she smiled immediately after the patient realized.

"Will you check and tell me if Michael Stull, s-t-u-l-l, is not here?"

It took a couple seconds for the secretary to check the charts, she looked up at Bailey and told her, in confidence, that she should probably go see the chaplain, and that she was sorry, but couldn't say more.

Bailey leaned back, reading the lie as soundly as she expected one.

Nothing changes... a voice whispered tiredly inside her.

Bailey didn't believe that—not unconditionally. It did appear to be true in this case. So she was only wasting time. Most the time a "lost cause" only requires a different approach. Fatalism is for broken people and quitters. Detective Jacobs refused to be either.

She left the desk and went to the nearby elevator, all her personal things were under lock and key downstairs, because they included weapons. There were two people from one of the higher floors, already waiting inside the faux wood lined elevator. Bailey greeted them, almost soundlessly.

There wasn't time, after saying their own hellos, to ask if the patient was alright before the elevator doors opened on the first floor and she departed for the front desk. They assumed, if something was wrong, the people there would help.

"May I please use your phone?" she asked the ancient volunteer in a green smock, behind the desk.

The old woman hesitated.

"I'm a detective—I need to check on my partner," subconsciously including both Nate and Michael in the role.

The phone rattled as the atrophied arm settled it on the counter before the troubled woman.

Dialing again.

Something felt wrong—someone should have answered a phone—someone should have woke her.

"Damn it," she bit back tears, at the expense of her trembling lower lip. No answer from Stull or Treuer. "Come on…"

She tried to regurgitate numbers modern phones no longer required a person to know by heart—the captain, lieutenant, maybe…

"Curtis?" she didn't mean to say as loud as it came out, when his voice came on the line. Her knees gave slightly and she dipped a few inches until her arms decided they'd help hold her up. Again, a hand flew to her mouth, only now to cover the grateful smile that broke across her pallid face. Joy and or adrenaline bloomed pink high up on her cheeks—or perhaps again, all she got was relief.

"—and had to have a special team go through the house. Bought Detective Stull enough time to bring over your friend from Boston."

"Nate—why?"

"Like I was saying, the house was rigged with traps."

Bailey had missed most of that, he'd been talking so fast.

"Wait—bring him where?"

"To the hospital," he told her.

The woman's fingertips creaked as they clutched the marble laminate countertop.

"Why?" was all she could say.

"He's alright—he had to have replantation surgery. Where have you been?"

"I had—I had—"

"Those guys almost killed me—I'm waiting for you to wake up, so I can see you. I fall asleep. I wake up to a yell, the balloon's reflection startled Nate, the door slams open and Stull's yelling— 'What's going on?!'—I'm startled awake, Nate's hit with the door. I drop everything in my hands. We realize you're not there. The surgeon arrives, Nate is paged to OR. We go to look for you—some macho supervisor starts getting after a housekeeper to clean up Stull's blood trail. After an exchange, Stull cleans up the mess—kinda—and throws the rag in the guy's face. Gives him hell about interrupting people working and runs down to get his hand stitched up before going back to canvas the scene. It was my job to find you. Have you looked outside? Lanester is in chaos."

"How did we do?" she pressed.

Curtis fell silent and, after a few moments, went on to explain how they lost the officer at the back door, noting that the arrest turned out pretty costly in that.

"I'm so sorry," she stammered against the mouthpiece. In sleepy little towns like Lanester, most officers go to work every day without worrying if they will be coming home. It made her sick to think Bad Penny managed one last victim—even as he was being arrested.

"He was a good cop—there was a reason he was at the door first—someone needed help—that's all there was to it for him, or other guys like him."

Bailey nodded slowly. She had been lucky enough to know the type. There are two kinds of officers you want to help you…

She answered with silence—almost always the closest translation for what goes on in her heart or in her mind… or in the secret place where they meet— that she liked to think of as a soul.

The technician thought he understood what the quiet meant. When you know someone well, what you hear in what they don't say often speaks volumes over what they do.

Sometimes it's just that simple.

The hospital stayed in lockdown for more than a week after the arrest and rescue.

By the end of the month, things were more or less back to normal in Lanester, Massachusetts. The "Home Away From Home" small town tucked into the tangled estuary of the Annisquam River.

School shootings, terrorist depravities, celebrity scandals and makeovers, and the global zombie obsession making the news night and day and night again made it easier for the town to crawl out from the shadow of Bad Penny. He was, as far as most people were concerned, a short lived nightmare that was quickly snuffed out. Bad Penny would turn up a

few times, months down the line, especially when
the trial began, but was ultimately old news after the
first month or two of utter sensationalism.

The sensationalism went stale for most the
officers and citizens after the first few days. After a
week, even Michael Stull was sick of answering
questions. The big time magazine cover he graced,
and thought he would frame for a wall, ended up
tucked away as a memento.

After a couple days recuperation, Stull went
back to work with his old partner—even though, he
told Detective Jacobs, he would have been okay with
them staying a team.

Nate was supposed to be out for recovery a few
weeks, with several weeks of physical therapy
following that. Some ninety-percent of digital re-
plantations are successful, though most patients
enjoy only fifty-percent of the mobility they once
had. He planned on being back at work in no more
than six weeks. He would be back in three.

There are only two ways officers like him leave
their responsibilities.

Off of bed rest and standing at the living room
window, where he could see the briny Annisquam
River and the woman sitting beside it, Nate Treuer
felt like he was about to abandon responsibilities he
had to her. He didn't know how to leave her and
didn't want to.

While not one for small talk, to begin with, he
found her growing quiet in a way that made Bailey
feel out of reach. The silence, before, belonged to
her thoughts and anyone that needed her to listen.
The silence, now, belonged to thought alone.

Unbeknown to Nate, Detective Jacobs quietly
made arrangements for her father to be cremated,
after making a list of every reason for or against

burial or cremation, based on what she knew about the man.

Even though father, daughter, and whole town knew that Bailey was no Douglass—she had a blood test done and had it made ash with the body, that maybe the truth would let his spirit rest more than the shame and anger of what everyone assumed.

Bailey could never bring herself to look at the results. Not that the truth could harm her, but because it meant nothing to her.

For no other reason, but to make them scatter as far and wide as possible, "The Wall's" daughter poured his ashes off the Annisquam Bridge. It felt horrible to let him go, again, but he would not want to be kept, by her or anyone.

There Bailey could visit all she wanted. In his life or death, being there for and with her father was, indeed, all she ever asked.

In an effort to move on, Nate thought she should sell her dad's house.

Even after all these unoccupied months, it still looked like home, to Bailey. It still looked lived in, having lived there, having nothing—not even the stained coffee cup where the path of a hundred thousand sips permanently browned a section of the rim—been altered to suggest otherwise. Ultimately, she didn't feel she had any right to, in the back of her mind thinking how mad her dad would be. Maybe it was just too soon to accept he was gone.

It was not uncommon for Nate to find her, feeling secure in her privacy, weeping as quietly as humanly possible into hands rarely free of tremor.

He tentatively crossed the snowy yard to reach the woman reclined almost like a mermaid on the same rock where she always sat. Her gleaming copper hair spilled over her shawl and flapped loosely in the cutting breeze. When near enough, he gathered it in his hands, winding it carefully and tucked it back inside the thick wool wrap.

"Trying to catch your death?" he asked the unmoving woman.

Her eyelids lowered with lowering eyes that seemed responsible for her face descending to also face the water. She shook her head.

"I'm going to be able to go back to work soon." She swallowed hard.

"Are *you*?"

Her lips pressed lightly, it seemed she might say something, but only shrugged.

"You are needed out there, Bail."

Her sea-water eyes flicked toward him, written with so many troubles that no one was clear for the others, like writing over writing, over writing, until it all just looks like scribbles.

"You know that," he figured and sat on the rock where he always sat. "Well, maybe you should have forgot that."

A look of surprise lit on her face and this time he knew she was going to say something, but he spoke first anyway.

"Leia Redding's killer is locked up. Your father has been laid to rest. There's no family and no phantom to move you. You serve somewhere you don't want to be, but now you feel responsible for them and you haven't ever stopped feeling responsible for the people of Boston or the unit you worked with…or maybe your partner," he looked out across the churning ice-gray water. He felt her eyes on him, but didn't feel strong enough to meet them. He suddenly didn't feel strong at all.

"I feel guilty and I feel torn," she muttered under the wind.

He looked at her helplessly.

When he finally responded, he tried to be careful and provocative, "I asked you once what you would do in this situation and you didn't really answer me."

"Maybe I knew I couldn't find an answer."

"Is that what you've been looking for?" he put his feet up on the side of her rock so he could lean on his knees. "Maybe you were disappointed that Stull went back to his partner?"

Bailey shook her head and half-smiled for merely the hint of a second, "I surprise myself every time I even wonder about him." She sighed. "By the end, he was alright."

Nate nodded, but would never agree aloud.

"Do you want to stay here?" he pressed.

She shook her head emphatically, but felt like a traitor to say out loud.

She was once told that when you save a life, it in some way belongs to you—as you have invested your free will in changing God's plan—you are responsible for that person forever. So what happens when you rescue a town or towns from an unrelenting butcher? Coming, going, staying…was all about obligation.

"There's nothing to be here for—" she confessed. As he'd seen her do a dozen times since all of this began, she covered her mouth in her hand and pushed down the feeling trying to break out. He imagined a little girl spending all of her childhood and youth doing that. Again, it was all he could do not to touch her, to hold her.

"Then why stay?" he asked.

"I asked for this," she reminded him, meeting his eyes steadily.

"Other places will need you—you're with the county now, remember," he pointed.

It hadn't escaped her.

Then he thought of something else.

"Are you sorry you didn't get to collar Bad Penny?"

Without falter, she held his gaze and answered, "The only thing I wanted was him caught. How could anyone want more than that?"

"It was personal," he gently answered.

Her face softened thoughtfully and was nodding again.

"Maybe I wanted him caught more than some. The only reason I return to that night is to wonder if things might have went different if I hadn't been hurt at the bridge... or maybe things might have went worse. A person can't help, but think. Especially when a life is lost and you want to reason it out, down to how it could have been changed. If, in some small way, you share responsibility with every other point on the secret chain reaction that led to whatever went wrong."

He found a reclusive strand of penny-red hair and tucked it behind a pink ear. For a brief moment, when he drew that hand away, his hand lit against her fair cheek, but didn't dare linger at the incidental meeting and drove his hands, which were actually very cold, into his jacket pockets.

Her answer didn't surprise him. He remembered the one time when she defended her personal time and needs to him—needs that didn't really serve her either. She didn't know how to be selfish yet or to stop doing the one thing she believed was at the core of every act of service. Caring.

She was supposed to be taking time for herself, for recovery. Everything about Bailey Jacobs was reserved for other people—while having been kept at a distance since infancy, she really had no idea how to be close to society or if it was even safe to try. He guessed she was so goddamn good at being a cop because she spent so much time watching, listening, and trying to understand others. Sorting the motivations for cruel jabs, or shy kindnesses. The reason behind a mother leaving and a little girl's violent death.

Was it uncanny or conditioned that Bailey could wander a crime scene and see and make sense of abnormalities invisible to everyone else? Bailey spent her life a ghost, no wonder that she should operate so well around death.

How do you make someone feel alive?

How do you remind someone they are?

Not by arguing that you don't need to care about someone who died—especially if there was no one to want you to. That anyone was better off to have the only person in her life dead. He felt like every other piece of crap in Lanester, like every cold shoulder, every bully, every reason for self-doubt.

He couldn't make up for every self-righteous asshole. He couldn't take back any of the things he said. All he felt he could do was ask for something no one else ever had to consider.

"I want to know what you're feeling, Bail," he confessed into the snow below his legs.

In silence, long and lasting, man and woman were taken by a stiff, wintery gust and the smell of a sea bed dragged up by churning waters. There is something about the ocean that offers escape and freedom—and has long since been the road to countless peoples' new beginnings.

Bailey's hands lay still beside her. She drew a steady breath from whatever the wind didn't steal away. Across the water, in a cluster of trees, a gathering of stones. There, people asked nothing, because they wanted nothing, anymore. To whatever promise indebted her to the spirit of a little dead girl—of the debt and the deed she thought:

It's done…

And perhaps, permanent as it felt, would also in her consciousness be true.

Until then, other people would need her.

There may be someone as yet unseen, laying still and waiting for someone to champion their untimely passing.

She would.

She exhaled slowly, raised her radiant blue-green eyes to whatever horror chanced before them today, tomorrow, and any other tomorrows.

She who can be forced has not learned how to die…

At risk of exposing herself to questions in return, the almost six year detective of homicides looked at her ex-partner and asked him something she always meant to—to slowly decrease the long list of possible regrets, if only one at a time:

"Can I ask you something, Nate?"

He looked up at her through brown hair tossed and tangled by gusts. His eyes read an answer even as one came without hesitation.

"Sure," he said.

"Do you even like coffee?"

ACKNOWLEDGEMENTS

. . .

Alice would like to thank everyone who purchased, read, means to read, or gifted someone her first detective novel.

A wise writer once said, "The difference between fiction and nonfiction is that fiction has to make sense." The truth in this she finds cruelly intimidating—foregoing stories such as this for ones which do not demand as much calculation, climax, or the pressure of a startling conclusion.

Hardcore crime readers are often halfway to criminal investigators themselves—to these she pins her hopes of thought provocation and reading pleasure, as you may be the greatest test in gauging the quality of this manuscript. You are the nightmare overshadowing every moment of this novel's creation.

To all other readers, Alice hopes no disappointment finds you and thanks you kindly for your interest in her writing. It means the world to her.